ASHES OF REBELLION

MICHAEL JECKS

Boldwood

First published in Great Britain in 2025 by Boldwood Books Ltd.

Copyright © Michael Jecks, 2025

Cover Design by JD Smith Design Ltd.

Cover Images: Shutterstock and Heralder/Wikimedia Commons

The moral right of Michael Jecks to be identified as the author of this work has been asserted in accordance with the Copyright, Designs and Patents Act 1988.

A CIP catalogue record for this book is available from the British Library.

Paperback ISBN 978-1-83703-282-2

Large Print ISBN 978-1-83703-283-9

Hardback ISBN 978-1-83703-281-5

Trade Paperback ISBN 978-1-80635-322-4

Ebook ISBN 978-1-83703-284-6

Kindle ISBN 978-1-83703-285-3

Audio CD ISBN 978-1-83703-276-1

MP3 CD ISBN 978-1-83703-277-8

Digital audio download ISBN 978-1-83703-280-8

This book is printed on certified sustainable paper. Boldwood Books is dedicated to putting sustainability at the heart of our business. For more information please visit https://www.boldwoodbooks.com/about-us/sustainability/

Boldwood Books Ltd, 23 Bowerdean Street, London, SW6 3TN

www.boldwoodbooks.com

This is for my friends at Tinners' Morris
For, mostly, their support:
with wine, constant bickering,
arguments, rude comments about my dancing,
timekeeping,
unreliability,
forgetfulness,
and yet still being
best of friends.

BOOK 1

THE VINTAINE

1

BIHOREL – OUTSIDE ROUEN

January 1358

He stood beneath them, gazing up at the bodies. Four of them, hanging intermixed with the more recent common criminals, who were already decomposing. The four were hung about with the rusted links of the chains that suspended them from the gallows while, set on lances fixed in the gallows' beam, were their heads, wizened and distorted, blackened with the sun and wind, eyes gone to the crows and other birds that congregated still, squabbling over their fresher meals.

It had been two years since they had suffered their fate, accused by King John II of betrayal to him, the King of France. The Count of Harcourt and the Lord of

Graville were both suspected of complicity in the machinations of King Charles of Navarre. The third, Guillaume de Mainemaires, had attempted to take the king's son, the dauphin, to Germany the previous year, in order to attempt a coup.

It would be natural to think that the fourth man was their leader, the infamous Charles of Navarre. But no, Navarre was too senior in the aristocratic ranks to be subjected to such a fate. Instead, he had been taken away to the Châtelet in Paris, with two of his closest advisers, Friquet de Fricamps and Jean de Bantalu, where all three were interrogated. Later, Navarre would be imprisoned at Arleux.

No, the fourth victim on the gallows was a mere esquire: Colin Doublet. He was in the service of Charles, and had deprecated the sudden arrival of King John's men during the dauphin's meal and drawn a knife. He was immediately disarmed and held for drawing a weapon against his king.

Later, a curfew was declared in Rouen. The streets were emptied as the two carts bearing the four rode through the city to the Champs-du-Pardon, an open space where the horse fairs were held. There the victims were beheaded by a forger who volunteered in exchange for a pardon from his own death penalty. Unused to such business, he had got himself blind drunk before picking up his weapon. By the time he was told to go through with the executions, he could barely see his victims.

Their deaths were not good.

* * *

Thomas de Ladit nodded to himself at the memory.

It had been hideous. The felon had been so drunk, he could scarcely grip the axe, let alone strike with precision. Afterwards, the bodies were taken on the same carts up here, to Bihorel, the hill overlooking Rouen. No one could escape the conclusion that King John would not forgive those who tried to wrest power from him.

Now, at last, they were to be taken down and given a decent burial.

* * *

The executions had been madness. There had been the one attempt at a coup, certainly, but to execute the leading noble aristocrat of Normandy without even the semblance of a trial did not give other aristocrats the sense that their king was anything more than a brute, a despot who made decisions on a whim. A fool

who thought that because he was strong and courageous, he could hold the realm in his fist. But by doing
so, he had alienated all the noblemen of France.

Perhaps that was why, in the midst of the combat at
Poitiers, the middle battle of men had deserted the
field, leaving King John alone with his youngest son to
fight to the bitter end, until both were captured by the
English amid the bodies of their men-at-arms.

Was it true that the Duke d'Orléans had deliberately taken his men away to leave King John in an impossible position at Poitiers? Perhaps. Thomas didn't
care. All he knew was his own master, Charles of
Navarre, had been captured and held, and these four
had been murdered when all they were doing was
trying to protect France and themselves. The king was
a tyrant.

The men were coming now. He could hear the
carts rumbling along the roadway and, as they arrived,
he directed them to the victims to be cut down.

King Charles of Navarre was free once more. Supporters had gone to his place of incarceration armed
with ladders and grappling irons, and he was welcomed as a saviour as he made the journey to Amiens.
He was the unifying character, the one man who could
bring together the nobility and peasants.

After all, who else could lead the country? The dauphin acted as regent, but he was only eighteen years of age. He was not strong enough to control the aristocracy. Knights wandered the kingdom demanding money from those who worked the land, robbing abbeys and churches as well as merchants, because the dauphin could not restrain them and their depravity. And of course, then there were the English. His father, King John II, was held prisoner in England, and all France must collect money for his ransom, but even as the Estates General in Paris discussed how to pay for his release while also supporting enough men to hold back the marauding English, the noblemen of France took advantage of the king's absence to enrich themselves.

In such a time, a strong hand was needed, and Charles – King of Navarre – was the strongest in the realm.

Today he was showing his contempt for the dauphin. The dauphin had agreed that Navarre could cut down these bodies and see them buried without fanfare. It was his father who had ordered that they should be hanged here, their heads on spikes in this contemptible fashion. Well, Charles of Navarre would set matters straight.

Navarre would not adhere to that arrangement. He

had sent his most loyal servant to see to it that the dauphin's wishes were ignored.

And meanwhile he was collaborating with the English and allying with them to depose King John of France.

* * *

Thomas could see him on his horse, directing the men with the arrogance of the knightly class through the ages. Pointing to each with his riding crop, watching as each of the four was cut down and removed from the chains, while men clambered up onto the gallows beam to retrieve the skulls. There was some confusion as to which belonged to which skeleton, but that dispute was soon ended as Navarre selected which head belonged to which torso – did it matter which was which to King Charles? Thomas wondered – and then they made their way back along the road down which the bodies had been brought two years before, just as the light was fading.

Later, Thomas would recall that evening and the next morning.

Once in the Champs-du-Pardon, where the four had been executed, the main ceremony took place. A hundred torches were lighted, and a requiem mass was sung over the bodies, before they were carried back to the cathedral on tumbrils, and once there, installed in state, the crowds filed past them through the night, persuaded by the men Charles had brought with him. It was hardly the quiet removal of the bodies that the dauphin had envisaged, when he had agreed that Charles could cut them down without ceremony.

Worse was to come. The following morning, Charles gave an impassioned speech to the populace of Rouen. He itemised all the unreasonable suffering to which he had been subjected, the lies told against him, the unfair judgements, and referred to these victims of King John as 'martyrs'. He was giving all the reasons justifying his alliance with the English.

And the English were wasting no time in taking full advantage.

2

VINTAINE

'My holes have got holes in them,' Dogbreath said mournfully.

He was sitting on a rock beside the roadway, his boot in his hands, an expression of distaste on his face as he upended it and watched the dust and grit pour out.

'It must be the noxious fumes from your feet,' Peter said, grimacing.

'Nothing wrong with my feet,' Dogbreath scowled, and held out his unshod foot to Peter's face as evidence.

Peter winced, wafting away the odour with a desperate hand. 'It smells worse than your farts!'

'Aye, your arse is more fearsome than the last

trump,' Seth said.

'There's nothing wrong with my arse,' Dogbreath said, frowning now.

'There's nothing at all wrong,' Gervase agreed. 'So long as it's considered in the same light as any other weapon. Point it at the enemy, and it's fine. Just keep it away from the rest of us.'

'That,' Nick said, 'is the point. It's like an arrow. Deadly, but you don't want it pointing at your friends.'

'Eh? It's so foul, I wouldn't point it at my enemies,' Ingram said.

'Aye, ye're all just bastards,' Dogbreath said. He stared disconsolately at the boots once more. The hole in the sole was enough to tempt him to throw the boot away, but if he did, he would have to go barefoot for... how long? There was no telling when he would be able to liberate another. This had lasted for many months, since he stole it from a French man-at-arms after Poitiers. 'It was comfy, too.'

'We'll find you a new one,' Peter said.

'Won't be the same. This was good quality, this.'

'Such good quality that it has a hole the size of a penny,' Nick said.

'Even the best of shoes must suffer from a long march,' said Fulk, the Swiss.

'Not the way Dogbreath uses them,' Saul said. 'He

rides everywhere on his pony, like the good hobelar he is, so it must be something about his feet that makes his boots fall to pieces.'

'Aye. It's the foul stench from them,' Peter said.

'You say that? Ach, you smell worse than a midden or a cesspit,' Dogbreath said. He tugged the boot on again. It was a tight fit, but at least it was more or less shaped to his foot. 'I need a new one.'

'Perhaps at the next town we'll find a cordwainer,' Hawkwood suggested.

'Or a merchant with a foot as dainty as yours,' Peter said.

'Dainty?' Seth said. '*Dainty* is suitable for a lady, for a woman of style and elegance, not for a tatty git like him.'

'Tatty git? Who're you calling a tatty git?' Dogbreath snarled.

Seth looked at him with a mixture of amusement and distaste. 'I'm calling *you* a tatty git, Dogbreath, because, well, you are very tatty-looking, and you're a right git too.'

Dogbreath took a deep breath, but then glanced down at his hosen. They were badly faded, and there were three long rips in the right leg. His shirt was stained and worn, and the boot still had a hole in the sole. 'Aye. I suppose so. Not that you're any better.'

That much was true. The entire vintaine had been affected by their foray into France. Since the battle of Poitiers, they had been travelling almost constantly, taking small villages, two castles, and any number of farms and hamlets along the way. France was full of riches, and the English were there to farm it to the best of their ability, taking what they wanted. There was no one to prevent them. The French king had been captured by the Prince of Wales and was held in England, and the nobles who should have upheld the rule of the king's laws had been slaughtered on the fields at Poitiers. The English and their allies were able to wander as they wished, and take what they wanted. There was no army, no king's host, to stand in their way or protect the common folk.

Hawkwood stood and grimaced as a muscle complained. He went to his pony and patted his muzzle. The beast was rested.

'All right. Time to mount up,' he called, and Robin nodded, taking up his horn and blowing a short, sharp note. Hawkwood had no authority over the others, but Robin and Peter tended to accept his leadership. He had a little more experience, and his general approach had so far proven to be successful.

Gradually, the men gathered. Hawkwood's fifteen men, Robin's twelve, Peter's fourteen: forty-one men altogether, all that was left of the three vintaines. There should have been sixty, but they had all been understrength even before Poitiers. Several had died there, and afterwards many had left to return home with their profits from ransoms and plunder. The boys were at the rear, where they would lead the overladen sumpter horses, the beasts used to carry their booty. Each had a simple wooden frame on its back with bales of clothing and sacks of silver and gold, while two held quivers of arrows and waxed bags with spare bowstrings and spare bow staves.

The men stood, some scratching at flea bites, others staring into the distance, fiddling with packs or retying bootlaces. A mingling of scruffy, unwashed soldiery, each with a short riding sword or long knife, a small eating knife, a horn, a leather pocket at each belt, water flask hanging from a shoulder. Each had been in their vintaine for over a year, and each knew his job.

They were archers, here to despoil the country.

* * *

It was tedious. William, esquire, looked out over the lands from the hill at Okehampton and felt his face twist into a grimace of disgust.

He had friends who were achieving things. They had followed the king to France, where they were serving him honourably, winning glory and honours, and money, while they helped him win back his French possessions, unreasonably stolen by the pretender-king, John II of France. Except all knew that King Edward of England was the rightful King of France. His mother, Isabella, was the daughter of the French King Philip, and when Philip and his sons died, leaving no heir, the crown should have passed to Edward.

But the wily, duplicitous French refused to allow that. Instead, they changed their law to ban inheritance through the female line, allowing them to hand the crown to the Valois. It was a source of outrage throughout much of England, the idea that this pretender-king could have taken the crown that was so plainly the inheritance of King Edward.

Not that Edward would allow it to be stolen so flagrantly, and that was the cause of the eruption of war. It was the war of possession. King Edward and his son, the Prince of Wales, were determined to retrieve that which had been stolen from them. During battles at sea and battles on land, the two Edwards, father and son, had prosecuted their campaign to bring France to heel. They had put their trust in God, and God had rewarded them with their victories at Sluys, Crécy and Poitiers. Now, with the latest French king, John II, safely held prisoner by the king, surely soon God would reward their campaigns with the submission of the whole of France.

Meanwhile, William was here, in Okehampton, staring out over the valley, past the deer park, up the hill towards the cold, windswept moors. An esquire desperate for action, for the chance to prove himself, the opportunity to win his spurs like his father, Sir Baldwin de Furnshill. William dreamed of glory and honour, but he was stuck here in Devon.

But today his life would take a new turn. He saw the cavalcade appear along the river's road, the banners declaring the arrival of Sir Thomas de Courtenay: *Or, three torteaux, a label of three points azure.*

This was his chance. William hurried down the steep slope from the keep to the main courtyard and waited for the knight to enter the barbican.

* * *

That morning they were planning to ride south and east, but on their way they spotted a small farmstead, and, on seeing it, Hawkwood detailed Dogbreath and

Fulk with four others to go and view the place and make sure there was no risk of an ambush.

Dogbreath dropped and called for the boys to come and take their ponies, handing the reins of his to Arn, and soon both Arn and Rat had three mounts each, the other two boys standing and waiting in case there was an ambush and they had to take other horses. The boys acted as grooms, servants and weapon carriers during battles, and now they stood watching while the six men trotted off cautiously towards the buildings, each carrying his bow and a handful of arrows, all except Fulk, who gripped his halberd.

The farmstead was little more than a single peasant house with a barn at the side. A dog howled as they approached, and Dogbreath nocked an arrow as he went. He could hear a clucking from hens, and he licked his lips at the sound. It was a while since he'd eaten chicken, and it also meant there must be eggs nearby. He liked eggs. With luck there would be ale or wine. It was some time since his comrade Clip had died, and without Clip the vintaine suffered from a lack of the foodstuffs that Clip had inevitably discovered for them. He had an infallible sense of where villagers would conceal their food stores and farm creatures. Dogbreath missed Clip – his airy declaration that they'd all die was irritating, but at the same time somehow reassuring. They had all felt sure that Clip would be the last man to die if there was any disaster. Yet died he had.

The farmstead was utterly still, apart from a few chickens pecking at the grit of the track. Although the dog still complained, there was no sign of it. Dogbreath guessed that it was shut up in a shed or some form of makeshift kennel. The main point for him was that there was no evidence that the brute was free and roaming to take a bite out of anybody foolish enough to trespass on his owner's land.

With his bow ready, Dogbreath moved along the line of a fence, his eyes darting about. Stepping on a sharp stone, he stifled a curse, hopping on his good foot. That hole in the sole would have to be mended. He knew from long experience that the others would all be similarly aware of every movement. They too would have arrows fitted to their bowstrings, Fulk with his great weapon ready to slash or hack at any enemy. They had all searched plenty of other villages and farmsteads in the past to know what each must do, how each of the others would respond to any threat or danger.

Dogbreath moved along to the rear wall of the house itself. He glanced about him quickly and saw that his companions were all close behind him. Darting forward, he reached the door and thrust it wide, peering in cautiously without entering. That was the risky part, opening a door, only to be struck by a crossbow's quarrel, or pushing inside and finding a man concealed behind the door, where he could stab the intruder safely.

He kicked the door, just to make sure, and as it slammed back against the wall, he entered the building.

There was a sharp cry, and he ducked, listening intently. A muffled noise from the back of the room, and then a scratching, and he went through the room to where it emanated.

'What are you doing here, eh?' he said.

3

The Rat shivered as the men went into the village. He often shivered now. The cold ate into his feet and seeped through the thin leather of his jerkin. Movement was the only way to keep warm.

He had memories of warmth, but they seemed as ancient as the old crone who used to live in his village – a toothless old hag, she had been. Once she saw him at her apple tree, stealing a handful of fruits, and she screeched at him. It was terrifying. All the boys in the village knew that she was a witch, that her words could kill, and when she cursed someone, that person would immediately weaken and begin to fade away, death a certainty.

But those apples were food. His family needed them. The famine shouldn't have hurt them so much, but his family was struggling, and his mother had grown pale, giving up all the food she possessed to keep her two sons and their father fed. And when she got the pestilence, she was too weak to survive. She and Rat's brother both succumbed. Rat's family had nothing to eat. He had stolen the apples so his mother wouldn't fade away any more.

A fresh shiver racked his frame. At about ten years old – he wasn't sure – the memories of the hag's screeching at him were still a source of horror. She haunted his dreams.

Not that his theft had helped. He was sure that it was the old hag. She had cursed Rat and his family, and that was why his mother died, and his little brother too. That was why his father took him to France with him to fight.

Rat was all alone now. His father died assaulting a town, and since then Rat had scratched a living like his namesake. This English company had adopted him.

There was nowhere else for him to go. The world was scary outside the company.

* * *

She was dead. Auffroy crouched at her side in the middle of the town, his hand over his eyes to conceal the bodies from his view.

How could this happen? How could she do this to herself, to their son? She had been complaining, weary, miserable, but to do this? How could God allow it? Was it the arrival of the English that had pushed her over the edge? Why would God permit English murderers to come and cause such horror that a young woman would kill herself and her son?

God, he prayed, *bring justice, bring peace, and bring back my woman and son!*

But He was not listening. There were too many voices clamouring for His attention as the English plundered, burned, and slaughtered across the land; He had no time for the villagers here, for the men and women slain, and not for Auffroy's lover and their child.

* * *

Perkin Puttock was working at the collapsed pigsty when he heard the clattering of hooves on the road.

It was a dry day, thanks to God, but cold. The ice had melted, but the mud was thick and cloying, the red soil covering the yard area. His boots were already smothered in it. He could feel the chill seeping into his toes through the thin leather.

He unbent from his toil, the adze heavy in his hand from smoothing the timber for the door frame. Cupping a hand over his eyes, he peered along the road. A small party: perhaps a single rider, he thought. It was not a cause for concern, of course. This was England, and since the famine, many years before Perkin was born, the kingdom had been at peace. Not in the borderlands of the Scottish and Welsh marches, but here there was little need to fear outlaws and murderers. Especially in January, when the roads were icy and sleeping rough was likely to kill a man.

'Who is it?' Simon Puttock called. His father was sitting on his favourite seat out near the chickens, wrapped in blankets. His hearing was as acute as ever, but his eyes were blinded with age, and he turned his head this way and that to discern the rider's direction.

'Just one rider, Father.'

Simon grunted. 'No doubt some blasted traveller demanding bread and ale before our fire,' he grumbled.

Perkin nodded – pointlessly, since his father could not see – and continued staring, hand over his eyes against the sun's glare. For him, any visitor was a source of interest and news. Here, on the outskirts of Sandford, some miles from Crediton in the county of Devon, it was rare to see men who were not from the scattering of cottages nearby. The nearest news from farther afield came from the sermons given by the priest at Mass. Not that there was ever much. Only the usual complaints about the devious French stealing the crown from King Edward.

The way the rider came on at a brisk canter was familiar. He rode loosely, at ease in the saddle, and as he turned down into the track to the house, he stood up in the stirrups and waved.

Perkin broke into a broad grin as he recognised his friend William of Furnshill. 'It's Will.'

Simon grumpily pulled a face. 'So, no bread but we'll soon be dry of ale.'

* * *

Gadiffer found Auffroy at her side, and the two stood over the two bodies. Auffroy racked with silent sobs.

'How could she?' he asked.

'She was despairing,' Gadiffer said.

Auffroy picked up the tiny bundle at her side, the linen wrap still damp from the boy's blood, clutching him to his breast. He pushed his face into the little figure, his grief overflowing. 'She knew I loved her, and him!'

'But she couldn't provide for them. And with the English coming closer, what did you expect? The townspeople couldn't offer to support her and him. She knew that. Just as she knew that without admitting who the father was, she would be deserted. You should have admitted to being the father!'

'I would have, if I'd known she was...'

'But you *didn't*!' Gadiffer snapped. 'And *that's* why my sister is dead: because you wanted to protect your good name!'

* * *

'You want to do *what*?' Simon repeated, disbelieving.

Perkin and he had invited Will into their home, and Perkin had enthusiastically built up the fire. Simon sat on his chair before it, the blankets thrown from his shoulders and hanging over the back of the seat, so he could feel the flames on his face.

'Yes.'

'Your father will have plenty to say about that,' Simon said.

'He will not like it, but I have to do this,' Will responded. 'I have to seek my fortune, and the best place to do that is in France. Others are going and finding treasure and glory, and I must too. My Lord de Courtenay has given me permission, and I'll go as soon as may be.'

'Well, I'll wish you godspeed,' Simon said. He yawned, and his chin fell to his breast. Perkin was not certain how old he was, but he thought his father must be nearly seventy, and Perkin gazed at him affectionately as he began to snore.

'He looks tired,' Will said.

'Aye,' Perkin agreed. 'He's an old man now. Everything tires him.'

'How is your sister?'

'Well enough. Busy with grandchildren, mostly.'

'She was always a good woman,' Will said.

'What are you getting at?'

Will's face radiated innocence. 'Me?'

'I know you, Will. I know the way your mind works.'

'You're too suspicious, Perkin.'

'Yes, well, it's easy to be suspicious of a man like you.'

Will put on an offended expression. 'That's unkind. What have I ever done to deserve that?'

'Oh, no!' It dawned on Perkin.

'What?'

'I'm not going to France.'

'I wouldn't expect you to,' Will said, hurt. 'Why would you think something like that?'

'I can't. Who would look after my father?'

'Of course you can't.'

'That was why you were asking about my sister!'

'No, no. I was just...'

'No. The answer is no.'

'That's fine. I quite understand,' Will said. And he smiled.

At the village, while the vintaine's men went in to search for food or treasure, the Rat stayed near the rest of the men, trembling in the cold. Arn was nearby, shoulders hunched in an attempt to keep the warmth inside him, but Rat knew it wouldn't help. He wanted to go and lie down in front of a fire in one of the houses, but he daren't go without the men here. The houses were too like the ones from home: small, dilapidated. He could see the little orchard behind a couple, and instantly thought of the hag who had cursed him and his family. All for a few apples.

When he looked at the clouds, sometimes, or

glanced at rocks in a wall, he saw her face staring back at him, as though she was following him all the time, watching him, waiting, ready to pounce.

It was not only the cold that made him shiver. It was the certainty that she was following him, that she would take revenge one day.

4

Dogbreath returned to the vintaine with his prize.

'What is *that*?' Hawkwood demanded.

'A boy. He's scared out of his wits, but he's not hurt,' Dogbreath said.

Arn and Rat eyed the lad with disdain. The men of the vintaine paid him little attention. They had all seen plenty of orphans in the last weeks. With so many companies wandering about France, there was no shortage of bodies. Many men had died in the French armies; more had died when companies raided in their area, killing peasants in their own homes or fields. Mothers were all too often taken and used, either raped as a town was captured, or kept as marching wives, joining the ever-growing party of camp followers, some of them happy to leave a miserable marriage and attach themselves to an English archer, others forced to against their will. It meant that there was an increasing number of children who had lost both parents. While mercenaries would often kill the children at the same time as firing the houses and slaughtering the parents, sometimes the orphans were left alive, to scrabble some sort of living from the remains of their homes.

'What do you want to do with that?'

'I thought you'd have a use for him. We need boys to look after ponies, don't we? This one could help. He can fetch and carry, can't he? Not as if the bratchet will eat much. He looks like he's never eaten more'n a spoon of oats a day, don't he?'

'If you say so,' Hawkwood said. 'What of the farmstead?'

'Empty. This boy's the only one left. There're bodies out back of the house. I reckon some company came here a week or so ago, killed the father and mother, and didn't find this 'un. They took all the food and wine, though,' he added despondently. Then he cheered up. 'But there's three chickens and I reckon must be eggs. And this dog. I'm going to call him Midden.'

'A dog?' Hawkwood repeated. 'Why call him that?'

'He smells like one.'

Hawkwood shook his head. 'Aye, well, hurry and catch the chickens. We have work to do. Arn, Rat, take this pathetic little bundle and look after him, yes? Don't let him run away or you'll get a thrashing. Go!'

* * *

They rode on for some miles, reaching a town that had already been assaulted. From a distance Hawkwood could see three buildings still smouldering gently, the smoke rising on the still, cold air and then flattening out, as if meeting a ceiling of glass that prevented it rising further. However, many of the inhabitants were still there, or had returned after fleeing for their lives.

It was a simple task to take the place. The people were in no mood to deny the vintaine's entry. Like so many French folk, they had already suffered enough and put up no defence as the cavalcade rode in, a group of men on ponies, with one dog following.

Peter and his vintaine went to the farther side of the town while Hawkwood and Robin entered from the west. The paltry imitation of a wall was no obstruction to the men – it had been started but never completed, and much of it remained as piles of stone ready to be used.

The usual weeping and wailing, the usual desperation, the usual resentment from the younger men, the
usual pitiful cries from the womenfolk. But in the
middle of the town there was a pair of bodies set apart
from the others.

'They died when the last routiers came through,'
the leader of the town said. He was a man of middle
years, with a receding hairline and prematurely grey
hair. He glowered at the vintaine, but made no effort to
protect himself or his town: he knew full well that any
such attempt would only lead to his own death, and
probably those of other townspeople.

Hawkwood frowned. 'And you haven't buried them
yet?'

'The murderers killed our priest,' the man said
shortly. 'We have no one to hold a funeral. And the
woman there, and her son, are not to be buried in the
village cemetery in any case.'

'Why so?'

'She killed her son, and then herself,' the man said.
He looked up at Hawkwood with a fierce resolution.
'You want her to pollute our cemetery?'

'What of her husband?'

'She has no husband. Her son was born in shame,
and she died in shame. She must be damned, and
cannot be interred here. We have to find a place to put

her body. A crossroads would be best, but we have to find the best place. The child too. He was not christened.'

'Take her now and find a place for her,' Hawkwood growled. 'Else I will see that others have to be buried with her.'

Auffroy wanted to go to him and punch and kick him for his words against Juliot and Jacquotin. He was close to marching to him and attacking him there, before the whole town and these latest English murderers, but Gadiffer's hand on his arm kept him back. Gadiffer was her brother – what right did Auffroy have to take revenge for the insult given to her? He had not had the courage to proclaim his love for her while she was alive.

If he had, if he had taken her under his roof, perhaps Juliot and Jacquotin would still be alive now. If not, they would both be eligible for their own places in the church's graveyard.

Whereas now, both were doomed. A suicide, and an unbaptised child. They would never reach Heaven. Their only hope was the symbol of Christ she bore about her throat. Perhaps that would be seen by an angel, and she would be forgiven and accepted into God's grace? It was his only hope.

When Gadiffer pulled him away, Auffroy yielded, stumbling like an old drunk. His life was gone, along with his woman and son.

* * *

Arn and Rat saw to the ponies with the other boys, while some of the men searched houses, and others sat in the tavern and demanded drinks. The host wore a face as long as a horse himself, serving men whom he knew would not pay. But providing drinks at least would mean they didn't attack him or destroy his tavern.

'What's your name?' Arn demanded of the boy from the farm. He gazed at Arn without comprehension, wide-eyed, and said nothing.

Rat tried, 'I'm Rat. Who are you?' But he received the same response. The boy seemed to shrink in upon himself as though fearing the two would shortly attack him.

'Fool!' Arn said, and slapped the boy on the cheek. He fell to the ground instantly, a hand to his face and sobbing silently, and Arn kicked him experimentally. The boy rolled into a ball.

'What you do?' Fulk demanded. 'Hey? Why?'

The two boys moved away quickly. The Swiss was huge, and terrifying in anger.

'Nothing, we just wanted... we asked his name,' Rat said.

Fulk strode to the boy and squatted before him, glaring at Arn and Rat and muttering, '*Unsinn.*' Fulk squatted before the boy, who was still weeping and snivelling. '*Qu'est ce que ton nom?*'

'*Suis* Henri.'

Fulk glanced round at the other two boys. 'This boy's name is Henri. If you cannot speak French, ask one of the men to help. Do not hurt him. Show sympathy, *ja?* He has had a hard life, just as you two.'

Arn and Rat gave sulky agreement.

'If I learn you have hurt him, I will see you beaten, yes?'

Both boys had respect for the Swiss. He was alarming to them: tall, fierce, and threatening, and when he frowned, they trembled. They did not want to upset him. Going to see to the horses, they left Henri to his own devices.

'Bet he won't last long,' Arn said with a grunt of disgust. 'He's too weedy.'

* * *

The town was resentful the next morning when Hawkwood ordered five of the townsfolk to dig a grave at the nearest crossroads and bury the two bodies in it. 'And make sure it is deep enough. I will come to see and if it's not deep enough, I'll have you dig it twice as deep and put one of you in there with the woman,' he added.

His words were accepted with grim discontent, but the men put the two bodies onto a handcart and soon were trudging off to the north with shovels and pickaxes over their shoulders. Hawkwood watched them go, and then signalled to Dogbreath and Saul. 'Go after them and make sure they do a good enough job. But keep your eyes open, and beware of ambushes.'

'Why me? Send Seth or Nick,' Dogbreath said.

'I need someone there I can trust,' Hawkwood said.

'You blame him? He doesn't want your feet stinking out the whole town,' Ingram said with a grin.

Dogbreath glared at him. Then said: 'I'll go, but find me some shoes for when I return. Either that or a cordwainer who can resole this one.'

Hawkwood nodded in agreement as the two went to fetch their ponies.

'Why you do this?' Fulk rumbled as Hawkwood

turned away from the sight of the men disappearing through the wall's gate.

'It is the way of things, of course. How else do you dispose of the bodies? The child wasn't baptised, so he cannot join others in a Christian cemetery; his mother was a suicide, so she can't either. They have to be buried at a crossroads, and she has to have a stake through her heart.'

'*Ja*. I understand. It is different in my canton.'

'Yes?'

'We believe that the self-murderer must be punished as any other murderer. The man, he must hang; the woman must be burned on a pyre.'

'In England we believe the felon will not walk and cause harm if the stake is driven through her heart,' Hawkwood said, confident in the superiority of the English system.

'I have heard of a town where they did not do this also, and there were months of bad weather,' Fulk said. He shrugged. 'They had to dig up the body of this woman and throw it into the Rhine. Then the weather, it was better again.'

'I don't know where the nearest river would be,' Hawkwood said lightly. It was not a matter that concerned him.

'*Ja*. I hope that you are right,' Fulk said.

'What do you mean?'

'Only that if the soul remains restless, you may have set it free to attack people here. Or follow us.'

* * *

Auffroy watched the men load her body onto a cart and set off on the road to the crossroads. It was not a great distance, and he wanted to follow to see what happened, but he knew that would be dangerous. Not that it was any less dangerous to remain here in the town while the vermin, these murderers, were in occupation. He saw the little group disappear on the road northwards, the handcart pushed by one man, the others resentfully carrying their pickaxes and shovels behind, the two mercenaries on their horses.

While they were here, he must remain. The English were known for their violence and brutality, and he should remain here in case there was a fight. He still had his long-bladed knife at his belt, and he could kill some of them before he died, he swore. 'Dear God, help me to see them die,' he pleaded.

5

Rat was disgruntled at being told off by Fulk. It wasn't him who kicked the boy, was it? No, that was Arn. If anyone should get told off or beaten, it was him. It made Rat angry that he was given the blame along with Arn. It wasn't *fair*.

Henri was squatting in a corner with a chunk of bread, which he scoffed quickly like a dog fearing another might take his food, and Rat was tempted to take it from him as a matter of principle, just to show that he was the bigger, stronger boy – but he didn't. It was not that he knew he didn't have to prove anything, it was merely the fear that Fulk would learn of it, and then his punishment would be severe. Rat could not even protect himself by threatening Henri, since the boy didn't understand plain language.

Rat left him and went up the road to where a house still smouldered. It was one of those fired by the earlier company before the three vintaines' arrival. The walls still stood, but the roof was gone, and the floor was a mess of scorched timbers and various belongings of the last inhabitants. He idly kicked at the ashes, searching for anything that could be useful. Remains of a table, broken shards of pottery, a wooden board, badly scorched, but then, beneath it, when he kicked it aside, he saw metal glint. It was a metal spoon, and he picked it up gingerly, using a corner of his shirt to stop it burning his fingers. The metal was still hot to the touch, and he rubbed at it and blew on it to cool it. He would keep that safe, he decided. His own spoon was a cracked wooden one.

It was outside that Rat first saw the man dressed in lead-coloured clothing with a hood and cloak of russet. At the time he thought little of it. The man was probably just one of the townspeople, he assumed, and put the man from his mind.

More important was his new spoon. It would last a lifetime.

* * *

Later that afternoon, when Dogbreath and Saul returned with the grim men of the village, Peter glanced at the road. 'All good?'

'They were as meek and well behaved as nuns in their church,' Dogbreath said. 'Not a word of protest.'

'And you saw them put a stake through them both?'

'The woman, aye. Seemed little point with the baby. They just threw him on top of her,' Dogbreath said. He wrinkled his nose. 'One of the men, the youngest, he was snivelling a bit. I think she was his sister or something, but they gave us no trouble.'

'Good.'

Rat was with them. He was still playing with his new spoon. It was bound now with a thong about the handle, and it dangled from his throat like a crucifix. He fondled it through his shirt, looking forward to eating with it. He was sure that the supper today would be a pottage, as usual, and he would be able to enjoy it with this symbol of affluence.

He was not the sole member of the company who was happy that afternoon. It was only a little later that he heard a joyous cry, and when he peered up the street, he saw Dogbreath capering.

Intrigued, Rat walked up to see what Dogbreath was doing.

A man was standing beside Dogbreath, mournfully looking down at his bare feet, while Dogbreath balanced badly, attempting to pull on the man's boots, standing on one foot, hopping as he almost fell. The little silver cross at his breast glinted and gleamed as he clumsily bounded about. His old boots lay discarded at his feet. 'Rat! Come here, you turnip! I need your help!'

Rat hurried to his side, when instructed, and stood still as the mercenary leaned on his shoulder, trying to pull the boot on. At last he gave up and sat on the ground to pull them on.

'Look at these, Rat, eh? Good enough for at least a hundred-mile march, I swear! I knew this town would be good for me!' he crowed. Then he paused and looked about him. 'Where's my dog? Where's Midden?'

* * *

It was hideous. Seeing the cross, Auffroy felt his world fracture about him.

His only hope had been that the cross might save Juliot's soul. It was the only proof to God that she was a good Christian. He almost drew his knife, intending to hurtle down the street and smite the filthy little mercenary where he balanced on his one foot, demanding that the boy should stand still so he could pull on the boot.

Why didn't Raymon stab him where he was? Raymon could draw his knife and stab the shameless murderer under the armpit, shove deeply and it should reach his heart, if the bastard had one!

But then Auffroy took his hand away from his knife. If he were to attack the English here, there would be reprisals against the whole town. The place would be destroyed. It had happened all over France, he knew, and he wouldn't have that on his conscience. No, he would have to get his revenge another way.

Auffroy would find this man alone. He would take the man's life, just as he had robbed other people of their belongings. These English knew only murder and plunder. They would pay for it in this world or the afterlife, but this man, he would pay first!

6

It was a good sight, Sir James Pipe reckoned. All across the Beauce, towns, villages, farms, were burning. The valley of the Seine was impassable for trade or travellers. The English and Navarrese companies had blocked off all the routes through it. Sir James had based himself at Épernon, with a clear path east and south, where he would bring fire and death to all the peasants.

There was news of more troubles in Paris. It was amusing, really, Sir James considered as he sat back in the great chair on the dais in the hall, drinking from a gilded goblet, his feet on the table before him. Yes, quite entertaining. The King of France, John the second, had been caught after Poitiers and now rested in

Windsor at the pleasure of King Edward. But he needed money to pay the exorbitant ransom demanded. Sir James didn't know how much it would work out to, but he knew that King John's son, Charles the dauphin, had nothing. From the men whom the English had captured and questioned, it was clear that the dauphin's regime was collapsing. He had no money. Even his garrisons, who were supposed to be protecting the realm from English and Navarrese bands, were forced to demand food with menaces from the populations they were guarding.

The peasants were growing restless under the never-ending demands of ever greater taxes to pay for the war, to pay for ransoms, and now to pay for the king. The government was itself crushed under the lack of finances, along with the loss of so many administrators and officials – they had died, slaughtered by English arrows at Poitiers.

Yes, France was now a ripe plum, ready to be plucked from her tree, Sir James felt.

There were rumours that the Estates General were meeting to discuss the financial catastrophe that was bludgeoning France into the ground. Some said that the currency was to be devalued, others that the city of Paris itself was growing radical, that they might refuse to pay for the king's ransom, that the city itself might elect its own government, even that Charles of Navarre might take over the government of France. He did, after all, have a strong claim.

That would be interesting, Sir James thought. He was proud to serve his own king, of course, but Charles was a good ally, and a man of foresight and courage might wax with the backing of a man of such authority and power.

Authority and power, plainly, would mean money and success to those who served his interests. Sir James lifted his goblet in a toast to money, success, and his own glory.

* * *

Arn gave a sudden shriek and sat up.

The vintaine was sleeping in the town still, and the boys had their own beds in the hayloft over the horses. It was cosy, and the boys all revelled in the comfort after so many days of living on the roads, making the most of any hollow they could with a blanket to snuggle in, generally keeping together for warmth. Now they could lie on their blankets and pull the excess over them and enjoy some space to themselves.

'What is it?' Rat demanded.

Henri and the other boys all looked about anxiously. One of the youngest gave a sharp cry, thinking that there was a fire and they would all be smothered in flames in the hay.

Arn shamefacedly turned to Rat. 'I think a mare came to me and made me dream of that mother and her son buried today. I had the feeling that they were coming here.'

'Why would they come here? *We* did nothing to her.'

'Wandering spirits don't need to know their victims,' Arn said. He was pale-faced in the dark loft, and with the silvery light of the moon, he looked as though he might be a wraith himself. That thought made Rat shiver.

'I don't know what you have heard, but I'm sure ghosts don't seek out strangers,' he said defensively, but he glanced about him quickly, just to make sure.

The other boys watched them with keen anxiety. Arn and Rat were the oldest of the entire party of boys at ten or eleven years. These were the fellows who would take the archers' ponies in battles, and perform the tasks of a groom at all other times. They were young, for the most part, some the sons of archers or the female camp followers, while some, like Henri, had been found along the way. All felt the same lurching fear deep in their bowels to hear that it was possible they might be hunted by a ghost.

'She was buried with a stake in her heart,' Rat said dismissively, with a certainty he did not feel. It was well known that often a mare would bring a dream that was a prediction, a foretaste of something to happen in the future.

'Was the baby as well?'

'Who cares? What could a baby do to us?' Rat said. His own mind was too filled with thoughts of the witch.

Arn was shivering, Rat saw, and it made him feel queasy. If Arn could be so scared, it was something that had really got to him. Rat looked about him uneasily, but there was no ghostly visitation he could see. 'Get on! You just dreamed it. 'Tis nothing.'

'I can see her coming,' Arn said and shuddered. 'She'll get us all.'

'She can't. She's been staked.'

'Her baby pulled it out.'

Rat didn't like the sound of that. 'The baby was too small, too young.'

'I don't know, but she's going to get us.'

'You're a baby,' Rat said contemptuously, but as he rolled over in his blanket, he felt the chill of fear lick at his soul. He saw that baby and his mother in their grave, and saw them claw their way out, walking swiftly together towards the town.

And behind them, he thought he saw the old hag again, smiling evilly, holding out an apple as if to tempt him.

He snapped his eyes shut and squirmed deeper into the hay.

Robin pulled the girth tight, and when the horse rolled his eyes at him, Robin punched it in the stomach. The horse jerked, and he yanked the girth another two notches tighter. 'You devious old bastard,' he muttered, but not angrily. It was just the way of this brute to try to keep the saddle looser and less restrictive.

He was going to ride about the town and check that the roads were all safe, but as he led his horse from the barn, he glanced up to see three of the boys peering over at him from the hayloft. 'What are you all doing this late abed? Come on, down the ladder, you lazy dollypolls! You have work to do.'

They did not immediately spring into action. Something about them was off, he realised. Two lads did reach for the ladder and descend – they were

Berthelot and Garnot – and then he saw Rat, before Henri and Crespin. Last of all came Arn.

The Rat, as all the vintaine knew, was generally a quiet, watchful type, whereas Arn was usually the louder, bullying sort. Arn tried to lord it over the rest of the boys, with the sort of cruelty that only an older boy would inflict on his inferiors, or those whom they considered inferior. While most of the boys scurried to their work, Henri included, Rat and Arn were reluctant to leave Robin's side, and that in itself was curious. 'What is it?'

Arn hung his head, and it was Rat who answered. 'Arn thinks that the woman buried yesterday isn't easy in her grave. He reckons she's going to rise and come and assault us.'

'You really think that?' Robin asked with a thin smile as he looked at Arn.

'She's coming. I'm sure of it. You know what they say about these souls who aren't proper pinned down? Well, I saw her rising from her grave. It was a message, honest. She's coming, and she—'

'Stop that!' Robin cut him off curtly. The boy was obviously terrified, and that was the sort of fear that could become contagious. It had plainly affected Rat as well. 'It's nonsense. She was properly staked. Dog-breath was there, and he saw it. She won't rise again.

Besides, if she was going to come back and haunt someone, she'd haunt the man who gave her the child, or the men who came and attacked the town. Not us.'

'Ghosts don't care who they hurt,' Arn said with desperate determination. 'Why would the mare give me this dream if not to warn me?'

'I don't know, but if you don't get on with your duties, you'll have a more alarming prospect than a wraith in the night. You'll have Hawkwood coming to find you,' Robin said, and the certainty in his voice was enough to send the boy mournfully wandering back to the horse lines outside to start their daily routine.

Rat glanced over his shoulder at Robin as the vintener led his horse out into the sunshine. But then Rat realised that his spoon was no longer bound about his neck. It must have fallen out of his shirt in the night while he squirmed in his sleep. He would have hurried back to the hayloft to find it, but the others were already about their duties. Besides, he thought, glancing up at the ladder to the hayloft, no one else would find it. No one else would know it was there.

* * *

Robin mounted, but before he left the town, he trotted over to where he saw Dogbreath sitting at a table, a hunk of bread and cheese before him, and a large pot of wine in his hand.

'What's that about your neck?'

'Just a little cross I found,' Dogbreath said defensively. He tucked it away in his shirt.

It was none of Robin's business. 'Dogbreath, tell me, when the men buried that woman and her child, they did stake her, didn't they?'

'Aye. I watched them, and they stuck it into her heart, just before they threw her into the grave. Baby on top of her. Why?'

'One of the boys had a mare last night, and believed that she had escaped her grave and was coming to get us all.'

Dogbreath sneered. 'Doesn't he know that a staked body won't walk?'

'Apparently not.' Robin spurred his mount, and was soon trotting easily through the town's streets.

He saw one man, a fellow in dark clothing with a russet hood and cloak, who watched him closely as he rode past, but Robin paid him little attention. All the inhabitants of this town were likely to stare at the English. It was part jealousy, part loathing, he knew, but they didn't matter. They were only sheep ready to be shorn.

* * *

Auffroy watched him go with the dull, unseeing eyes of the despairing. His life was ended, but now he was beginning to feel a rising fury against the smaller, wizened mercenary, the man who had robbed Juliot of her last possession and deprived her of salvation.

He must have his revenge.

And with that in mind, he began to talk to other men about the town.

7

As soon as he could, Rat hurried up to the hayloft, and began to hunt for his spoon. But it was not on his blanket, and when he felt in the hay all about it, there was no sign of it.

It was here, somewhere, in among all the straw, but finding it was next to impossible. They had picked this spot because the straw was so thick and deep, it would keep them warm, but its depth meant his spoon could be anywhere. It was as lost as it would be falling into the river. The difference was, back at home at the river, he would have been able to see it. Here, it was lost forever.

He sat back mournfully. It was only a thing. He had lost so much already in his life that one more thing was just that: one more thing. It was a spoon, not as important as losing his mother or his father, but it was something he had valued. It was precious to him, something that was his, and his alone.

He could feel the tears brimming, but he would not succumb to them. That would lead to ridicule, and he would not tolerate that.

Still, he could have wept.

* * *

William rode to the main door of the manor at Furnshill with a degree of trepidation. He knew that his father would be against his leaving to go to war, but he was determined.

His older brother was there in the doorway as he rode up and dismounted, handing the reins to a groom.

'Brother, I hope you are well? It has been many months,' Baldwin said.

'Brother, I hope you are too,' William said.

The two had never been close. Baldwin was named after their father and, as the oldest, would inherit Sir Baldwin's manor and lands, whereas William would have nothing, except that which Baldwin decided to supply.

The difference in their positions led to a distance between them. William would have liked to have felt more close to Baldwin, but there were too many years between them. Sometimes he felt that Baldwin would have liked to have confided in him, that Baldwin would have appreciated a loyal companion, a man in whom he could trust. But their paths had diverged from early on.

'How is Father?' William asked.

'He is well enough. He keeps himself fit with riding and practising with his sword, but he is old now. He will be glad to see you,' Baldwin said. His manner was stiff and officious. He truly had little idea how to communicate.

William smiled and stalked to the door, calling to the bottler for wine, and soon he was standing before the fire in the hall, his tunic lifted so the warmth could reach his buttocks.

'Father, I have news,' he said.

* * *

The disaster came the very next day.

Robin and Hawkwood had already decided that they had outstayed their welcome here, and it was a matter of common sense to depart before the townsfolk grew more restless. Yes, the company could have killed one or two to encourage better behaviour for the rest, but both men knew full well that it would take only a small spark to ignite the more hot-headed inhabitants into full-scale revolt, and while the English were very competent fighters, it was one thing to stand in an open field with longbows and defend against even men in armour, and quite a different thing to be forced to fight against a whole town in the narrow streets and alleyways, when overhead there was the risk of rocks being dropped on a man's head, and when people might suddenly appear from alleys or even windows to attack. Better by far to cut their losses and leave before the town rose up against them.

Hawkwood had taken the town's blacksmith as a hostage, over the protestations of his wife and the community's leader, but Hawkwood felt sure that the populace would regret much more losing their smith compared with any other member. He swore that he would release the man, provided that the townsfolk did not try to follow and attack the company. If they were attacked, the smith would be the first man to die. Hawkwood had the feeling that he might return here someday, and when he did, he preferred to think that the people would consider him a man of his word, rather than someone who was so feared that they might lose nothing by resisting him.

They rode out in good order, the camp followers close on their heels, and the way seemed clear ahead. Much of their route was in woods, and Robin kept a wary eye open among the trees for any signs of men laying an ambush for them.

'Look at them, fit almost good as the old ones,' Dogbreath said, holding up one boot to show off to a bored Saul.

'They'll soon rot, just like your other ones.'

'No, these are better quality. 'Sides, the last ones were on his feet in the rain for a day or two.'

'He was walking in the rain?'

'No, he was dead. I found them after Poitiers,' Dogbreath said, turning his foot this way and that to admire his latest acquisition.

'You stole a dead man's shoes?' Gervase asked, aghast.

'He din't need 'em,' Dogbreath pointed out, ''sides, the dead can't complain.'

'Suddenly the smell of your feet is explained,' Gervase said. He was a taller man, with the expression of a bishop with piles: pained but earnest.

Ingram laughed.

'Eh?'

'He means your feet smell like a rotted corpse,' Seth explained kindly.

Dogbreath's expression darkened. 'Oh, aye?'

'Wait!' Robin called, but the men weren't listening. Most were jogging along with smiles while Dogbreath summoned his linguistic skills to respond.

He found the words at last. 'You *bastard*!'

That was when the first man fell from his horse.

Robin bellowed, '*Ambush!*'

* * *

Robin kicked his feet from the stirrups and threw himself from his horse, quickly grabbing his bow and a handful of arrows from the canvas quiver at his saddle. He strung the bow quickly, nocking an arrow. The blacksmith, he saw, was already bolting for the trees, and Robin quickly drew, aimed, and loosed. The smith tumbled headlong with a clothyard in his back. Dogbreath and Saul both had their own bows ready, Fulk beyond them, while Hawkwood remained on horseback, shouting commands.

There was a flash in the trees ahead, but Robin didn't loose. He wanted a firm target. At last he saw one, a dark figure in the trees, who stood with a spanned crossbow. As soon as he saw the man, Robin drew and released, and he saw the arrow fly straight and true. The man disappeared, his bolt flying harmlessly high overhead. Robin already had a third arrow nocked, and when another figure appeared, he was about to loose when the figure disappeared, dropping back behind bushes. The undergrowth would deflect his arrow: better to wait for a more certain kill.

Glancing over his shoulder, he saw that Rat, Arn and the other boys were cowering near the carts. Robin urgently signalled them to remain where they were.

There came a shout from the van, and Robin saw Hawkwood, sword drawn, wave his sword about his head twice. Robin recognised the signal – Hawkwood was going to enter the woods with his vintaine. 'Loose at will!' Robin called to his own men, and they started a withering fire on the area with four arrows each, rapidly. As soon as the arrows were spent, Robin called for them to halt, and then led his men at a brisk trot to the edge of the woods.

With Hawkwood angling around to get behind the enemy, Robin and his own vintaine entered the woods to the front. Peter and his men had joined Hawkwood's, and there were already cries and screams. Robin got his hosen caught on brambles, but forced his way onwards, ignoring the scratches. A man appeared in front of him, and he was about to lift his bow when an arrow appeared to sprout from his breast, and he fell to his knees, hands clutching the missile with horror, his eyes moving from it to Robin.

Robin kicked him and the man fell over with a gasp, and Robin stabbed his throat with his ballock knife, jerking it up to sever the artery and his windpipe, then he was past him and heading towards the middle of the woods, his blade greasy with blood. The trees were tall and blanketed out the light and, as he went onwards, the undergrowth disappeared, and he could see groups of struggling men in front of him, another man running, too far for Robin to catch him, dressed in dark grey and russet, but Robin had others to think of. Seeing Hawkwood and Dogbreath struggling with three others, Robin ran to support them, slamming into the back of one, stabbing the second.

His arrival was enough. The man he ran into was spitted on Hawkwood's sword, while Dogbreath despatched the third, and then slashed the second's throat, his eyes wide with fury. 'Ambush me, would ye, ye murdering bastard! *That's* for scratching my arm!'

Robin knew better than to get close to Dogbreath when he was in a fighting mood. Just now he was likely to mistake even friends for an enemy, and Robin stood clear while Dogbreath stabbed again and again.

His victim was already dead long before Dogbreath had ceased his wild attack.

'Who were they?' Hawkwood wondered.

'They could be anyone,' Robin considered. 'They didn't seem particularly effective, so my guess would be locals called to defend the area.'

'Either that or another band of freelances,' Hawkwood said. He kicked at the nearest figure. 'Not that they would be likely to attack us. They'd surely realise we were professional.'

'Not necessarily. There are plenty of latecomers seeking enrichment,' Robin said. 'Perhaps these were some, and seeing us, they thought we might have plunder worth taking.'

'Possibly. *Dogbreath!* Leave him alone now. You don't have to carve the whole carcass. He isn't a bullock to be butchered.'

Dogbreath stared about him, panting, and then glanced down. 'Oh, the *bastard*! He's bloodied my boots!'

8

It had been carefully planned. They had waited far from the town, so none of the English, with their heads up their own arses, could have guessed that the ambush was from the men where they had been staying. Ymbelot and Helie should have waited, though. Ymbelot let off that first quarrel when it was far too early, the fool, and Helie should have been ready to back him up, but he missed, and when the mercenaries entered the woods, the other five threw down their weapons and tried to flee. They were all cut down, and only Auffroy and Huget had managed to get away in time, with Gadiffer leading their race away. Helie, Ymbelot and the others – all dead.

Auffroy sat down again, his head in his hands.

That foul one, the one who had taken Juliot and robbed and buried her, he was a very demon in battle. Auffroy had seen him, how he had whirled and spun, dealing death and then mutilating the bodies of his victims with the frantic ferocity of a devil, hacking and stabbing them until there was little recognisable.

He felt a fresh sob rising in his breast. It was not to be expected that these English killers would be easy to kill, but he had not expected them to rout his comrades with such ease. He had hoped to slay a few, and the rest to ride away. After all, people all said that the English were cowards as well as devils, and they should not have retaliated, nor sprung so swiftly to the attack.

Now he had lost his friends and the braver men of the town. Their feelings of guilt at not protecting the town against this company, nor the one before it, had spurred them to the attack here, and Auffroy's studied contempt had led them all to come here. And they were all dead apart from Huget, who would be halfway back to the town by now, and Gadiffer, who had lost his sister already, and was determined to help Auffroy avenge her.

Auffroy covered his face. He should return. This was a fool's errand. What was the point of following the company further? They would slaughter any group sent against them. Did he have the right to ask Gadiffer to join him in a foolish hunt like this? Gadiffer should go back and try to rebuild his life, the poor man. This was Auffroy's vengeance for the vile treatment of Juliot and their son.

The memory of Juliot's shameful death and the theft – which meant he could never see her again, even after death. No path to Heaven for her now. Not after that final indignity, which meant God and His angels would never be able to find her on the Day of Judgement, which meant that after his own death, Auffroy would not be able to find her or their child – that was enough to send a dagger of anguish into his skull like a sharp needle.

He would follow these violent, evil men, and he would have his revenge on that man. And if Gadiffer would join him, Auffroy would be glad of his aid.

9

NEAR ÉPERNON

February

They heard the screams some time before he appeared.

Rat ran and ran, his face red and blotched as he screamed, pelting through the undergrowth, scattering the twigs and branches he had collected, and out of the dark forest, falling to the ground as he reached the outskirts of the camp, still shrieking in terror.

They had moved on since the ambush in the trees, and now were in a new clearing at the edge of another forest, which gave the men good, clear views all about, and Hawkwood had detailed some men to keep just inside the woods as sentries. Meanwhile all the boys, once the horses had been fed and watered and rubbed down, had been sent in among the trees to fetch firewood. Now all the men stopped what they were doing as Rat burst from the trees, panting and blubbering, closely followed by the other boys, all petrified after hearing Rat's screams.

Fulk was first to reach him, the tall Swiss clutching his halberd in his right hand as he crouched, his left hand on the boy's shoulder, asking, '*Was ist's?* What is?' as the other men in the camp stood, weapons ready, moving together into fighting formation, the archers already nocking arrows to their bowstrings. They all had long experience of repelling attacks.

'What is it, boy?' Peter demanded, his eyes moving about the line of the trees, searching for any sign of danger.

'There, in there! I saw him!' the boy gasped, distraught.

'Who, boy?'

'The *Devil* himself. *He* was in there, and he killed Arn.'

* * *

Without any commands, the men had already formed tight arrowheads, triangles of men with bows ready, maximising their firepower with ease. Between them, the men-at-arms stood ready, weapons in their hands, forming a bristling hedgehog of spears and arrows.

No one came out. Peter and Fulk exchanged a look, Fulk still at the side of the boy, one of the camp followers, who snivelled and sobbed, his hands over his face. 'Calm down, Rat,' Peter said. 'Why do you say it was the Devil?'

'He was just like the pictures of him at church.'

'What does that mean?' Robin asked. He had joined Hawkwood and the trio, and now he crouched beside Rat, his eyes on the trees behind them. 'What exactly did you see?'

'A huge figure, with a dark grey tunic, and russet cloak and hood. He had horns, I think, and his eyes were red and... and – it was *him*!'

Robin and Hawkwood exchanged a glance over the boy's head. Robin was more than a little doubtful, and Hawkwood was certain that the Devil was unlikely to visit his company specifically.

'We go,' Fulk said.

Peter nodded, and the two crept forward, leaving the boy with Hawkwood and Robin. Peter drew his sword, while Fulk had his halberd gripped tightly in both fists.

The path the boys had taken was clear enough.

They had followed a track used by shepherds and goatherds. The undergrowth was flattened, twigs snapped from low trees and saplings, more twigs and branches collected by the two scattered at the side of the path, occasional hoofprints in the dry soil from tranters or other travellers.

The boy had said that the two were only a matter of a few hundred paces inside the woods when Arn had been grabbed and stabbed by the Devil. Fulk recalled what the boy had said: a figure in dark-coloured clothing with russet hood and cloak. Rat thought he was taller than a man, but that was from the perspective of a boy considerably shorter. The Rat was terror-struck, and it made Fulk step warily. He could understand why the boy might be terrified when surprised by a man in the trees, but that was different to saying it was the Devil who appeared and killed Arn.

The two men stepped cautiously, but at speed. Even a man-at-arms would be nervous in a thick forest where the trees could conceal a boar or a man with a ready crossbow.

'He said it was the Devil,' Fulk said thoughtfully.

'He's a boy. He was shit-scared out of his wits. Arn has filled his head with nonsense about the suicide in the town back there. I daresay he saw a black bird or a hog,' Peter said dismissively, ducking under a heavier bough. 'Or a big Frenchman who startled them, or who was startled by them.'

'Perhaps,' Fulk said. His eyes were fixed on the way ahead.

'You don't believe his story of the Devil being here?' Peter scoffed.

'I have seen many strange things in my life,' Fulk said. 'That suicide: Dogbreath, he said he had seen her with stake in the heart?'

Peter pulled a sneer but said nothing.

They had continued for some hundreds of yards when Peter saw the figure of the boy lying over a small bush ahead. He moved slowly to a crouch, eyeing the trees and bushes for any sign of a Frenchman with a weapon, but he saw nothing to alarm him. Fulk, at his side, was breathing heavily, both hands on his halberd's staff. The two rose at the same time, slowly making their way forward to where they could see the crimson stains on the boy's shirt.

* * *

The boy's shirt was beslubbered with blood. When Fulk peered, he could see the marks of the blade that had pierced the boy in so many places. 'The poor boy,' he said.

'This was no devil. This was a man with a knife,' Peter said.

Arn lay on his back, his hands crossed over his breast as though laid out ready for burial. It was a sight that made Fulk shiver.

'Not the Devil, then,' Peter said.

'Why you say this?'

'You think the Devil would willingly make the sign of the cross with the boy's arms? He might be clever and evil, but he wouldn't do that.'

'The poor boy.'

'Aye. Well, there are plenty of other boys suffering similar fates.'

Fulk nodded. Both knew the course of the various battles and fights that had swept over France in the last ten years or more. There were plenty of boys, young men, women and girls who had died in the various assaults against towns and villages. Villagers were just one form of plunder: objects to be used or cast aside. They were considered less than cattle. At least cattle could be eaten.

'The man who did this: *why*?' Fulk said. 'A dagger with a long blade, maybe.' He rolled the boy's figure over on to his back. 'Didn't Rat see the man?'

'I suppose he bolted as soon as he saw Arn

stabbed. He was so scared; that's why he thought he saw the Devil.'

'Arn must have cried out when the man did this to him.'

'Maybe,' Peter agreed. 'But you know as well as I do that a strong blow can take the air from a man's lungs. Stab him hard and fast, and he'll likely only gasp quietly. How much more true for a boy.' He gazed down at the figure, shaking his head. 'What a stupid waste. Arn was a good worker. Wonderful with the horses, reliable, mostly.' He sucked his teeth contemplatively. 'We'll have to get another boy trained to take his place. That new boy, Henri, that Dogbreath found, he'll have to learn fast. Come, let's take him back.'

Fulk nodded. As the larger of the two, he passed his halberd to Peter, then bent and picked up the boy, slinging him over his shoulder before taking back his weapon. He cast a look about him as he did so, suspiciously glancing at the vegetation for any indications of danger, but there was nothing evident.

'Is cold,' he said.

'You said you come from a country where the snow lies all year round,' Peter chuckled. 'And you feel cold here?'

'There is something,' Fulk rasped. 'Cold in the soul, perhaps.'

'Ach! You're just superstitious. It's a little chill, yeah, but that's because we're here under the trees. Come on!'

They started to walk back, Fulk glowering about him, fearing an attack at any moment. He had no idea what had happened here, but he could feel the flesh of his back crawling with anticipation. It was almost like running into battle, waiting for the strike of a bolt or arrow, but there was something else here. He could feel it. A shivering of evil.

* * *

'What happened in the woods, Rat?' Hawkwood asked.

He was squatting easily, the fire not far from him, and the boys all set about in a semicircle, with Rat in their centre.

Rat had the look of a boy petrified of a birching. His eyes moved from Hawkwood to Fulk and Peter, and then back, before dropping to the ground. 'We were all looking for sticks and branches, and I was looking on the ground for more, when I saw the Devil appear and stab Arn.'

'What did he look like?'

'He was tall enough, I suppose. Like you, sir. But he

had dark clothes, all black, and a hood of red and a cloak the same,' Rat said. He shivered like a man with the ague, and he kept licking his lips and blinking. His fists were clenched to stop them shaking. He had a sickness deep in his bowels, and he felt the terror once more, the stomach-chilling fear of death and revenge. The witch's face came to him again, and he shuddered like a birch in a gale.

'Have you seen this man before?'

'No! It was the Devil!' Rat shivered. 'Arn said he had been given a dream that the woman in the last town would come to get us. She must have called on the Devil to do it.'

'Why would he kill Arn?' Hawkwood said.

'He wanted to take his soul,' Rat said.

Hawkwood grunted. He was not prey to superstitions. In his time in France, from Calais to Poitiers and more recently, he had seen plenty of men who deserved to be taken by the Devil, but he had seen little enough proof of their souls' capture.

He looked over the rest of the boys. 'What of you? You were there with Arn and Rat, weren't you? Did any of you see this man?' He repeated the question in French for the boys who didn't know English. Henri was not alone in knowing few English words.

The boys shook their heads, all apart from one. It

was young Crespin, a pathetically under-nourished boy Saul had discovered in a town some weeks before. He looked so spindly and feeble, it was a miracle he managed to stay on his feet.

'Crespin, did you see someone like Rat described?'

'Y-yes, sir. Dark, dark clothes apart from his cloak and hood. I saw him. He was creeping along quietly, like he'd escape being seen or something. He had a dagger in his hand, and he scared me, so I ducked down so's he couldn't see me, but then I heard Rat roar, and followed him back here.'

'I see. Did anyone see where he went after he killed Arn?'

Rat shook his head. 'I ran. I was scared.'

Henri and Berthelot admitted that they had not waited to learn more when they heard Rat's screams of terror, and had both fled the woods in great urgency.

'It was the Devil,' Rat stated with certainty.

Hawkwood said nothing, but when he cast his eye about the vintaines, he saw that several of the men, those who were newer to the company, wore expressions that spoke of their own uncertainty.

'The Devil isn't following us,' he said irritably. But he was aware that his words had little impact on the men.

***

Gadiffer listened, but his face showed his concern.

'I miss her too. Juliot was such a bright, lively thing, and she was so happy when she fell pregnant, but after the birth, she grew despairing – you know that.'

'It wasn't my fault!' Auffroy declared. 'I still loved her, but it didn't matter what I said or did, she was so... so despondent.'

'Yes. She was more and more irritable, and anxious all the time. Even when she had a good sleep, she was exhausted the next morning. We did all we could, but it wasn't enough. When she heard that the English were near, it was enough to drive her to... to that.'

'And they buried her at the crossroads with a stake in her heart and stole her cross – her only hope of salvation,' Auffroy declared. 'Will you help me find it and kill the man who stole it from her?'

10

Later that evening, Hawkwood spoke with Robin. 'What do you think? I know Peter reckoned this is nonsense, but Fulk is less certain.'

'Dogbreath is sure that the body was properly buried, so it wasn't the ghost of the woman walking and summoning the Devil. It's more likely that it was a man, as the boy Crespin said. I don't see it as likely that this was some fallen angel or anything. The knife used to kill Arn was real enough, so the man was, too.' He paused. 'Rat was clearly terrified. I think the boy fears he'll come back.'

'He may. We must keep a wary eye open just in case. And when we find him, we'll kill him,' Hawkwood said.

Robin frowned. 'I recall seeing someone like that in the last town. A man of middle height, with russet cloak and hood. I didn't think much of it at the time, but it could have been the same fellow.'

'You think he could have followed us all the way here?'

'It wouldn't be a hard route to track, would it? We didn't conceal our passage. Anyone could have followed our hoofprints and wheels.'

'Why would he want to follow us – and why kill a boy like Arn?'

Robin mused, 'Maybe he stumbled over Arn and decided to kill him to keep him silent, but when Rat set up his din, he had to bolt?'

'Why kill anyone? All he need do was walk on as though he was a traveller passing by.'

Robin looked at him. 'You think any Frenchman seeing a party of English like us would think to stop and pass the time of day?'

'According to Crespin, he was already armed as though seeking to murder.'

'He likely wanted to protect himself. I doubt the boys were quiet. You know what they're like, chattering and squabbling like rooks in a rookery. No one could miss them. He would hear them from a long way off, so he knew that there were people about there. Approaching, he would just hear all that noise and think it was some more dangerous gathering, perhaps? He saw the boy, realised there were lots more people about, so killed Arn and made his escape.'

'He heard the row made by a few boys, and thought to draw a dagger?' Hawkwood shook his head. 'No. I think we are being followed for some reason, and I don't like it. Whoever this man is, I want him caught and killed for what he did to Arn.'

This was not territory Peter's men knew. The whole district was new to them. Fulk was sure that he could sense the presence of devils. It made him stare about him firmly, watching for any signs that could herald a vampire or demon.

There were plenty of men in the company who were fierce enough, he knew. The wizened little man everyone knew as Dogbreath, Robin the bowman, Saul, Hob, Seth, Nick, and others who had been with the Black Prince through many of his campaigns: men who knew no other task than war, and who were left at a loose end when the Prince left France to take his captive, King John II, to England.

Fulk had joined the company in the days before

Poitiers, but he had remained. His home was in the cantons, but here there was money to be taken, and there was nothing to take him home again. France was rich in gold and treasure, and he hoped to plunder enough to return to buy a small farmstead, marry again and raise a fresh family. He sighed at the memories, his Ilse, their child Jacquet. Both gone. It was much the same for so many others. One of the vinteners, John Hawkwood, had said as much. His brother had inherited all when his father died, and there was nothing for him there in England, so he had come here for adventure and profit. He had gained both.

There was evil everywhere in this country, Fulk felt, torn as it was by the warring groups, the peasants terrified of their own shadows, the effective lawmakers and upholders all gone, their servants and vassals slaughtered with them on the battlefields of Crécy, Poitiers, and more recently by the peasants and merchant classes who believed themselves betrayed by the nobility. Paris had risen against the dauphin, the heir to the throne. Those who had been at the battle of Poitiers, and those who survived, were viewed with disdain and often handled violently. More than one injured warrior had been attacked on the road, accused of cowardice – or of participating in a conspiracy against the people.

In the last months since he'd joined the English, he had seen that they had raised forces from England, Britanny and Guyenne. There were Brabants, Navarrese and even many French from the various regions. With his company, Fulk had marched east towards the middle of the country through areas accustomed to their plundering. Abbeys and priories emptied as news of the armies' advances spread, the occupants taking valuables and hiding them in specially created storage, whether it be a freshly dug cavern, or carefully hidden behind a false wall in the buildings, showing ever greater inventiveness in the face of the depredations of the English. Often one monk would be left to feed the animals and hope to preserve the buildings themselves, although all too often drunk English soldiers would set them alight from a plain, destructive impulse. If it was too heavy to move, or not valuable as a tradable commodity in exchange for wine or women, it would often be destroyed.

Fulk did not like to see such wanton destruction. For him, a house was a home for someone. To burn it to the ground was wasteful unless there was good reason. He did not understand the compulsion to destroy. Sometimes, he wondered whether there would be a reckoning for all this harm. Perhaps the death of poor Arn was just the beginning. A judgement, a payment for their desecration. It was a thought to make him shiver.

* * *

William of Furnshill had enjoyed a good evening. He was at the Sign of the Bear in Crediton, and there was a fair party of friends with him, drinking his health and cheering his valour at travelling all the weary miles to France, when all at once the noise died, and William looked up to see a familiar face in the doorway. 'Perkin!'

'I could hear your singing from Sandford,' Perkin said sternly. 'You make enough noise to waken all the bodies in the graveyard!'

'Well, they can join us, then!' William said.

'Don't say that, not even in jest,' Perkin said.

A barmaid approached Perkin, smiling. 'You want ale? I brewed this myself.'

Perkin took the drinking horn from her, a cheap pottery cup, and raised it in mock salute to William. 'Here's to the bold warrior, the fool who thinks he will make his fortune in France.'

'You'll see,' William said. He smiled broadly to conceal his increasing agitation. In truth, he was sure that this journey would make him find glory and honour. He wanted little more than a sum of treasure and his knighthood, and both would surely come to him. But there was still that niggling concern about what he would find in France. Would it be glory – or death?

'Yes, I will see.'

'I will send a messenger to let you know how I fare,' William said.

'That would be pointless,' Perkin replied.

'It would be a courtesy.'

'Will, you are a fool,' Perkin said.

The room was suddenly still.

'A fool? And you are a bastard!'

'Perhaps so, but at least I was born that way!'

Helena, the barmaid, gave a nervous laugh. Behind her, the host of the tavern had already reached for his blackthorn club. Giving insults to a trained esquire was a sure way to start a fight.

William glowered, and then grinned. 'Come, I won't have an argument with you today. Tomorrow I leave for France.'

'I know. And because you are a fool, and so inept you would clamber aboard a fishing vessel and be captured by slavers, I suppose I have to go with you and make sure you actually reach France safely. And there you'll need a man to guard your back.'

'You will come with me?' William said, his mouth falling open.

'Who else could be trusted with your safety?'

'More ale, Helena!' William shouted, and he embraced Perkin.

'Get off me,' his friend said. 'You're drunk.'

'So will you be, soon!'

* * *

The company was riding along a narrow track between tall trees, when Rat cried out, and the whole company wheeled to face whatever the threat might be, Dogbreath swearing loudly, and Robin springing from his horse to string his bow.

'What is it, boy?' Peter bellowed, alarmed.

'He was there! I saw him!' Rat said, pointing with a trembling finger. He had clearly caught sight of the russet material as the figure moved between the trees. Was it the Devil come to fetch him?

Robin stared into the wood, wondering. He thought momentarily that he saw a movement of russet or something similar, but assumed it could be a deer or fox, for it seemed very low to the ground. 'Who?'

'The devil from the woods, who killed Arn,' Rat

blurted, trying to control the sobs that threatened. 'It was him again, I'm sure!'

Hawkwood signalled to Robin to keep a close watch, and sent Fulk and Dogbreath in through the undergrowth, and although they continued on in the route indicated by Robin, they found nothing.

'It's like a ghost came down and watched us, ain't it?' Dogbreath said in a conversational tone.

Fulk said nothing. His feelings of wary awe and concern made him keep his eyes wide open, and his every sense alert. It was a relief to return to his horse, mount and be on his way.

It was no devil, he was sure. But equally, he was not convinced this was a human.

11

When they came to the top of a little hill, Hawkwood gazed ahead. There were a number of smaller farmsteads and villages, and he studied them with a professional's eye, taking in the appearance of each, assessing the likely value of the inhabitants, the type of property, the number of pastures, the way the buildings were laid out.

Here, some thirty miles south of Paris, some abbeys and priories were still open to the invaders, he knew. They mostly wanted to invest in their protection. The populations spent money on fortifications, but each town wanted to preserve itself against attack. Each had levied taxes on its populace, but that meant treasure was being spent in penny packets over lands that held hundreds of towns and villages, hundreds of churches, hundreds of castles and forts, thousands of small fortified houses. If John Hawkwood had been responsible for these territories, he would have used the money more wisely. It could have been used to protect cities large enough for all the locals to rush to and find accommodation, where they could congregate and form armies that could hold the English at bay; instead the money was frittered away in small sums at every municipality, perhaps to increase the height of the town's walls, filling in holes in the outer perimeters, acquiring new weapons for the men who needed them most.

But it was no good. The money raised by each town was never enough. The cities could afford better protection, but there was little time for them to spend all they needed.

Hawkwood could understand the desire of every man to protect his own house and lands, but it was a fruitless approach.

For all that, there were Frenchmen who were determined to defend their lands against the English. Some formed their own bands of a strength large enough to threaten smaller English war parties. Even with their greater size, they were no match for the professional fighters from England, who had already been fighting for up to ten years, and who were experienced.

But not all Frenchmen sought to fight the English. Some were happy to make money from other countrymen's misery.

* * *

From the shelter of a thick bush, Auffroy watched them closely, barely breathing, eyes slitted, his hood over his head. He and Gadiffer had hurried after the company with all speed. The men on their horses were hamstrung to the speed of their carts, and with the fords and hills, they were slowed. It took little effort to catch up with them.

When the English withdrew and reformed their column, slowly making their way eastwards, Auffroy made his way back to where Gadiffer was waiting.

'They continue.'

'You are sure it is the same company?'

Gadiffer watched Auffroy closely as he nodded. Juliot had been certain that this man was the one she would marry, and there was no doubt in his mind that if Juliot had lived, Auffroy would have married her in time. He was entirely devoted to her, and he was desperate to avenge her death and the demeaning treatment of her body, but Gadiffer was fully aware that he was no warrior, and neither was Auffroy. Gadiffer was a farmer, and Auffroy the son of a smith. What could they do against the arms of men such as these English?

'Come!' Auffroy said, and the two rose and made their way after the company of warriors. Auffroy was still filled with the righteous determination to win back Juliot's possession, Gadiffer with the fear that they were marching to their doom.

Hawkwood and the company rode down the gentle slope with the three vinteners out in front. The men had already strung their bows, and now they were cantering along, the four boys scampering behind, riding for the small town that lay ahead.

The town was good-sized, but today it was not barred against them. Robin and Peter allowed Hawkwood to lead them through to the town's centre, slowing to a trot as they went, all alert in case of danger. No mercenary enjoyed riding down narrow streets with buildings on either side. It was the ideal place for an ambush.

There were plenty of people. Women with hard

faces pulled their children to them, keeping them away from the motley riders, with the younger women either hurrying behind doors or standing in the streets and watching the men, especially Fulk with his long, fair hair and strong features. There were few men, but that was normal. As Hawkwood knew, many had been taken by the nobleman of the area to serve in his force when he marched to Poitiers, and few had returned from that slaughter. Many women were considering a future without a husband or protector. In such cases even English mercenaries held appeal.

Hawkwood rode straight to the tavern, where he dismounted and had Rat and the boys run forward to take the reins of all the men as they entered the tavern, Hawkwood leading the way.

'Master,' the tavern keeper said, nodding respectfully to Hawkwood as Peter and Robin took their seats from where they could see the main entrance. Some locals were already there, and one old man eyed them coldly, then spat on the floor, drained his cup and walked out without looking at the English.

'God keep you, Alardin,' Hawkwood said.

After the usual greetings, Hawkwood walked with the host through to a chamber behind the main bar. Here Alardin produced a flask and two cups. 'It has been a while, Master Hawkwood.'

'Yes. We have not been this way for some months,' he agreed. 'Do you wish for silver?'

'I can always make good use of plates and jewels,' Alardin said with a grin.

Hawkwood called to Seth, and a short while later Seth and Gervase appeared, both carrying the sacks from their sumpter horses. Rat entered carrying a bale of clothing that was almost as heavy as he himself, and Crespin and Henri carried another between them.

'This has been a successful venture for you,' the host said, eyeing the sacks and bales and trying, unsuccessfully, to conceal his eagerness to see what was inside.

'We have not had a bad time of it,' Hawkwood agreed.

The contents of the bales and sacks were studied, costed and haggled over, but Hawkwood, with his men at his back, knew that he had the upper hand, and finally he had a sum that was acceptable to him. The two shook hands on the arrangement. Before long the silver would have been taken to a smith the tavern keeper knew and smelted, the golden cross stolen from an abbey would be resold to a monastery, the rich silks and furs would be made available at the market, and Alardin would be considerably wealthier. For now, Hawkwood was content with the weight of the purse Alardin passed him.

'It is good to do business with you,' Alardin said, fingering a soft ermine pelt. It would have cost a vast sum, he knew. It was tempting to keep it, but there was a risk in keeping hold of valuables that a nobleman might consider beyond his means. Better to let it go, and enjoy the money in these troubled times.

'And you,' Hawkwood said.

'I hope to see you again before long.'

Hawkwood nodded. He had no feelings for Alardin; the man was useful, nothing more than that. While the company had need of money for wages and to buy food, replacement weaponry and clothing, a man like Alardin was convenient. He would buy all the mercenaries had taken from others, and resell them for his own profit. It did not make him a friend or ally, but it did make him useful.

When they walked from the tavern some little while later, Fulk and the others went to their horses. The boys had been given wine and bread while the company had been entertained inside, and now Henri and Crespin were grinning and giggling. The Rat still looked downcast and fretful. He kept glancing about as if suspecting that some spirit or ghoul was about to leap out at him. It upset Fulk to see the boy so discontented. In some ways Rat reminded him of his own little Jacquet. The boy was older, but had similar features to his son. On a whim, he called out, 'Come, Rat, you can ride with me.'

The boy looked anxious at his words, but then nodded nervously, and Fulk climbed up onto his mount, holding out his hand for the boy. Rat took his hand and Fulk pulled him up, seating the lad behind him. It would not be comfortable with the saddle's cantle sticking into his belly, but it would be better than walking.

The men were prepared to ride when Fulk noticed the Rat was staring up the street past the tavern. 'What is it, boy? You have seen a ghost?' he asked roughly.

'I... I thought I saw a man,' Rat stammered. 'A man with grey clothes and a russet cloak, like the Devil wore when I saw him kill Arn.'

Fulk followed Rat's gaze. 'There is nothing. You imagine much, boy,' he said, but as he wheeled his mount to follow the rest of the company, he felt for his long dagger and eased it in its sheath, even as he glanced over his shoulder.

That feeling of evil pursuing them would not leave him.

12

He *had* looked like the Devil he'd seen in the woods, Rat thought. He hunched his shoulders as if it would make him disappear, fearful of being seen. Was it the witch who had sent him? Or was it the ghost of the woman as Arn had said? No, she would not want to hurt Rat. He had done nothing to her. But the witch, with her curses, she could have directed the woman to come and take his soul.

The hag was surely responsible for all his fears. All because he had tried to keep his mother alive, he thought. Yet she had still died. He felt his eyes brimming again at the memory of those happy days, when both his parents had still lived, and he and his brother had worked in the fields, playing when they could.

But that was all over now. His prized memories were all that remained of those days. He had to be brave now, like this big man from the mountains.

As if he could read Rat's thoughts, Fulk put an arm about him. 'Don't worry, boy. You are safe with me.'

Some miles short of Épernon, Fulk's mind was to be cleansed of fears of evil. Instead more prosaic concerns took over when they met with a group of armed men.

Peter was the first to see them as he rode over a hill heading eastwards. There, in the roadway before him, was a gathering of men with weapons and armour. He heard a shout, and saw the men scurrying efficiently enough to form up and prepare to repel an assault, or to ride to him and capture him. The rest of his men were still behind him and concealed, but as he halted and took in the formation ahead, he could tell that these were English. There was a calm steadiness in the way that they moved into position, and he could see archers with longbows on the wings, men-at-arms dismounted in the middle, a small contingent behind as a reserve.

He waited until his own men had appeared behind

him. John Hawkwood trotted up to his side and studied the men before them. 'Aye, English,' he said.

'I think so. They're no peasant force, for certain,' Peter agreed.

'Best keep the men easy,' Hawkwood said. 'We don't want any sudden outburst leading to a fight. They have plenty of archers.'

Peter nodded, and only then did he move down the hill towards the force blocking the road, a hand held high in sign of peace. There was no indication that the archers were drawing their strings, he noted with relief. These may be English, but that counted for little when all English were here to plunder what they might. If these thought that Peter's men had a wagonload of valuables, any vague consideration of fellow feeling in the form of patriotism or common blood would soon dissipate.

'English?' a voice called.

'Aye,' Peter responded. 'Who's your leader?'

* * *

Sir James Pipe was a man of medium height, with dark hair shot through with silver. He had a steady gaze as Peter and Hawkwood joined him, and although he didn't rise, as for an honoured guest, he yet welcomed his visitors graciously enough in the hall of the house he had commandeered, his boots on the table before him.

'God save you. Wine?'

'That would be good,' Peter said.

'You are *tard-venus*?'

'No. We fought at Poitiers, and when the army was disbanded, we didn't know where else to go.'

'Ah. So you are fighting on your own account?'

'Yes, sir. You?'

'I used to serve in the retinue of the Earl of Stafford, but when he took little part in the fighting here, I joined the Duke of Lancaster. I've been here since. We came down from Honfleur last year, and I've based myself and the men at Épernon. It is a good town, and gives us access to the lands south of Paris.'

'How many men do you have?'

'Over a hundred, but of course we could always accept the help of more. And you have how many?'

'Three vintaines, but understrength. Total of forty, all told. We lost one on the way here. They are mostly men we commanded at Poitiers.'

'What are your plans?'

Hawkwood tilted his head and gave a short shrug, grinning. 'I had planned to ride to the south, to see what I might win. I've heard tell of rich lands and towns.'

'True enough. Much of France has never experienced war,' Sir James said. 'If you wanted useful employment, I could offer that to you here. You need not travel so far.'

'What tasks would be here?'

'I am here working to serve the duke still. I protect his territories. But I am also commissioned by King Charles of Navarre. He has been released from prison, and now he makes common cause with our king. Navarre wants his lands and properties returned to him, and the dauphin has failed. Oh, the dauphin is a weakly, unhealthy boy, and he has no money, anyway, but that won't stop Navarre. He wants the kingdom, I think. If he can take power, he will – and who can stop him?'

Hawkwood nodded. It was one reason why he and the other groups of fighters had remained. The collapse of law and order meant there were rich possible pickings. The French government was destroyed at Poitiers. Those most involved in governing the country were slaughtered or captured, and now only some few remained with the competence and knowledge to try to maintain the government. The taxes that were collected were kept by the towns and villages, to be used for their own defences; nothing was sent to the Louvre for the dauphin to use to raise an army to defend against the depredations of the various companies rampaging across France now.

'Will he succeed?'

'He might, if he can take over Paris, and by all accounts he could. He has the support of many citizens there.'

Peter exchanged a look with Hawkwood. Hawkwood gave a slight shrug. He didn't care whether they remained here or continued south. 'We could stay here for a period – see what the profits might be, and decide to carry on south later,' he said.

'If you stay, you will be serving our king as well,' Sir James said. 'We maintain the structure of power here. We keep the peace.'

'How?'

Sir James gave a wolfish grin. 'We don't rob or murder if the villages pay our *pâtis*.'

* * *

The tavern was quiet this early in the morning, and the tavern keeper was hardly welcoming as Auffroy walked in and asked for a small jug of wine. Gadiffer remained at the doorway, watching the roadway with anxious eyes.

His attitude was worrisome. Grunting his assent, Alardin took up one of his smaller jugs and glanced at him before he turned to the wine barrel, thinking he might have to grab the oak cudgel from its place beneath his bar. He turned the tap, watching the red wine flow, and as he did, he felt the chill of the dagger's blade at his throat. His eyes widened as Auffroy said, 'Turn it off.'

Alardin slowly turned the tap off and stood very still and careful. 'What do you want? I don't have money.'

'You have given it all to the English? Take me to your storeroom.'

'I don't know what—' His words were cut off as the blade moved. He could feel the keen edge slice into his flesh. 'You *bastard*! I'll see you—'

The blade moved again. 'Now.'

Alardin put the pot down and, with the knife still at his throat, he walked carefully out to the curtain that shielded his storeroom from the bar. Inside were the bales and sacks brought by Hawkwood and his men. 'This is all mine,' Alardin said.

'Shut up! You support the English. All they steal and kill for, you support them by buying it. Without greedy traitors like *you* they would have been forced to leave before now.'

'I only...'

The knife was taken away, and Alardin tried to turn, to move away and put distance between him and his attacker, but before he could, a slamming blow struck his head and he was knocked to his knees. A second clout drove him to all fours, and he didn't feel the third, but fell to the ground. Auffroy took his hands and bound them securely with a strip of cloth from a bale, and stuffed a thick ball of linen into Alardin's mouth, and then methodically began to go through all the items on the table, and emptied the sacks to look through them.

Gadiffer joined him, gazing down at the recumbent figure snoring on the floor with wide eyes. 'Is it here?'

'No.' Auffroy swore, and seeing Alardin was stirring, he kicked the tavern host viciously, twice.

They would have to continue to follow the mercenaries.

13

The keep at Épernon was a massive square block that almost looked as if it had been carved from a huge rock, the individual sections fitted together so perfectly. At the gatehouse, Peter looked up and around, always aware that too often men had been enticed into secluded areas where a trap could be sprung and all the men killed, but today there was no need for concern. The inner courtyard had few fighting men, but several grooms and stable boys to look to their mounts. He gladly dropped from his saddle and passed the reins to a young boy who patted his mount's neck. Peter retrieved his pack from the saddle's thongs and threw it over his shoulder, watching the rest of the two vintaines as they grumbled and complained, before going to the main doors to seek a drink.

Hawkwood remained outside with his men. He had the same reservations about entering a castle that he didn't know, and his eyes were on every doorway and the castle's walls, looking for any sign of danger. His bow and arrows he kept with him, as he did his sword, and while he could see nothing to give him concern, he was aware of a heightened tension.

He took a while, watching his men as they grumbled and complained, dismounting and gazing about them. Fulk, the tall Swiss with his halberd always at his side; Dogbreath, probably the longest-serving member of the vintaine; and the leader of the third group, Robin of London, the master bowman. Then there were Saul and Nick, Hob and the others, each of them competent with their bows, but as quick with their barbed comments to each other.

'My arse feels like it's been battered by a giant,' Saul was moaning.

'In that case you won't want to sit on a bench,' Dogbreath said.

Robin was eyeing the castle in much the same way as Hawkwood. 'Perhaps they'll have some nice, soft cushions for you to rest your backside.'

'You think so?' Saul said hopefully.

'Don't be a berk,' Hob said. He had taken his own bags from the saddle and now made his way to the door to the keep, shouldering bow, bag and quiver. 'Any soft cushions would have been taken by the first folk here. And we aren't first.'

'Surely they'll show compassion for a man suffering like him?' Robin said.

'They'd make up a first-rate bed for him, I've little doubt,' Nick called, grinning.

'Aye. In the pigsty, where he belongs,' Hob said.

'That's nice,' Robin said. 'He can keep Dogbreath company.'

'Ballocks to that. You think I'd share a bed with him?' Dogbreath said. 'I'd need a room of my own, me.'

'Admittedly,' Gervase said, 'sharing with a litter of pigs would be less unpleasant than sharing with Dogbreath.'

'Oh, aye. You reckon! When we win some money, I'm going to find a tavern full of women with bouncing bubbies and shag them stupid. I might buy the place, and when I do, I'll bar all of you bastards.'

'It wouldn't be difficult to shag them stupid. They'd have to be stupid to think you'd be able to afford them.'

'I'll make my fortune, you see if I don't,' Dogbreath said confidently.

'So, no, Saul. I don't think you'll be finding any nice, comfy cushions here,' Robin said. 'I fear you will need to make do with a blanket on the floor like the rest of us.'

Hawkwood grinned to himself as the men picked up their belongings and carried them to the main door. Before he followed them, he saw the figure of the boy, Rat.

The lad was still only a gangling youngster, with the arms and legs of a boy who was some years off adolescence. His arms looked like twigs that would be easily snapped. His tousled brown hair stuck up vertically, and he looked alarmed when Hawkwood beckoned him.

'Rat, I know you're worried. You're safe enough with us here.'

'Yes.'

'The figure who killed Arn scared you, I know, but you'll be safe here with us.'

'It was the Devil. Must've been. Never seen thing like it before.'

'What made you think it was the Devil?'

'Had a black tunic, and hood, and his eyes were all red, and his cloak was like wings, great red wings.'

'Where did he come from?'

'Suppose he was at the side of the path. We got there, and Arn was picking up sticks for the fire – me too – and then I saw this thing come up from beside the road, and he just jumped on Arn, and I ran. I couldn't do anything. I just ran to get help.'

'You did right, boy,' Hawkwood said. The lad's eyes were huge and round as he spoke, and it was plain enough that he was still scared out of his wits. Hawkwood had no doubt that Rat had seen a fellow; not the Devil, but a French peasant who deprecated the arrival of the men of the company. It was understandable. A man who was, perhaps, guarding a local village's treasures, moved away from their church or manor house, to a place in the forest where they thought it could be secreted safely, only to find a party of English mercenaries appear as though to steal the valuables? The boy saw a man dressed in black – a priest or monk? – and probably the man himself was as terrified of the appearance of the English as the boys were to see him. It was all too common for those who lived in fear to respond irrationally to imagined danger, rather than considering the situation with dispassionate calm.

Too many died for such reasons.

As he had the thought, a germ of inspiration grew and flowered in his mind. What if it was a priest or

monk? Such a man might be there in the woods because he was standing guard over a monastery's hoard.
There might be gold and jewels in among those trees.
That thought gave him pause for a moment. Perhaps
he should go back there one day?

'Boy, I am convinced that you saw just a man.' He
tried to explain his reasoning, that the fellow was just
a villager protecting his wealth, or a scared peasant
terrified that the English might find him and kill him,
but he could see that his words were not impressing
the boy. Rat remained convinced of what he had seen.
It was there in his eyes, in the way his gaze moved
about the yard behind Hawkwood, the way he bit his
lips. He was petrified.

Hawkwood waved him away irritably. If the lurdan
wouldn't listen, there was little Hawkwood could do to
persuade him. He directed Rat to the stables to help
the grooms, reflecting on the story the boy had told.
His tale had been consistent, and it left Hawkwood
wondering: could those woods hold a hoard of treasure that was guarded by a nervous peasant, priest or
monk, or was it just a panicked peasant who saw
strangers and struck out, fearing to be discovered?
Hawkwood might have to return to the woods and
spend some hours searching for it. He and Robin had
wandered among the trees looking for the mysterious

stranger since Rat's flight from his friend's body, but they had found nothing.

Yes, he should return and have another attempt, he told himself. But for today, just now, the main thing he craved was less gold and jewels, and more a pint of strong wine.

* * *

Paris

In the streets, Thomas de Ladit felt that the atmosphere was growing febrile, like August, when tempers tended to flare and minor altercations could all too often turn into battles.

This year it was not the terrible summer heat leading to warm words and the inevitable drawing of weapons. In the last month, the dauphin's treasurer had been murdered in the street, his killer running to claim sanctuary in a nearby church. It availed him little. An armed guard went to him, and dragged him away to be hanged.

The citizenry was divided, many starting to wear the red and blue hoods of the city's colours. These were the supporters of Étienne Marcel, the Provost of the Merchants. Thomas felt he had the status of lord mayor of the city. Marcel claimed that he represented change and revolution. The city had been engulfed by debt, he declared. The system of government was corrupt and incompetent. It was time to throw it out, to create a new regime, one in which the people had power to administer their own lives. Enough of the rich and nobles arranging the government to suit themselves, it was time to take control.

Under his authority, the city had refused entry to an army supporting the dauphin, who were even now encamped in the suburbs and outside the city walls.

But things were changing. The atmosphere was deteriorating rapidly, just as King Charles had hoped.

It was not easy to be King Charles's observer. Often Thomas found his loyalties split. He was sworn to the King of Navarre, but at the same time he felt an affinity for the French nobles. It was unthinkable, he felt, to desert the French in their time of most need. When so many honourable families had just seen their lords, their knights, their children slaughtered on the field of Poitiers, when the entire country needed leadership and support, King Charles saw only an opportunity.

This was made clear when Thomas met with Charles of Navarre's emissary to the dauphin. The man arrived craving an audience with the son of King John, and, when it was granted, the urbane ambassador demanded castles and territories that King Charles felt had been unfairly taken from him, as well as tens of thousands of *écus* in compensation. In response, the dauphin stated starkly that he owed the King of Navarre *nothing*. He would not accede to such demands.

The meeting ended as politely as any challenge to a duel after the gauntlet had been thrown down.

King Charles was already negotiating with King Edward of England. Thomas knew that, as did, likely, the dauphin himself. This embassy was merely performative, intended to prove that King Charles had tried to use diplomacy with all his power to avoid joining the rebels against the dauphin and his father. It was not a genuine offer, but a political move to demonstrate he was unfairly treated by the dauphin, that he had just cause for raising his flag against the royal family, although everyone knew – or guessed – that he had been hedging his bets for weeks, offering to aid the English in exchange for influence, land and money. Thomas knew all this, but King Charles still needed Thomas in Paris to keep him advised of the situation.

Thomas could tell him that now the die was cast. The Estates General – the parliament of the French government – had received details of the proposed English treaty, and they were ghastly. In order for the

King of France to be released on parole, the French must pay vast sums to the English, give up huge swathes of territory, and consequently accept ever higher taxes to pay for the king's freedom.

Heeding their objections, the dauphin had pretended to agree to the demands of the Estates General, agreeing to purge the government of certain officials controlling the provinces, accepting the imposition of new taxes, while demanding arrears from the previous year also be paid. The Estates General did allow for the amelioration of taxes for those areas currently suffering the worst depredations of the English and other free companies, but now Thomas had learned that even though the dauphin had agreed to signing their requirements into law, he intended to discard them and snatch back power for himself. It was not only Thomas who had learned this. Marcel and the Estates General had also discovered the truth, and Marcel was furious, as were his supporters.

Thomas saw the men of Paris gathering, and he kept well away. There must have been three thousand men there, all of them armed, and they forced their way into the palace grounds. From what Thomas heard, the guards had little choice but to let them in. With Marcel at their head, the mob made its way up the marble staircase and into the dauphin's chambers.

There they found Jean de Conflans and Robert of Clermont, two marshals, with the dauphin. The men under Marcel set about these two, hacking and stabbing them to death, even covering the dauphin himself in their blood, before dragging their bodies out and hurling them into the courtyard.

Later that day, Thomas went to the Place de Grève, where a great crowd had gathered, and they listened while Marcel told them that he and the others had acted for the good of the realm. The two marshals were evil. They were false, treasonable men, and he begged the mob to support him and the men of the Estates General, who were acting in the best interests of the city and the kingdom.

The shouts of approval were deafening. Thomas felt himself beaten back by the roar as though it was a solid wall of sound that hammered against him. The people had chosen. And he was unsure what the outcome would be.

He knew that Charles of Navarre would be interested to know of all this. Paris was the key to France. Whoever owned and controlled Paris would control France.

Charles must come to Paris.

14

CALAIS

March

There was no doubt that Ed was a competent apprentice. In fact, Archibald the gynour reckoned the lad was perfectly capable of his own affairs. He didn't need to remain with Archibald. His apprenticeship was all but complete. He knew how to mix the powder, how to slowly grind it, how to reduce it to the flakes that served to fill the main barrels, and how to grind up the finer powder ready for the vent hole to ignite the gonnes.

Better, since he had been working with smiths, Ed had a good understanding of the bronze and the making of the barrels themselves, the individual staves of bronze, the cooperage binding them together like those of a great water barrel, how the hoops were made, heated, and allowed to cool on the barrel to tighten and hold the gonne's shape before heating the entire barrel to fuse the staves together to contain the explosion of the powder. Yes, there were occasional accidents. At Crécy one of the gonnes had shattered, unable to hold the immense force of the detonation, and men serving the gonne had died, cut apart by the immense splinters of metal that flew through the air, but a properly made gonne with the correctly mixed powder, that was safe enough.

However, Ed would not leave Archibald. When he was only a boy, Ed had witnessed a French pirate raid on his city, and had seen both his parents slain. He'd joined King Edward's army to come to France and take his revenge all those years ago. Now he was a grown man, but a man without purpose, other than learning his trade. At Poitiers the woman he had loved had been killed in battle, and since then he had shown no interest in leaving Archibald. It was as if he looked on Archibald as his father. The only remnant of his family, the one stable figure in his life for the last twelve years or more.

He was young enough, bright enough, to make his own way in the world. Ed should be breaking away from Archibald now, finding a woman, setting up on his own... but he wouldn't. Ed had already lost so much; he was like those who had suffered through the plague years, who had seen family and friends destroyed by God's pestilence, and who clung desperately to anyone who reminded them of security, of home.

They had come here, to Calais, in the hope of finding a new company in search of men with their skills, but so far there was little enough work. In the past, the army of the Prince of Wales had been keen to make use of them, with the great gonne that Archibald petted so enthusiastically, but in recent months, there had been little interest in gonnes of that size. It was difficult to lift them, site them, and load them. Smaller ribauldequins were easier for mobile groups of men.

But as matters stood, few seemed to think that Ed and Archibald were reliable enough – or perhaps safe enough.

There was still the ridiculous superstition that their powder was Devil-inspired and evil. It was the smell given off by the gonnes when fired; that whiff of brimstone was enough to persuade so many that the weapons were not Christian. With that odour, they had to have been derived from the Devil.

It would be some time before Archibald could find a new sponsor. The money he had earned after the fabulously successful *chevauchée* that led to Poitiers was almost exhausted now, and he needed a new patron, someone who would take him and Ed on another march across France. Everywhere people were talking about the fabulous sums men could earn in a single journey. France was ripe and ready for harvesting. Men who left England's shores as impoverished peasants could earn enough to buy a house and a plot of land after only a few weeks of work. If they could capture a knight or baron, so much the better. The ransom for nobles ran to fortunes.

All he needed was a new captain, someone like Sir John de Sully, a man who saw the potential of Archibald's and Ed's little toys.

* * *

The vessel had arrived in the afternoon, and William and Perkin climbed off the cog as soon as the shipmaster told them they could. Amid the noise of creaking timbers, straining hemp, and the constant slap and hiss of waves striking the harbour walls, the two could barely hear each other speaking, and besides, they were both a little alarmed by the numbers of men all about them.

'Let's find a tavern,' William said.

'That's your answer to everything.'

'Well, we have to find out where we should go to find a commander,' William said reasonably.

'First we have to get our horses stabled and their gear stored.'

'Oh, you practical Puttock! Very well. Let's go find where we can leave the horses.'

It took a little time to find a stable that had space. Apparently there was a constant flow of mounts as men-at-arms arrived in Calais and sought to arm and equip themselves for joining one of the companies under the war heroes who were riding over the whole of France.

Leaving the stables, Perkin grimaced. 'I still think we should have offered ourselves in England before coming on this wild goose chase.'

'You just wanted to stay and get inside Helena's shift again.' William laughed.

Perkin's expression soured still further. 'I could barely escape the wench. She would not take "no" for an answer.'

'You didn't mind her saying yes after the last feast.'

'Yes, well, after three quarts of ale, things seem different,' Perkin said defensively.

'There must be a ratio of beauty to the number of ales drunk,' William said with mock-seriousness.

'Go swyve a goat!' Perkin said.

There was a tavern not far from the dock area, and the two shouldered their packs and made their way to it, peering in through the open doorway. It was filled with shipmen and local workers. William and Perkin exchanged glances and when Perkin shrugged, William led the way inside.

It was warmer inside, with a fire roaring on the hearth in the middle of the floor, the thin smoke rising to the blackened timbers of the rafters overhead before seeping out between the wooden shingles. Some rough benches were scattered about on the rushes, and old ale barrels served as resting places for cups and drinking horns. The host of the tavern was a broad man who, from the look of his belly, enjoyed his own produce to the full. His beard was thick, his hair thin, as if it had migrated, and he had a scar across his nose and up to an empty eye socket, but for all his grim appearance, he was friendly enough as the two approached the bar.

'Two quarts of ale,' William said.

'Aye.' Two leather jacks appeared shortly after, and

the host stood eyeing them both speculatively. 'New to Calais?'

'Yes, we arrived today,' William said.

Perkin threw him a glance. In a new town like this, he was sure it was better to maintain a certain caution before giving information to strangers.

'Joining a company?'

'We hope to,' William said. 'We don't have indentures yet, but we hope to quickly. My friend and I are keen to join in the adventures.'

'Aye, and make your fortunes, I'll wager,' the barman said.

'Of course,' William said with a certain hauteur.

'I did. That was back in the days after Crécy, of course. I was riding with Sir Gaston of Boulogne then. We had a good time of it. That's where I won this,' he said, indicating his scarred face. 'Bastard Genoese managed to scratch me before I killed him. Still, I made good money, enough to buy this place.'

'It is a good tavern,' Perkin said.

'Should be. Another man made his money after the siege here, and was awarded it by the king, so I heard. His family died in the pestilence, and he left to join one of the other companies down south. I found it empty, and managed to buy it. It's every old soldier's dream,' he added with a faraway look in his eye, 'to have a place like this. Wines, ales, and women. What more can you ask for, eh?'

'Indeed,' William said.

'Well, gentles, I'll leave you to your ales. Shout if you need anything more.'

As he walked away, Perkin rounded on William. 'You fool! Don't tell everyone our business here.'

'Why not? If you want to find a position in one of the companies, we will have to make ourselves known to those who might be aware of commanders looking for strong young recruits. We need to get papers and go with one of the captains.'

'I'm just saying that it may not be a good idea to let tavern keepers know our desire for positions.'

William laughed. 'You're too serious. You see dangers and plots around every corner!'

'With good reason. You forget, my father was twice keeper of the port of Dartmouth under the abbots of Tavistock. I grew up around men like these shipmen, and I know what they can be like, some of them. If they learn you have money, or see it on you, they'll like as not pull a dagger and cut it from you. And if they think you might argue the toss with them, they'll stick you.'

'You fear too much, old man!' William said with a

cheery toast of his cup, finishing his first quart. 'Let's have another.'

They had another jug each, and halfway down the second, Perkin's mood did improve. He unbent so far as to smile as two young women came to introduce themselves.

In truth, he was lonely. It was a long time since he had lain with Helena, and the younger of these two was a tall woman, with a roguish eye and a lot of curling hair that escaped the confines of her coif to frame a round face with readily smiling eyes and mouth. She was a sorely tempting distraction.

'We cannot stay here,' he protested when William suggested a further jug each, and perhaps wine for their new companions. 'We have to find rooms, William, and a captain who might employ us. Our money won't last forever.'

'You're seeking a place to stay?' the taller woman said.

Perkin acknowledged that the two were recently arrived from England, and the woman smiled prettily, glancing at her friend. 'We know just the place. Come with us when we've finished our sups, and we'll take you there.'

'Will they have spare rooms?' William asked.

'Well,' the second wench said with a sly little side-long glance at him. 'If not, perhaps you could share with us.'

It was enough to persuade the two. After a third jug each, and one which their new acquaintances shared, the four left the tavern. William, glancing back, saw the host standing behind his bar. He barely acknowledged William's farewell.

15

The two women were plainly the type to share their favours for a fee, but that was no concern of William's. A little pleasure with them would be welcome.

He was twenty-two, the son of a knight. His father, Sir Baldwin de Furnshill, was Keeper of the King's Peace, occasionally a Justice of Gaol Delivery and member of parliament. In his life, William had known little of war or foreign lands, but he had trained from the age of eight in all forms of martial art, and he was confident of his ability and prowess. There was no one in this city who could best him in a fair fight, he knew, and although the city was daunting, with many thousands of citizens, and a preponderance of martial types, he was sure that any building where two attractive young women could find lodging would be perfectly safe for a couple of men like him and Perkin.

Perkin was the son of his father's best friend. In their day, his father, Sir Baldwin de Furnshill and Perkin's, Simon Puttock, had worked together as keeper of the peace and bailiff, but Perkin and he had often felt constricted in the little towns of Devon where both were brought up. They had sought excitement and adventure, not to mention treasure.

Neither of their families had been keen on their coming here. William's father himself had been highly antagonistic. 'You don't know how dangerous such travel is,' Sir Baldwin had grumbled. 'I've been to France and beyond, and it's not like travelling in England. Besides, the country is ravaged with these free companies. If you go, you are as likely to be slain by ruffians on your way as by French men-at-arms. You are not well enough versed in the ways of the world, boy.'

'I am no *boy*! I am twenty-two! And you have no idea what it might be like. You haven't left the kingdom in thirty years or more!'

His father was right in some ways. William and Perkin had not travelled. It had not been possible.

Both had hoped to join the king's forces in one of the previous chevauchées, but with the unsettled situation in England at the time, there never seemed a good time to take up arms. Then, of course, there was the pestilence, which ravaged the kingdom, and in the face of that catastrophe, travel was all but unthinkable. Some had said that it would be better for him to remain at home and protect his father's lands. His father was so old now, at over eighty years, that he needed support – not that the old fool would admit it. But he had plenty of servants, and very loyal men-at-arms who were there with him, and William was not really needed. Especially since his older brother, who would inherit the manor anyway, was there.

But William had been chafing at the bit. He couldn't stay in the quiet countryside of Devon when there was adventure and profit to be had in France. Besides, he and Perkin were well trained in fighting. Both could handle sword and spear, while Perkin himself was highly competent with a bow, too, although he was reluctant to be considered an archer. He wanted to remain at William's side if they were to go to war.

They had followed the two wenches along a high street, and turned right. This took them into a small maze of alleys, where they were led right again, and eventually down another, narrower alley. The taller woman was holding Perkin's hand as he paid her fulsome praise for her elegance and comportment. William himself found his companion slipping her arm about his waist, and he smiled down at her. She was pretty, in a pale-complexioned, dark-haired sort of way, and he felt himself warming to her.

He was just about to lean down to kiss her when the blow struck his skull, and he felt himself tumbling forward, so it seemed, into an immensely deep, dark well that suddenly opened at his feet.

* * *

Perkin groaned as he opened his eyes. It was an error.

There were little sparks and whirls of blue and red stars about him, and he felt as though each of them was pelting him as he tried to roll over and sit up. He pushed himself upright, his back against a wall, and peered about him with narrowed eyes.

William was lying a little way away from him, his mouth wide, snoring roughly, a small dribble of blood running from a cut in his scalp down to his temple and thence to his cheek. They were in the same alley where they had been walking with the women, but of them there was no sign, just as there was no sign of their packs. Two men were running away at the farther end of the alley, but Perkin was in no fit state to give chase. When he felt at his belt, he found that the thongs holding his purse were also cut. He groaned to think of all the money. It was gone. No doubt the two men and the women would be sharing it between them shortly.

Climbing to his feet, he had to pause and blink, a hand on the wall beside him, trying to shake off the dizziness that assailed him. It was some moments before he could walk to William and rouse him. His friend grunted and moaned as he opened his eyes, and then stared up blearily at Perkin. 'What happened to us? The girls, what...?'

'They led us into a trap,' Perkin said. 'We're lucky they only cut our purse strings and not our throats.'

'You think they had something to do with us being attacked? No, they seemed kind-hearted. They were taking us to a place where we could rest.'

'We've lost our packs, our purses, and our friends. The women brought us here, to a place where we could be knocked down and they could steal everything from us,' Perkin said bitterly. 'We were led here by our tarses, and the women knew it.'

'We have to find our way back to the tavern,' William said, struggling to his feet. 'We cannot let them get away with this. There must be a constable somewhere near here, or a bailiff. Someone we can tell of this assault. Go find them and get our money back.'

'And what good will that do? What was the name of your woman? No, I don't know the name of mine either. We were dupes, William. We were shown the entrance to the trap, with the enticement sitting within, and we both swallowed it whole, the hook as well.'

'Be damned to that!' William rasped and, tottering slightly, made his way back along the alleyway. As they left, entering a broader thoroughfare, where there were more people about, the two were aware of curious eyes gazing at them.

It was clear enough why. Both were rolling in their gait, both were marked and besmottered with refuse and muck, and could have been any form of vagrant.

However, the way to the tavern was plain enough. They came upon the main street once more and immediately turned left, following down the track to the sign of the bush, and there they pushed their way inside.

'Host, where are the two women who left with us?' William demanded.

'I don't know – you took them from here. I was hoping you would buy them drinks and perhaps a meal, but you all left together, didn't you? Why should I know where they went after that? There are many taverns and stews down nearer the sea. Shipmen go there, and two wenches like those will always find gainful employment there.'

'You know them. I saw you looking at them,' William said heavily. His hand strayed to his sword's hilt.

'Careful, master,' the tavern keeper said, and from beneath the bar he brought up a blackthorn cudgel. 'I don't want any trouble in my bar, and them as try to cause it can win a broken pate anytime they fancy it.'

'They robbed us!'

'Oh?'

'They took our packs and purses,' William said.

'Really?'

'What will you do about it?'

'Me? Nothing! What, did they rob you here in my tavern? No, and you know full well that I have no control over the streets. Keep your hand from your sword, master, or I'll knock it away.'

William lowered his head, but he was certain that this tavern keeper was no slouch when it came to handling his blackthorn. He had the look of a man who would not hesitate to use it on a patron's skull. 'At the least give us some wine or ale for our injuries.'

'Aye. As soon as I see your coins, master.'

'We've been robbed, damn your cods!' William said.

'Then, fuck you, master. Piss off out of my tavern.'

'I will buy them an ale each,' a man said.

And that was how William and Perkin got to meet Archibald.

* * *

'You were taken for fools,' Archibald stated as they took their seats at his table. 'You thought two women like them were attracted to your good looks?'

They had introduced themselves, and Archibald sat with his back to the wall as he drank his pot of cider. The other two had ales again, and although the flavour was the same as before, this third quart tasted more tart to Perkin. 'We were fools,' he admitted bitterly.

'This is a city of thieves and mercenaries,' Archibald said. 'Let me guess, you are here to try to join a company, are you?'

'That was our intention,' William said. He gulped more ale. His head was sore, and he was feeling slightly dizzy.

'Well, you are in the right part to find one, although I cannot tell you which captain would be best.'

'Have you been involved in the fighting?' Perkin asked doubtfully, looking at his bald head and grey beard.

'Me? I was with the king at Crécy, I served here to win this city the year after, and I was at Poitiers, too. But I cannot help with the names of good captains. The best men I knew then are gone now. One died in that battle, and the best vintener chose to cease fighting and took holy orders. Others, they went their own way, down south, I think, but where they might be, I don't know. You latecomers will have to make your own way.'

'Not easy without our packs or money,' William said.

'Well, you'll have to do it somehow with neither, my friend. They are gone forever. The good host here was quite right. It's not his responsibility if you decide to accept an offer of entertainment from young wenches who lure you to a trap. Anything happening outside his tavern is nothing to do with him. What have you lost?'

'Everything, bar what you see on us now. Purses and packs, all gone. Spare clothing, food and money,'

Perkin said. 'Luckily our saddles and accoutrements are all with our horses at the stables.'

Archibald pulled a face. 'Ach, well, you can come and rest with me and my companion, if you wish. We have a dry barn and some straw for bedding. If you need, we can share some food too, not that we have much.'

16

The scream cut through the men's sleep, and they roused quickly, Fulk springing up and snatching at his halberd, before slumping down again.

It was not the first time. Just now, in the middle of the night, when the darkness was at its thickest, it was natural for those with the most violent mares attacking them, giving them dreams of horror and terror, to mutter, moan and sometimes cry out. And when they did, Fulk and Hawkwood in particular would bestir themselves, although others who had taken more to drink the night before might stay lying on their benches or on the floor in the bailey's great hall.

'Boy, are you well?' Fulk asked now, his hand on the Rat's shoulder.

The boy was shivering, his eyes wide, and he clutched at his blanket as he stared up at the Swiss. 'I'm sorry,' he said. 'I saw him again. I couldn't...'

He saw that figure again, the man from the woods, who had looked so like the Devil, and behind him, he was sure that the witch was there, directing him. They kept returning to him in his dreams. The woman with the blood at her breast had retreated, the farther they travelled from the town where she and her son had been buried. Perhaps they were only threatening Arn. But this man, he scared Rat, just as did the witch.

'The Devil, yes?'

'He was so big, so quick, his knife...'

'You must sleep,' Fulk said, not unkindly. As soon as he could, he returned to the bench he had taken near the fire and rolled himself up in his blanket once more, his halberd on the floor beside him.

'His dreams are getting worse,' Hawkwood grumbled.

'He is unsettled,' Fulk said. 'A boy seeing a demon, it is natural.'

'If he's going to keep on waking us up in the middle of the night,' Hawkwood said, 'he'll have to find somewhere else to sleep.'

'He cannot. He is only young. What happened in the woods scared him. He will take time to heal. He will not heal if you leave him in another room where he is alone and more scared.'

'Then he'll have to learn to deal with it. I won't have my sleep ruined every night because of a boy with mares,' Hawkwood growled uncompromisingly.

Now, in the cold light of morning, Fulk watched the boy as the men broke their fast with bread and cheese. Rat was eating a thin gruel with his metal spoon. 'Come, tell me, how did you come to join this company?'

Rat licked his spoon clean before carefully stowing it away under his shirt. He would not lose it again. It was his only valuable possession, other than his knife. Those two things were all he had in the world. Everything else had been lost when his mother died. That memory brought a tear to his eye, which he quickly dashed away. 'My mother died. My father had a sister, but she died in the pestilence, so he brought me here to France to fight. He told me to work with the followers and be useful.'

'Where is he?'

The boy's eyes brimmed. 'He died when the company attacked a village. They stormed the walls and my father was one of the first up the ladders, but he was cut down and fell all the way down. I saw it...'

'I see. I am sorry, boy. What is your name?'

'Aldred. It was my father's name.'

'Well, Aldred, you have to try to calm yourself at night. If you keep waking the men, they will send you out from the hall when you sleep.'

'I can't... They mustn't send me out! I'm scared of what the Devil will do if he finds me all alone! He'll kill me like he killed Arn!'

'I won't leave you alone, boy,' Fulk said.

* * *

It was a week after their arrival in Calais that William and Perkin heard of the company that was heading towards Paris.

Archibald and Ed were in the barn testing their barrels of powder when the visitors arrived. Perkin and William watched, Perkin with a keen interest, William with a degree of boredom. It was, when all was said and done, he felt, a black powder like charcoal. It held little fascination for him.

'I am looking for the gynour, the man who can work with serpentine powder,' the visitor said as he entered their workshop with three men at his back.

'And who would you be?' Archibald asked. He did not look up, for he was gathering a small sample of powder from the nearest barrel.

'I am Sir Reginald de Tony.'

From the pride in his voice it was clear that he felt sure that any Englishman in the city would know of him.

Sir Reginald de Tony was not a significant nobleman, but by reputation he had been successful in winning good profits for those who served under him – and survived. It was true that he had been forced to replenish his men at regular intervals after unsuccessful escapades in the past, but now he had a larger force, and he had heard of the treasure that lay about Paris and further to the south, and he was keen to gather up as much as possible for himself.

'Oh?' Archibald said, still concentrating on his task.

Ed saw Sir Reginald frown. 'I am seeking a man who can join my company. The rewards will be great, and the risks small, but we will be riding very soon. Would you join us?'

Archibald shrugged. 'It is possible, I suppose. What would the terms be?'

'For a master gynour like you?' Sir Reginald had clearly considered this beforehand, and now he held out his hand to one of the men behind him, a clerk, apparently, for he passed an indenture to Sir Reginald. 'Here, Master Gynour. These are the terms.'

Archibald listened to the clerk's offer of terms and conditions of service, and then nodded to Ed. 'I will need my assistant as well. Ed is a very competent worker with the powder, too. And then there are these two. The fools' – and here he pointed with his chin at William and Perkin – 'are keen to prove themselves in battle and win great renown or something. Would you have an indenture for them too?'

'I can always use competent fighters,' Sir Reginald said, eyeing them with a keen interest. 'Who are you?'

'William de Furnshill, esquire, and Perkin Puttock.'

'Furnshill? I know that name,' Sir Reginald said.

'My father has been Keeper of the King's Peace in Devon.'

'Ah, I am from Devon myself. What of you, Master Perkin?'

'I come from Devon too. My father is a farmer near Crediton.'

'You will both do, then,' Sir Reginald said.

His clerk asked for a clear space on a table, and made out indentures for William and Perkin. Once written out, with a full description of their duties and their remuneration, the clerk carefully tore the pages in half, deliberately ripping them in different patterns. Each contract was individually shaped, such that only the two originals would match perfectly. One half was kept by the clerk, the other halves given to Perkin and William as proof of their agreement.

'Well, Master Gynour?'

Archibald nodded. Ed replaced the lids on the barrels they had tested, and then the compact was agreed. Archibald and Ed would once more go to war. Archibald looked at Ed as he took his half of the indenture. In their last battle, Ed had lost the woman he had loved like a sister, poor Béatrice, killed when a gonne had misfired. Now Archibald wondered how Ed would respond when the gonnes began to roar again.

Sir Reginald took the company at a swift pace through the countryside.

'Our objective is to get to Paris and then we'll head to the south and find our pickings down that way,' he said. He appeared to be interested in William, and William felt sure that it was due to proximity, since William's birthplace had been not many leagues from Sir Reginald's home.

'What then?'

'We'll see what we can learn. That will guide us. As things stand, I understand that the French king has agreed a ransom with King Edward, but the French are unwilling to submit the funds. It may well mean that he brings another army over here to lead another series of raids on French towns and cities, but I doubt it will come to that. The French lost so many noblemen at Poitiers,' Sir Reginald said. Then: 'It is difficult for them, you understand. They relied on so many of those men to run their government. Those who kept the peace, those who led in war, are gone. But there are many others, the men who ran the bureaucracy, those who collected the taxes to be submitted to the government, they too are dead. The dauphin, the king's heir, is in place as regent, but he has little authority. The man is only eighteen, and has to rely on his own council, but who are they? Two of his favourite advisers were murdered at his side last month. Two marshals, hacked to death at his side in his own chamber, so close to him that he was all besmottered with their blood. It was the people of Paris, it is said. So the city itself is rising against the lawful rule of the dauphin. Where will it all end, I wonder? The people of this sorry country are milling like sheep before a wolf, none of them knowing how best to protect themselves.'

His face took on a sly look. 'But, of course, that means we have the best opportunities, too. While the dauphin finds it impossible to gather taxes, none of the towns will be protected. He cannot pay an army, and while the towns demand taxes, they keep it for their own defences, but it won't be enough for any of them. So we can ride down and take any number of places and plunder them to our heart's content.'

William nodded enthusiastically. 'That is what I was hoping for!'

Perkin was riding a little behind them, listening. It grieved him to hear the excitement in William's voice. His friend was keen to test himself in battle, Perkin knew, but it was strange to him. He had always liked William's father, who was a rather austere man who possessed a strong sense of justice and fairness. Perkin knew that Sir Baldwin had been against the idea of his son coming to France.

'I recall France,' he had said one day when Perkin had been staying with Sir Baldwin and his wife, Jeanne. 'I had to visit the south, at Avignon. It was the sort of country where a man would be happy to give up the life of struggle, and join a monastery.' He had worn a sad expression then, as if he regretted not having taken up the opportunity when he was there.

'You travelled widely when you were young?'

'Yes, I did.'

'But you don't want me to share your experiences,' his son said.

'William, you don't realise how dangerous it is. Since the pestilence, and without the great nobles since Crécy and now Poitiers, the land is in turmoil.'

'You cannot tell how bad it is! As I've said before, you haven't been there in thirty years!'

His father shrugged as if the passing years were the mere blink of an eye. 'That may be true, but that does not mean I am wrong. It is a dangerous place to visit, with the threat of death and capture at all points. I have seen war, and it is not a pleasant experience. I would prefer you not to go.'

'If you hadn't stopped me last year, I would have been with the Black Prince at his battle, and I'd have come back with riches after that.'

'Or you would not have returned at all,' his father said heavily.

'I will take part in the next great battle,' William said. 'You cannot stop me! I want to do the same as you, and fight for the king. Just as you did against the traitor.'

'I know,' Baldwin said, and he sighed. 'Since your sister died, I had hoped you would remain here. But if you are determined, I will not prevent you.'

That, of course, was the main difficulty that William's father had raised. He did not want William to die. Perkin had heard his own father say often enough that losing a child was the most tragic event in any parent's life. Perkin had lost two brothers, both dead before they were four years old. He never knew his older brother, but thought he vaguely remembered little John, who died when Perkin himself was only three years of age. His mother never truly recovered from that death. It marked her for the rest of her life, until the pestilence took her.

'Then I shall go,' William said, and thus was their fate sealed.

The company had been planning on riding to a neighbouring village to extract more food and *pâtis*. Hawkwood and Peter's men rode from the castle in the middle of the morning, taking the road towards Paris, and as they rode, the men began to see dribs and drabs of other men riding away. Sir James Pipe was tempted to send men after some of these, but it hardly seemed worthwhile, as his sergeant said.

'They may be carrying valuables with them,' Sir James muttered.

'Why would they be riding away from Paris, though?' was Hawkwood's comment.

It was a matter of some consternation, Hawkwood

could see, among the company members. If they were riding from Paris, what did that mean? Any number of people would flock to the city, because it had the strongest walls, it had the largest population, with stores of food and weapons to defend against a siege. Leaving the city was lunacy, since it would mean travelling to a smaller location with weaker defences that could be easily overrun. The companies had proved that all over France already.

It was not until they reached a village near Arpajon that they heard the latest news. A herald came to Sir James and craved a meeting.

'Who sent you?'

'I am sent by the dauphin, to ask you to halt your raids. Will you agree to a truce?'

They took their rest at a small village, and when a tavern keeper was forced to broach a barrel of wine, they sat with the herald to discuss terms.

Sir James shook his head. 'I would be happy to have a truce, but you see, I have over a hundred men to think of. They will grow restless without food and drink, and how can I pay for them, when I am prevented from claiming *pâtis* from the people about here?'

'You would threaten the poor peasants of this area?' the herald asked sorrowfully.

'Of course not, but if the peasants refuse to accept our King's Peace, and instead continue to try to thwart his will, I have no choice.'

'I had heard that your king has sent emissaries to beg you to stop your actions here.'

'Ah, yes. I did meet with them. But, you see, their warrants were not correct. I could not confirm the validity of their authority, so obviously their mission was not convincing. It was impossible for me to halt my efforts on the whim of two men whose positions were dubious.'

'The dauphin is prepared to offer you money.'

Sir James sat back in his seat with a broad grin. 'That sounds better. How much?'

17

The march was tedious for William and Perkin.

Travelling at the speed of Archibald's oxen made for a long, slow journey, and although Sir Reginald continued to state that his interest lay in quickly entering the fray on behalf of the king, his actions seemed less ambitious. The company made a leisurely advance towards Paris, the oxen lumbering along, but their need for regular halts to feed and chew the cud meant they could only travel a few miles every day. William found himself fretting that they would never reach any area where they could experience the action. He had come all this way to *fight*, not to plod along at the speed of Archibald's oxen!

However, all along the way, he was impressed by

how docile the populace was. They were definitely cowed, he reckoned. He mentioned it to Perkin, and Archibald overheard him. The gynour was less enthusiastic about their apparent acceptance of whatever strictures were laid upon them.

'They have suffered much,' he commented.

William was unimpressed. With all the confidence that his twenty-two years gave him, he declared, 'It's more that they accept the authority of their rightful king.'

'You think so?'

'Of course! *Look* at them. When we arrive, they come and give us food. They don't attack us, they just submit, as they should.'

'Look at them, William. They have suffered enormously, from our men, from brigands, from their own noblemen, from the taxes levied to ransom their king, and what do they have to look forward to? Everyone robs them. Me, I feel only pity for them. Their lives are all but unendurable.'

'They dare not even rise up to defend their lands.'

'How? They have done, and each time, our professional soldiery has massacred them. Not only the peasants here in the country, but their noblemen too. They have no leadership, no money, no food, no hope. Yes, I pity them. But if they should ever decide that they can bear no more, then I would be worried. Very worried indeed, for then we should have many hundreds of thousands against us.'

'A few English can fight even many thousands,' William scoffed.

'Don't be a fool!'

'You call me a fool?' William demanded, his honour impugned.

'Take your hand from your sword, master. Yes, I called you a fool. I have seen battles all the way over France from Guyenne to here, and I tell you now, yes, English archers and men-at-arms are strong, organised and effective against larger forces, but the whole English army would not suffice if the entire kingdom of France rose against us. There would be no protection against that. So, yes, I pity them, but I fear them in equal measure, for if they were to realise their strength, we would be the ones fleeing.'

William took his hand away from his weapon, but his face remained cold. 'Perhaps so, but they would soon catch you, if you were to try to run. Your oxen would barely outrun a snail.'

'I have fought often enough. With my gonnes, I could hold them off for a while. If they were to surround you, with ten against you, I wonder how long you would survive?'

William shrugged and trotted a little further on, away from the rattling wagon. Perkin kept his mount at Archibald's side. 'Do you think there is a risk that the peasants might rebel?'

'I haven't seen any try, but next time you meet with them, when you pass them in the road, when you see them in their fields, look at them. You see it in their eyes.'

'What? Resentment? I have seen that in the eyes of some English peasants before now.'

'Yes, in some. But here? There is a sullenness and anger in them. They feel their government has failed them, that their *bellatores* are not fighting for them, for their livelihoods, and yet they still tax them even after they have been plundered by us and other *routiers*.' Archibald hunched down on the board of the cart and shook his head doubtfully. 'I would not gamble money on their continued acceptance.'

In the end, Sir James's company held to the truce until the second week in March. As soon as it expired, the company rode out. On 12 March, they took Arpajon and Montlhéry, and from there, they continued on almost as far as Montereau. Fulk and Hawkwood were happy to see more towns and villages fall to the arms of Pipe's men, and there was a great deal of food and drink that could be plundered from the locals.

This was a land of plenty, Fulk considered. It had been an area of relative peacefulness and calmness, a vast territory that had filled the grain stores and butcheries of Paris for two hundred years, and now Sir James and his men were reaping the benefit.

But they were not alone. Every so often, the company would meet other freebooters from England or elsewhere. Many fighters who had once been warriors for King John of France, who now had no employment or income, had also come to take what they might. Hawkwood and Peter were keen to prevent as many as possible, and when they found other parties encroaching on the lands, they considered their own fierce little skirmishes could ensue, although more commonly the French bands would disperse hurriedly. They had experienced the firepower of English bows in battle before, and were not enthusiastic to repeat such an adventure. Once a man had seen his comrades pinned to the ground with a rash of arrows, he was not keen to risk putting himself in that position.

Today, Hawkwood and Fulk were riding together, leading a small column of Pipe's men past a little wood, when they saw the glint of steel ahead, and Fulk and Hawkwood both reined in, warily eyeing the roadway between the trees. Fulk's horse made his own feelings known, lifting his tail and defecating.

'What think you?' Fulk said.

'Hard to tell, but I'd guess men-at-arms. That looked like a lot of steel,' Hawkwood said, and soon they were organising the men from their group, dismounting and stringing bows before having Rat and the other boys lead the horses to safety. There were only thirty men all told, but with twenty archers among them, Hawkwood was convinced that they were more than a match for even three times that number of French soldiery or a force of impressed peasants.

Fulk had his halberd in hand, and took the left-hand side of the road, organising the archers at the rear of the company, while Hawkwood took the front. They had worked this ploy before, deploying the archers along the one side of the road. Fulk's men would despatch the lead riders as they came close, and while the group panicked, Hawkwood with his men would attack the group's rear, enclosing the survivors in a milling horror of bodies and death. They would invariably surrender, and then the English could decide whether to ransom the survivors, or merely rob them of all valuables and let them pass on their way.

The riders were approaching at a steady, if slow, pace, and Hawkwood could see them now. The foremost rider had armour, and while he didn't wear a bascinet, he looked ready and prepared for action, with two outriders before him, and a strong party behind. The rumble of heavy wagons came to Hawkwood clearly, and the hooves of the horses were a constant clatter.

On they came, the outriders moving comfortably on their mounts. One was a little ahead of the other, and when he was close to the small wood, he stopped, indicating to his company that they should halt too. Very slowly, he walked his horse forward, his eyes all over the trees. He studied the branches and undergrowth on both sides of the road, then trotted back to the main party. All at once the man-at-arms barked an order, and the men behind dropped from their horses and deployed on both sides of the roadway.

Hawkwood saw them stringing their bows, and made a quick decision. He called, 'Wait! We are English – are you too?'

'I am Sir Reginald de Tony. Who are you?' the knight replied.

Hawkwood indicated to his men that they could ease their bows, before standing and walking from the trees. 'I am John Hawkwood, Sir Reginald. I serve Sir James Pipe. He's a few miles behind us.'

Sir Reginald studied him cautiously, but although he did not order his men to settle down, he was suddenly surprised by a shout from a wagon.

'*John*, is that really you?' Archibald bellowed. 'God give you health!'

* * *

April

Today Fulk bore the Rat on his mount with him.

The company covered many miles every day. Now, since they had met with Sir Reginald's party, they travelled more sedately, at the more leisurely pace of Archibald's oxen, which was easier for the boys, but even so, lads as young as Crespin and Henri could barely keep up, pattering along on their bare feet. Especially now, in the darkness before dawn. They had been installed in Archibald's wagon to rest.

Fulk rode with one arm around the boy, gripping the reins, his halberd in his right hand. The butt resting on the stirrup. Rat was dozing again, and Fulk occasionally glanced down at the lad's face. It was perfectly at ease, much like his own Jacquet when he had been asleep. Rat was older, at ten or eleven, but harsh living had made him look older. Now, asleep, at peace, he could have been only seven or eight, like Jacquet. There was something utterly engaging about a young boy's face at rest, Fulk thought. It brought a little lump to his throat to recall his own child.

Jacquet had been a joyful little boy. Eager, into everything – Fulk had been forced to take his belt or a switch to the fellow all too often, but he was yet a good companion. He made Fulk feel whole and entire; the simple presence of the small figure who was so dependent upon him for protection and food was enough to warm his heart. And these boys made him feel the same. He had failed Jacquet, but he wouldn't fail these boys.

They were riding towards another little town. Fulk eyed it with the dispassionate gaze of a man viewing a rabbit and deciding whether to capture this one, or the next. It was no difficult task, only one more step on the way to plunder. He hefted his halberd, and the small figure before him grunted and snuggled deeper into Fulk's arm, whimpering and squirming as he dreamed. It made Fulk smile.

The company had already taken many others, but this little walled town was appealing. The fact that it had walls indicated that people thought there was safety behind them, and that might mean that people from miles about could have gathered up their valuables and brought them here to be safe. Which also meant it was a choice target for the men of Sir James's and Sir Reginald's companies.

Fulk gently stirred the boy and helped him to slide from the horse. Rat and the other boys, yawning and rubbing their eyes, took the reins from the company, moving away, while the men trudged quietly forward.

Under cover of darkness, the men advanced to within a bowshot of the walls, and now, in the chill light of morning, with a gentle mist about them, they formed into their vintaines.

Fulk had seen many little towns like this in his time in France. It was no different to any other, but he could see that some of the men had little experience of such assaults. The two new men in Sir Reginald's force looked excited, but trepidatious too. Fulk saw that the esquire, William, was glaring at the walls as if he could force them to tumble with his will alone.

And then they attacked.

18

In reality, William's show of ferocious calmness was intended to conceal the roiling in his stomach. This was his first action, and he had no idea how he would react to the reality of battle. He glanced over at Perkin, who looked concerned as well, and said, 'Here we go, then!'

'Yes. I'd prefer to be in the tavern in Crediton just now.'

William gave what he hoped was a bold and courageous grin and shrugged. 'Only because of young Helena!'

'More because of the ale,' Perkin said. He gripped William's shoulder. 'Godspeed, William. God save you!'

'And you!'
And the trumpets blew.

* * *

It was a mad, thrilling rush, William thought. They ran, full tilt at the walls, three men to each of the ladders, all of them assembled quickly in their sections, so that they could be thrown against the walls at speed, William and Perkin in the second group immediately behind the big Swiss.

Perkin went before William, clutching the ladder in his left hand, his right gripping his sword. It was lunacy, exciting but terrifying. Perkin had never been in a real battle – his fights had been struggles in taverns and one riot in a street. In his mind's eye he saw men he had known who had been in wars, men with lost limbs, one with an empty eye socket, men with scars over their faces and breasts, men permanently hobbled, men with arms that would not lift or hands that couldn't grip. It made his stomach feel greasily loose, as if he might empty his bowels at any moment, and that made him panic, fearful of shaming himself in front of all these men.

A crossbow bolt slammed into the ground near him, and he yelped in quick alarm, then bent his head and tried to force the ladder and the other men with him onwards, but then the ladder stopped, and when he looked up, they were at the town's walls, and the ladder was being pushed up and up, until it went past the vertical and slammed against the wall, and two men were already climbing up at speed, bellowing their defiance at the men on the walls hurling rocks at them. The topmost man was struck on the head, a glancing blow that tore a flap of skin from his brow, and he shrieked in crazed fury, pressing on upwards, until he reached the top and defended himself against a man with a spear, but by then Perkin was on the ladder himself, clambering up, only to see the first man cough, clutch at his breast, and then fall back, off the wall, plummeting to the ground with a quarrel in his breast. There was a loud crackle of breaking bone as he landed on his back.

Perkin was the fourth man on this ladder, William immediately behind him, and the two scurried up the rungs as though they were chased by all the demons of hell.

But hell was at the top. Perkin sprang over the battlements to the walkway, and there he stumbled on a man's arm and entrails. It reeked of iron and shit, and he hurriedly stepped away, grimacing, shaking his boot to clear the muck from it, and as he did so, a sword flashed in front of his face. It struck a spear aimed at Perkin's face, knocking it away, and Perkin looked up into the face of a wizened little man gripping a sword. He laughed, grabbed the townsman's lance and pulled it away from him, thrusting his short sword into the man's throat. Blood gushed, spattering Perkin, and he felt he wanted to heave, but there was no time. He wanted to thank the man for saving his life, but the fellow was already haring off along the walkway to the steps, flying down them and making his way to join the knot of English at the gate, attacking the guards there, and then pulling the bars free to let in all the rest of Sir James's and Sir Reginald's men into the town.

'Good God,' William breathed beside him. 'That was wonderful!'

Perkin looked at him, then down into the town, at the bodies lying sprawled, at the men who were still alive, weeping or screaming with pain, at the women hurrying away, desperate to escape the inevitable.

That was when he vomited the first time.

* * *

Gadiffer stood trembling at the sight. From here, a half mile from the town, the two could hear the screams and see the flames rising from the buildings. It was a town being despoiled. He knew what that looked like. No Frenchman could have any doubts as to the savagery now being inflicted on the populace.

He didn't want to be here.

Juliot, he thought, *why did you do it? We're here because of you, to try to win your salvation, but can we?*

Auffroy was determined – that was true. But Gadiffer was less certain. Retrieving the cross stolen from Juliot's body might mean that God would look more kindly on her. They would have to regain it, and then take it to her grave and place it on her breast. That was a horrible scene to think of. Auffroy would do anything to try to save her soul, to be reassured that he would see her in Heaven, but Gadiffer was unsure. Juliot had committed the sin of self-murder, of slaying her child, of having her child out of wedlock... Even if the two succeeded in winning back her cross, would that change anything?

* * *

William sat at the fire's side drinking wine. The drinks were flowing easily here tonight, and he felt satisfaction at the efforts of the day. His arm was stiff from wielding his sword, and there was a long scratch on his left bicep where an opponent had raked it with a dagger, but he felt well enough. One of the archers had spread egg white all over it, and the pain had faded to a mere annoying itching, with occasional flarings as if a hot blade was being dragged over it again. He would live.

The town was full of the cries of widows and children, with some men screaming as they were invited to share the location of their treasure. It was all natural, if a little disconcerting. William tried to put it from his mind. He was a man-at-arms, the son of a knight, and he couldn't allow himself to be distracted or upset by this kind of matter. The class of noblemen of which he was a part had a duty to be firm, resilient and relentless. People like these townsfolk, who stood in the path of armed forces, had to pay the price for their defiance and insubordination.

He stood, finished his drink, and went out to the tavern's rear yard, standing at the wall to empty his bladder. More screams and laughter from the roadway made him wince. This was far from his quiet home in Devon. A pang struck him as he recalled his father's manor. His older brother, Baldwin, named for their father, would inherit that. It was better that he should. It was curious, when William thought about it. His own uncle, his father's brother, had inherited the manor when William's grandsire had died. Then, as his father had said, his father had left England and travelled to Outremer, the rump of the lands that had been the Kingdom of Jerusalem. There Baldwin had fought the Saracens in the last battle, the siege of the city state of Acre, before the Christians were evicted from God's own lands.

It had been a disaster for all Christendom. God had taken His lands from His people, and the whole of Christianity felt that slight with horror. If God was so appalled by His people, the end of the world must soon be upon them. William's father said that Christians across Europe were keenly aware of their failings, yes, but no one had expected Him to deprive them of the solace of protecting His city. Dire predictions were made, of famine, war and plague, and by all accounts they had come true: there was an appalling famine in 1316 lasting for five years, when many died. Then there came the wars, and most recently the pestilence. William remembered that last, although the famine was long before his birth.

In any event, when his father had returned from the crusade, he had discovered that his brother had died while he was away, and the manor was now his. It was a shock to a man who had expected to receive nothing, to be suddenly elevated to become a magnate in the county of his birth.

William rehitched his hosen and tunic, and returned into the tavern to cross the screens passage out into the road, and it was there, before the tavern's door, that he saw Sir Reginald and Sir James squaring off against each other.

'I do not recall indicating that I would serve under you,' Sir Reginald said firmly.

'You joined my company,' Sir James responded.

'We agreed to ride together for a period. I did not agree to become your sergeant.'

'If you do not find the position to your taste, you are free to leave at any time,' Sir James said. He moved slightly, planting his feet more firmly, his hand dangerously close to his sword's hilt.

'Good sirs,' William said, hurrying to stave off a dispute that could lead to bloodshed. 'Wait! Surely we can all continue as we have, riding together for mutual advantage and profit? There is no need for an altercation. Come, there is wine in the tavern, why not share a cup in good humour? We have much to celebrate, don't we? We've had a great success in taking this town, after all. Let's celebrate, eh?'

'I suppose so,' Sir Reginald said. After a moment or

two, he held out his arm in sign of peace, and Sir James, after a brief hesitation, took it, before the two followed William into the tavern. There, the three sat and drank to each other's health. But William did not feel that the truce would last. These knights were strong-willed and ambitious. Sir Reginald would not tolerate another commanding him, and Sir James would not want a second, rebellious knight in his company.

19

Perkin had not enjoyed his first experience of battle. He was uninjured, which was a blessing, but he had seen too much violence that day.

He had brought up his stomach's contents after the town was surrendered. Still feeling weak, he left the men of the company as they ran riot through the streets, some taking women they found cowering under tables or concealed in cupboards. Others were keen to find wine and ale, or money, or food, while still more seemed to delight in simple destruction, breaking into buildings and setting them on fire. Even now, as the light faded, sparks flew into the air with every gust of wind, and as he stared along the line of the wall on the upper walkway, the screams and cries from the town appalled him.

He saw, from his high position, a woman fleeing a group of men, her chemise torn, and one arm over her breasts as she fled. In the streets there was a woman sobbing and keening next to a figure covered in blood, while only a short distance behind her a pale-coloured dog nudged at a man's body.

It was not at all what he had anticipated. For some reason Perkin had thought that this first battle would blood him, like a boy on his first hunt, and that as soon as the blood flew, he would feel the same exhilaration, the same joy, that he had experienced when his hounds caught the first fox and his face was blooded by the master of the hounds, cutting off the tail and giving it to him as a reward, marking both cheeks with blood to show he had taken part in his first chase. That initial hunt had been alarming at first: both daunting and fearsome. After that, though, he had learned to thrill to the sound of the hunting horn, to feel the excitement deep in his belly as his mount lurched forward into the gallop, the hounds hurtling along, baying their enthusiasm... He had known after that first hunt that it would become a passion for him. Just as certainly, he knew that assaulting a town or city would never give him the same pleasure.

'You seek silence?'

The voice intruding into his reverie made him jump in surprise, and he turned to see Archibald. 'I was leagues away.'

'I could tell. You had that look of a man who is like as not about to walk over the end of the path and fall to your doom,' the gynour said, peering over the edge of the wall. 'It would be a sad end, falling there. You'd land in that cesspit, I fancy.'

'I wasn't thinking where I was going.'

'Your first taking of a town?'

'Yes.'

Archibald nodded, his mouth curved like a strung bow. 'It is not pleasant, this after-effect. I know how it affected me, that first time.' He could recall it with perfect clarity. Once a monk, he had left his order when he was persuaded that the religious life was not for him. Fascinated with black powder, he had taken on the role of serpentine, making his powders and using them to propel stones at men and cities. But then, that first time, he had been appalled by the sights, the bodies, the destruction.

Some had said to him after that that he should return to a convent and plead that God might forgive him his past and help him forget. He had spent much of that first evening weeping to himself, hidden in his wagon, trying to shut out the sounds of despair of widows and children. He had not succeeded.

'Come with me, master. I have found friends here. I will introduce you to them.'

* * *

There were some thirty men in the encampment. Perkin was introduced to the thickset man called John Hawkwood at the nearer fireside. He gave Perkin a cursory up-and-down look, like a sexton measuring a man for a coffin, before giving him a sharp nod.

'Hawkwood is one vintener of these men. This here is another: Peter. Robin is the last vintener. Anything you want to learn about a bow and arrow, Robin can teach you.' Robin – tall, lean, with mousy hair – looked up with an easy grin. 'Here is Fulk. He's from some place, he says, where the snow stays on the ground even in summer, high up in the mountains.' Fulk was sitting back with a young boy on his lap, who was snoring. He met Perkin's eye with disinterest. 'I think he's joking with us. This is Nick, and here's Saul and Dogbreath.'

'I know you,' Perkin said. 'You saved me from a lance up on the wall!'

'That was you? Aye, well, you looked like you was

about to get spitted,' Dogbreath said. 'Aye, those bastards on the wall were keen to see what you was
made of.'

'I am grateful to you.'

Dogbreath shrugged. 'Aye, well...'

Perkin was offered a space on the ground, and he
gratefully took his seat between Dogbreath and a
Frenchman called Gassot. A jug was passed around,
and the men all took a pull at it. It was full of good
wine, and Perkin began to feel less mournful and
sickly.

'It was a good attack,' Peter said.

'None of us dead,' Dogbreath said. 'That's a good
ending to the day.'

'Have you all been together for long?' Perkin asked.

'Too long,' Hawkwood said. 'I've been part of this
company since we were fighting to capture Calais. I'm
still trying to lose Dogbreath, but he's like a turd on
your shoe. Once he's there, it's difficult to get rid of
him.'

Dogbreath glowered at him. 'Aye, leastways I don't
hang back like some lovelorn vintener. I'm bold, me! I
go into the attack and get stuck in; don't matter who
the enemy is. I'm there.'

'Yes,' Robin said, explaining for Perkin, 'we let him
go in first, because with his breath he's likely to strike

all defenders with horror as he gets close. He is our sacred weapon, the man of foul breath.'

Dogbreath scowled. 'Aye, well, you're all lucky to have a real fighter like me with you. Without me, you'd all have got stuck at Poitiers. It was only me and a few others who held the line. Others like you were ready to run!'

'You went on ahead to see if you could get to the wagons in the baggage train of the French army.'

'Aye, well, there would have been good pickings in there,' Dogbreath said with a faraway look in his eyes. 'You know, a royal princess, a crown... That's the sort of thing I need. About time I was proper rewarded for all my efforts.'

'Why aren't you all in the town with the others?' Perkin asked.

Peter shrugged. 'When you see a company like the rest of the men here all going into a town, it's best to make sure that some stay sober. If there's a French company in the area, we may have to fight to keep the town, or fight our way through them to escape. Either way, it's better that we remain ready for anything. We have a couple of men in the church's tower keeping an eye out for any advancing force. If you hear a horn blast in the night, arm yourself.'

'You think some group might come tonight?' Perkin asked, alarmed.

'No. But that doesn't mean they won't,' Robin said lightly.

Archibald had seated himself with Ed a short distance from the rest of the men. He called out, 'Don't listen to them, Master Perkin. They like to talk about how important they all are; they would have you believe that they're all wolves, when in truth they are as much use as a collection of lapdogs in a fight. Besides, if there were an assault, I would load up my little toys, and we'd soon repel them, Ed and me, before this lot had stirred themselves.'

'Oh, aye, Gynour,' Dogbreath sneered. 'You and your toys wouldn't manage to load and fire a first barrel, lessen us archers had taken the enemy out from a quarter mile away. If we relied on you and your devilish machines, we'd still be stuck at Crécy, six feet under in a mass grave.'

'Your arrows can only hit one target at a time,' Archibald said comfortably, resting his back against the wall.

'Your stones can miss all targets every time.'

'My stones will strike ten or more with every blast.'

'Yes. Ten or more other stones, and miss the men.

Besides,' Dogbreath added, 'we know they aren't good for others, don't we?'

Archibald's expression changed. His eyes snapped open and he stared at Dogbreath. 'What does that mean?'

'You know, like at Poitiers, when...'

Robin said quickly, 'Dogbreath, don't talk about that.'

Archibald and Ed were both staring at him hard.

Dogbreath took in Robin's expression and his eyes widened, just fractionally. He shook his head. 'My mouth runs away sometimes, Gynour. That was an evil day. Clip, Grandarse, all those others. I didn't mean to upset you.'

'There's nothing to apologise for,' Archibald said, and Perkin saw him settle back again. Ed, too, visibly relaxed. It was enough to remind Perkin that he was among comrades, but they were still all archers and warriors. A quick mistake, a wrong word, could easily lead to someone pulling a sword or dagger and killing without thought.

He must be careful with these men.

20

___

MAY

'I will not see the village destroyed,' Sir Reginald said.

'I order it burned,' Sir James countered.

The two were standing scant feet apart, and the animosity was clear between them. William stood near, anxiously moving from one foot to the other as the two men stood off. Perkin had moved to his side as the shouting began, and the men of the company were watching with sombre expressions. None of them liked to see their commanders in dispute.

William left the two knights arguing, and made his way along the lane to the approaches to the village.

It was an unimpressive little hamlet. Small peasant houses huddled together as if for warmth near a small church, two barns and a storeroom for the village's cart. Chickens had been walking about, pecking, but all were now in sacks ready to be plucked. There were no other animals, only a cat, which watched the men with the cold indifference of a god. Why would anyone want a place like this? William wondered to himself. It was too small to bring in much produce, the fields were overrun with weeds and thistles, and the houses were in a sorry state of dilapidation. It was obvious that the small community was both poor and under-populated, that they had not the manpower to farm the land effectively.

He was standing surveying the weed-infested strips of the communal fields when he noticed a flash in the hedge about the southern edge of the place. Carefully, so as not to give away the fact that he had seen the movement, he kept his face away from it, but he kept his eyes on it carefully all the while. There was another flash, a short movement of a pale figure, and William turned and walked away, his spine tingling with anticipation.

It might be a crossbowman, or an archer, and at any moment he might feel the stab of a missile, or per-haps he could be felled by a bullet from a sling. They were very effective weapons at shorter ranges, and he had no helmet to hand. He walked further, down to the roadway, which led through the hedge, and then he crouched and peered up along the greenery. There was no sign of a force of men or cavalry, to his relief, but he was convinced that the movement was that of a figure. There was a man or woman up there. Quietly, he began to follow the line of the hedge. It encircled the hamlet, a defence against wild animals, made of thick, thorny plants, which would deter foxes and wild dogs, while also keeping in any cattle or horses near to the village.

It was thick enough that a man could lie within it and watch, William thought, and as he stepped silently towards the spot where he thought he had seen the figure, he slowed cautiously, pulling his sword from its sheath.

There was a hollow beneath the hedge, which indicated that there was a run for rabbits or other creatures, but this had been widened, and now, even as he came closer, he could see a bare foot protruding.

He tapped the flat of his sword against the ankle and stood back.

Rat squirmed in his sleep.

The men had marched a long distance, and although Fulk seemed to be fond of Rat for some reason, it was more comfortable for all the boys to sit and rest in the bed of the wagon with Archibald.

Since that first ride with Fulk, Rat had become more confident. Before that, his dreams had been haunted with visions of ghosts – the woman buried at the crossroads, the hag, Arn – but gradually now, after the months of travel, as no ill befell him, he began to feel more secure. It was sad that Arn was gone, but the men all believed him when he spoke of the Devil appearing. It still made him shiver.

The attacks on towns and villages were scary, yes, but somehow he felt sure that the mountain man and the others were almost impervious to danger. They seemed to be immune. Even running across open fields with scaling ladders, few were injured. Fulk had said that it was because all the Frenchmen who were capable of fighting were already dead or injured, or had been impressed into the local hosts, preparing to fight for their king or their lords, and only the elderly and infirm remained.

It made no difference to Rat. All he knew was he was safe. Fulk would protect him, and Fulk was greater than any of the men in the company or the French army. The hag was no longer a threat. She had tried to deprive Rat of family and belongings, but he had outwitted her. She had no more power over him now.

He had not felt this secure since his mother died. Even his dreams were calmer.

* * *

The man was barely seventeen, William reckoned, and built like a wraith. He was so slender, every muscle stood out like whipcord, perfectly visible under the thin flesh of his arms and breast. Eyes the grey of aged steel stared at William from a shock of pale fawn hair that stuck up in all directions from where the twigs and branches had caught it as he withdrew from his place of concealment.

'Do you live here?' William demanded, his sword at the man's neck.

He stared, and William thought he was about to spit at him, but then he pulled a grimace and shook his head. '*Non.*'

William nodded. 'Nearby?'

'Yes.'

'What were you doing here?'

'Watching.'

'Us? Why? To tell others where we are, what we do?'

'No, to make sure our homes are safe enough. You

English burn everything. You murder, you plunder, and you destroy! We know about you!'

'Where are your noblemen to protect you?'

'They hide in their castles, and come out sometimes to capture your knights so they can ransom them.'

William frowned. 'But they are the third estate, the *bellatores*. It is their duty to defend you.'

'They do nothing. Our lord was injured at a battle, he says, but he remains in his castle where he is safe. We have nothing. No one will defend us. Who cares about the peasants who give them their food?'

William felt his sword's blade waver. This man was much like a number of the men who worked his father's manor. He had the same appearance, with his unkempt hair, his worn hosen and torn shirt. 'Does your lord not have men-at-arms to come and defend you? We have seen none since we arrived here.'

'A great lord? Come to risk his life for the poor *bonhommes* in his fields? No. He sends men when he increases the taxes to make sure we pay, not to help us. We have lost half our village to the plague, then when the English came we lost more, and now we have less than half our people, but the lord wants to increase our taxes again. *He* pays no taxes, but he forces us to. He collects everything from us, like all the nobility. But there is no compassion, no sympathy. We exist; he thrives.'

'It is the way of things. God gave us the three estates,' William said, haltingly. 'The *bellatores* to fight and maintain the peace, the priests to save our souls, and those who labour to provide the other two with—'

'At our own lives' cost! We struggle and work ourselves to the bone for a pittance, and all our efforts are stolen! Well, it won't carry on much longer! There are men who will overturn things. There will be a great bloodletting, and the rich will be destroyed,' the man said, his chin high.

William was tempted to run his steel over the man's throat. He stood there, so defiant, so contemptuous, the dollypoll – it was a struggle to withdraw his sword and sheathe it. 'You believe that?'

'The *Jacques Bonhommes* will punish them all. God is on our side!'

William felt his face crack. 'You think that peasants can rise against their masters? You fool, it would only lead to a great slaughter!' He chuckled.

But there was something in the lad's expression that stopped his laughter. There was no humour in his face as he said, 'The peasants together will form the biggest army in Christendom! You think a few nobles can stand against us?'

William frowned now. This peasant was quite serious, he thought. 'Go,' he said. 'Go with God.'

The man's expression changed. The defiance was
replaced by confusion, a look of doubt, as if suspecting
that this was nothing more than a ruse, but William
took a couple of paces back, away from the fellow, and
as soon as he was out of sword's reach, the man turned
away and bolted. William watched him. The stained
and filthy hosen and shirt ran all the way to the encircling woods, disappearing in among the trees, but he
was not alone. As he ran, William saw a second man,
someone dressed in dark grey, with a russet cowl and
cloak. He stood at the edge of the trees, observing
William. As the first fellow was swallowed up by the
woods, this second one slowly followed, his attention
fixed all the while on William.

It was curious. William returned to the village in a
deeply contemplative mood.

* * *

While the men shared their meal in ruminative
silence, Archibald and Ed tested the powder to make
sure it was still dry and functional. Perkin joined them,
his face betraying his anxiety. 'What will we do?'

Archibald carefully tapped the lid back on the

small barrel before answering. 'They will separate, I believe. Sir James is determined to keep going, I think, to the east. But his ambition is to destroy all the lands of the Île-de-France. He calls himself the lieutenant of King Charles of Navarre. Sir Reginald wants nothing to do with destruction.'

'What will you do?'

Archibald glanced at Ed. 'What do you think?'

Ed scratched his head. 'I think we should stay with the larger party of the two. There is strength in numbers.'

'Aye, there is truth in that,' Archibald said. 'I have just the one concern, however, which is, when drunken sots play at burning villages, towns and cities, they are all too likely to start a fire they cannot smother, and that might mean our powders being caught. I would not like to be caught with smouldering grasses or too many sparks and motes flying about. I value my life.'

'So, Sir Reginald?' Ed said.

'Aye. I believe he would be the safer of the two.'

'What of you?' Ed asked Perkin.

'I don't know. William and I were keen to join the battles for the land, but there are no great armies now. We are the latecomers.'

'Yes, you *tard-venus* are unfortunate,' Archibald

said with a dry chuckle. 'You missed all the profit, missed all the excitement, and now you are come, you discover a devastated land, with few crops, little livestock, and the country denuded of peasants.'

It was true enough. The fields had been burned, the monasteries, abbeys and convents closed, their valuables taken away for safekeeping, and the farms and hamlets contained few remaining residents. Most had fled at the first news of the advancing English.

'What will Sir Reginald do?' Perkin asked.

'He will seek lands farther from Paris, I expect, where he can expect to win better returns. In his mind, the best scheme would be to capture a small town and hold it, taking *pâtis* and tolls from travellers. That way a man can enjoy a rich and fulfilled life. He could rest himself on a comfortable seat while the money rolled in. No more burning villages, no more death, just regular milking of the peasants.'

Perkin nodded. He was unconvinced by the argument. To him, remaining with the larger party made most sense, but it would be good not to be involved in more war by terror. When he had heard that the English war in France was largely composed of *dampnum*, the deliberate destruction of entire communities, bringing home to all the peasants that their king could do nothing to protect them, he had believed it was a necessary task to bring about the end of the war. It should be effective. He knew that. The peasants should accept that there was nothing their king and his officers could do to save them; the people should understand this and agree to come into King Edward's peace, accepting his overlordship.

But instead the peasants remained mulishly reluctant. They left their farms to the English assaults, fleeing to the nearest towns and begging to be permitted to enter – not that many towns wanted extra mouths to feed. Yet, the stronger peasants, the men with strong arms who were used to wielding axes and mattocks, were snapped up. There may be little food stored by, but more to the point, the towns needed men to garrison their walls.

Since the black death, the population had not recovered. There were already fields that were fallow, with trees starting to colonise the spaces, and many houses were empty even before the English advances. The towns had little enough food stored to support their own population, without considering all the peasants from about them.

Whether to go with Sir James or Sir Reginald? He would have to discuss their options with William. For his part, he already felt more a part of Sir Reginald's

company than Sir James's. Besides, he held their indenture.

* * *

From deeper inside the treeline, Auffroy had watched
the tall, heavyset man as he stood staring at the trees
as young Gadiffer ran over the grass to the woods and
past Auffroy himself.

The man was a different one. Auffroy had not seen
him before, but no doubt he was one of the new co-
hort of men who had appeared.

It made everything more difficult. Auffroy had
hoped that he might be able to get close to the thief
and capture him, or merely waylay him and stab him
when he least expected it, but no, the man was always
with others, and even though Gadiffer was keen to
help Auffroy, neither of them was a trained warrior,
whereas the vile little man who took Juliot's cross was
a highly skilled fighter with weapons of all types. Auffroy had seen him practising with bow and arrow, and
had witnessed his ability with a sword when he
watched them from a safe distance as they stormed the
last village. If Auffroy was to attack him, Auffroy and
Gadiffer would probably die unless there was some

form of ambush that incapacitated the devil. But now, with a larger force about him, that was even less likely.

He rubbed his face. He had come all this way following the company, and he was no nearer achieving his aim than he had been at the town itself when that man had gone with the townspeople to bury them both, his woman and his child.

At his side, Gadiffer pulled his cloak around him more tightly. He was anxious. Auffroy was resolute, and Gadiffer sought to help Auffroy avenge his sister, but with every town captured by these English devils, his confidence in his ability to catch the thief diminished.

What could the two do against so many?

21

A week later, the dispute almost spilled into violence.

It was an ordinary morning, with the company riding from one town to the next, and when Sir James saw a small farmstead, he commanded a couple of his men to go riding out to investigate. They cantered off to the buildings, and before long, screams could be heard, and the men returned, one with his lance blooded. Behind them, when Perkin looked, he saw that a column of thin smoke rose from the farmstead. Soon it changed to a thick, oily yellow smoke with orange flames licking up as if to join the smoke and fly away.

'Sir James, what was the purpose of that?' Sir Reginald demanded, riding forward to the vanguard.

'We are here to destroy the land and all the farms. This is our task,' Sir James said calmly.

'This is damned stupid! Go and seek what may be stolen, yes, and then we can find a strong town or castle to fortify, and go about the countryside raiding, and take whatever food and treasure we desire, and return in a few months to fleece the peasants again. If you destroy everything, we cannot return. What would be the point? What, will you burn the whole of France just for a whim? This is madness!'

'You can leave at any time,' Sir James said loftily. 'That is your concern. I am here to serve our king and King Charles of Navarre. They command that we should destroy all that we can here, and that I intend to do.'

'The king would hardly be glad to know that all those he claims as his subjects have been tormented and slaughtered!'

'You don't know our king very well, do you, Sir Reginald?'

'I know him well enough, and now I know you too, Sir James,' Sir Reginald snapped, and he wheeled his horse about, calling in a voice that could be heard by the whole company. 'I will not continue on this route just to destroy all in our path. I will take those who wish to join me. We shall establish our own order in a castle and with that as our base, we shall ride about the kingdom like lords. No more destruction, only farming the peasants as lords should. Who wishes to join me?'

Perkin was surprised to see some of the men falling from the main column, especially when he saw that one was the tall Swiss with his halberd, and then Robin and Peter, who joined him. Soon, Dogbreath and Hawkwood, Nick, Ingram, Saul and the others from the archers' group. In all, perhaps thirty-five men joined with Sir Reginald.

'What of us?' he said to William.

'Look!' William said, pointing. There, at the rear of the column, was Archibald leading the oxen of the wagon, Ed kneeling on the bed. They were leaving the column and plodding on towards the archers. 'Even the good gynour is joining them.'

'Well?' Perkin said.

'Well, we are indentured to Sir Reginald,' William said. 'We can't just leave him. Come on!'

* * *

'What now?' William asked.

He and Perkin were flanking Sir Reginald. He had an esquire with him, and a boy riding a gentle-tempered palfrey behind him. The esquire, Giles of Holborn, was a man of perhaps four-and-twenty, with straw-coloured hair and a ready smile.

'Well, Master William, I intend to ride to the next town and see whether it shows promise. What I wish for is a good, strong fortress of some sort, in which we can base ourselves, and then conduct military sweeps around, taking money from the locals and, if we are fortunate enough to find one, sacking a manor or monastery. There are always rich pickings in such locations.'

'But Sir James is covering all the lands south of Paris with his men,' William said.

'Yes. So we shall go to the north. Amiens is a great city, too great for a force this size, but we may meet with other like-minded men on our way. We can see whether we can absorb some of them.'

His hope was soon to be put to the test.

When they met with this new company, William was initially convinced that they must be enemies. Their weaponry and armour was less like that of the English, and he felt sure that they must be Frenchmen, coming to attack.

Sir Reginald himself was also suspicious at first. It was only after a brief conversation that he gave a roar of pleasure and shook hands with the commander of the men. 'This is Sir Martin, and he is a loyal servant of Charles of Navarre,' he explained. 'They are riding about Paris to see how the situation is.'

William felt Perkin ride to his side as Sir Martin spoke of the situation in Paris. 'It is madness. The city has rebelled, and demands to control its own affairs. They want to destroy the nobility, and have already murdered several men. Even two marshals. So the dauphin has taken hold of two castles on the rivers feeding the city. With the ring of fire caused by English and Navarrese all about the city, it is difficult to see how they can survive.'

'What do the two castles matter?' Perkin asked.

Sir Martin glanced at him, rocking gently as his horse cropped grass. 'It is important. Paris depends on river traffic for food. The dauphin now can stop all food passing by those castles. There is only one last route for food to enter the city, and that is from the north. To the east, west and south, our forces control all roads and rivers. East and south-east, the dauphin's own forces have cut off Paris. Our King Charles is with the Parisians, and we shall join him there as soon as we may.'

'We would ride with you for a little while, until our paths diverge,' Sir Reginald said.

'You would be very welcome,' Sir Martin said. 'The roads are not as safe as once they were. Beware the red and blue hoods. That is the sign of the revolution.'

'We won't approach Paris,' Sir Reginald said with a chuckle.

Sir Martin was not smiling. 'You will see the hoods all over, north of Paris,' he said. 'The peasants, the townspeople, those from the cities; they all wear these colours to show their support for the revolution. And they have the ambition to kill all knights and noblemen, as well as all English. So, you see, it is best to keep an eye on the horizon, just in case.'

'We will bear that in mind,' William said.

'Do so,' Sir Martin said, but then he froze, staring ahead.

Following his gaze, William saw, a few hundred yards ahead, galloping like men chased by the Devil's Wish Hounds, a pair of riders. Seeing the company on the road before them, both slowed, turning in their saddles to gaze behind them, before cantering up more cautiously.

'Hold!' Sir Reginald said, his hand raised to halt them.

The two were men-at-arms, one with the insignia

of Clermont on his breast. He was a slender man, with strong, slim features under dark hair. He glared at Sir Reginald. 'Why, who are you?'

'Sir Reginald de Tony. I serve King Edward, and this is Sir Martin who serves King Charles.'

'I am esquire Galoys. I served Robert Clermont till his death. We are here because we were taking Saint-Leu, we and nine others, but we were set upon by peasants, and they slaughtered our companions and would have killed us too. We were fortunate that they had too few horses.'

'Peasants attacking men-at-arms? How did they succeed?'

'They fought on foot but, with spears and lances, they held us off until they had us surrounded and could kill us all. We were both in the van, and they could not catch us,' Galoys said. His head hung, dejected. No man-at-arms enjoys a reputation for cowardice, and fleeing from a group of mere peasants was an embarrassment. Any man would feel the shame. A real man would have stood his ground, even if it meant dying, William knew. A knight without courage was no man. William felt contempt for the two.

'Well, do not be concerned. They will pay the price.'

'Perhaps.'

'You doubt our ability to put down this rebellion?'

'The rebels are everywhere, Sir Martin. I hope we might be able to kill some, but in God's name, the lands here have burst into flame! There are risings in all the towns about here. They call themselves the *Jacquerie*, after *Jacques Bonhomme*, Jack Goodman, the peasantry of France.'

The very next day, William and Perkin encountered the after-effects of a rebel visit. At a little manor house some leagues from Paris itself, they rode into the devastation of a raid.

It was a pleasant setting, with a house not far from a spring that fed a channel where the horses stopped to drink, but almost immediately they shied and withdrew. That was when William saw her: a woman of perhaps sixteen years, her belly opened, her throat cut. She lay beside the spring, and her blood had polluted the water.

William dismounted and walked his horse to the remains of the manor. It had been fired, the roof all gone, and in the doorway were three bodies, a man and two women. In the yard itself were five small children, and William could feel tears pricking his eyes at the sight. They were all too young to be murdered. There was another woman, a servant girl, from the look of her, who lay on her back, legs spread wide. William averted his eyes from her, shocked.

'It is hard to see, is it not?' Sir Martin said. He had followed William, and now stood close by him. 'This is the sign of the rebels. They care only to kill noblemen and their servants. They think that they will have an easier life if they can kill all knights. Foolishness!'

William nodded, his eyes still fixed on the woman. 'What will they do? Could they attack a force like ours?'

'Unlikely, I should think,' the knight said. 'They are only peasants, after all. I would expect them to flee before us.'

'Galoys said that they had routed him and his companions, killing nine.'

'Perhaps that was bad luck. A small force of men-at-arms can always be overwhelmed by a larger force, but knights will always prevail against such men,' Sir Martin said comfortably. 'We have the training, the resilience, to succeed. These peasants, they have no courage, no *élan*. They cannot beat noblemen.'

'No,' William said. He glanced around to see Perkin, who was also staring down at the bodies.

Worse was to come.

22

It was a small convent, and the men rode in with a presentiment of evil. William could hear the intake of breath as some of the men saw the figures on the ground. Even Dogbreath was silent.

The women had all endured great suffering, apart from the mother superior, who was elderly and looked to have died quickly, a great wound at her shoulder and neck where a sword or axe had struck. William could easily imagine that she had accosted the men as they appeared, and they had slain her on the spot before ransacking the convent and raping the women.

He was staring at the body of a young blonde woman when he heard a stifled sob behind him.

When he turned, he saw that Rat was there, an expression of petrified horror on his face.

'Boy, go back to wagons,' he commanded curtly. The boy didn't seem to hear him, but remained where he was, staring at the dead woman. Then a slight, piercing keening came from his throat, and William quickly dismounted, crossing to the boy and, taking him by the shoulders, turned him away from the scene. He crouched down and held the lad's attention, staring at him firmly. 'Boy, go back to Archibald and Ed. Do you hear me? Go now.'

Fulk was behind the boy, and he nodded, taking the boy's shoulder and turning him away from the scene of horror. Rat's breathing made his small chest shudder, and he clutched at Fulk's hand. The Swiss pulled him away, past the rest of the archers on their mounts, to the wagons and Archibald.

* * *

Rat felt himself lifted into the wagon, and he knelt, staring ahead at the devastation. All at once, the memory of his mother's death came back to him. Seeing the nuns slaughtered like cattle destroyed the sense of security that had enwrapped him in recent days. This felt like the work of the Devil.

It was enough to make him sob with the horror.

* * *

William stared about him at the devastation, and felt shame – but more: the anger of such violence perpetrated against those whose only task was to protect the souls of all men. Yes, he could feel the rage bubble in his blood. It seemed to boil in his arms and shoulders, and then his breast as well.

His father, as he well knew, was a fierce opponent of injustice and cruelty. Sir Baldwin would have been determined to avenge such a crime. He spent his entire life fighting for the rights of the people in his jurisdiction as a Keeper of the King's Peace and Justice of Gaol Delivery. If he had discovered a scene like this, the needless slaughter of nuns, he would have sought out those responsible and brought condign punishment on the heads of all those who were guilty.

William had come seeking adventure and excitement. For him, participating in the fighting here in France, he had seen as little more than an opportunity to enrich himself, perhaps to take a manor of his own, a place where he could settle and find a wife, raise a family. It was the dream of many second and third sons, and many poor men too. John Hawkwood was the son of a tanner, William had heard, and there were many other examples of men who had come to France in recent years and become fabulously rich, earning glory and rewards beyond their wildest dreams, even though they were not of noble stock. Englishmen had courage, and they had the skill and training to take on larger armies.

But it was one thing to fight an army, and something quite different to see this kind of destruction. Wanton savagery for no purpose, inflicted on the brides of Christ. The English soldiery had come to France to take back the king's lands which had been unfairly stolen from him, but that was not the same as this *carnage*.

Who could have done this? Another company of English archers and men-at-arms? It was possible, and similar attacks had been perpetrated in the *chevauchées* before – the campaigns during which the English rode across France to bring horror to the population and cow them into submission.

How could any man think such treatment of nuns was justified? William felt his belly ignite with a fierce rage. He felt that he had a mission. Rather than merely plundering towns for his own profit, he envisioned a different future, one in which he emulated his father. Where Baldwin had been the Keeper of the King's

Peace, he, William, could become the same for King Edward's lands here in his French territories. He could take responsibility for swathes of land and the people living in them, help protect the monasteries and nunneries across a wide area. Pacifying the area after the violence of these murderers would be an honourable act.

But first he would have to establish himself. Both as a knight and as a government official.

It was not only Rat, Fulk realised. Young Henri and little Crespin were both also deeply affected by the sights at the convent. Fulk brought all three to the wagons and deposited them in the bed of Archibald's wagon.

The older man pulled off his coif and rubbed his bald head. 'That bad?'

'*Ja*,' Fulk said. He clutched his halberd in both hands. 'This was an evil attack.'

'They killed all the nuns,' Rat said. He was still shivering, Fulk saw, and he clenched his jaw, worried that the boy had seen too much death and violence in his short life. It was wrong for a boy to see so much. Most men would be appalled by such sights, he knew.

Crespin and Henri were just as upset. Fulk saw Crespin clutch at his breast, as though reaching for a cross, while Henri sat perfectly still, his eyes enormous and unblinking, like a small statue.

Fulk put his hand out and rested it on Henri's shoulder, but the boy did not seem to notice. He remained where he was, staring into the distance.

'It is the Devil,' Rat said. 'Like I saw when Arn was killed. He's following us, and he'll kill us all, like he has those nuns.'

'It is not the Devil. Just evil men,' Fulk said.

'I'm scared!'

Rat's words were so quiet, so filled with terror, that Fulk could not leave him. He pulled Rat into an embrace and it felt like his own little Jacquet all that time ago, when he was happy, and whole, and still living in the village with Ilse and their son. Happy times, joyous times. And all ended with the fire that took his house and home and family in that one conflagration.

'Do not be scared,' he said gruffly. 'I will not let anyone hurt you.'

'Even the Devil?'

Fulk felt those words like blocks of ice trickling down his spine.

* * *

'I don't know! I was just one of many!'

They had found him a scant half-league from the convent, a peasant man with the shoulders of an ox, the square, bronzed face of a worker, and the callused, scarred hands of a labourer. His shirt was spattered with brown stains of dried blood, one knee of his britches black from where he had knelt in blood. His hood was made of blue and crimson.

He had been snoring off the wine, which he had discovered in a farmhouse the previous evening, sprawled in the room where he had found the barrel. Now, with his hands tightly bound behind him, kneeling in the dirt of the yard outside, his face as mournful as that of a bullock taken from his mother, he stared up at the men with genuine terror in his eyes.

Peter was the one holding a knife before him. There was no need to rest it on the man's throat. The threat was all that was needed, as his eyes and the little patch of dampness between his legs demonstrated.

'How many were there?'

'I don't know. Hundreds.'

'Where are you from?'

'I came from just outside Paris. We attacked the castle at Beaumont-sur-Oise, where the Duchess d'Or-léans lived, but she had escaped before we reached it.'

'Whose idea was it to march on her castle?' Peter demanded.

'I don't know! It was our leader, Guillaume Cale, I suppose. He is the leader of the Jacquerie.'

William leaned forward. 'What is this "Jacquerie"?'

The man looked up at him with obvious bemusement. 'The *Jacques*. The *Jacques Bonhommes*, the *Jack Goodmen*, yes?'

Peter looked across at Fulk, who shrugged. Sir Reginald was sitting on a stool at a wall, listening, and now he rose and strode to the man. 'You claim to be a soldier in the French host? This is a term used for the common soldiery,' he explained to Peter.

'Yes, I am a Jacques,' their prisoner said with pride. 'We should have been at Poitiers, but the king in his foolishness decided that we weren't needed. Look at what he achieved! He led his men to disaster. If we had been there, the result of the battle would have been very different!'

'You think so,' Peter said quietly.

'You say your commander was a man called Guillaume Cale?' William said.

'He is the captain of the men of Beauvaisis. He will lead his army to war and destroy the nobility of France.'

'It takes a number of men to rise against the warrior class,' Sir Reginald said with contempt.

'We are thousands. All the men of the peasantry will rise against their oppressors. What do the nobles do for us? They demand our money for taxes, they force us to labour for them, they say they will *protect us*! *Protect us!* When do they do that? If they fear attack, they run away! Look at the Duke d'Orléans at Poitiers. Did he stand and fight? No, he ran from the battle like the coward he is. He let the soldiers fight and die, but did nothing to help them. The nobles, they are all the same! They take, take, take, and what do they give in return? Taxes! All they want is for this war to continue so they can make money from ransoms, and all the while they plunder the land, they rape our women and kill us men. All the peasants feel the same. The Jacquerie is growing, and rising. Soon we shall be a host ready to assault the dauphin and his entire corrupt government!'

'You think that mere peasants can defeat an army of noblemen?' Sir Reginald said, and his face registered his amusement.

'It is not peasants alone. Guillaume Cale has men under him who were noblemen. He has men with military experience. Besides, the towns support us. You think we are alone? The towns give us food and drink when we pass by, even as they close their gates to the dauphin's men. It is not some little uprising. The Jacquerie will take over France, for the good of France and all the French. And we will take back our lands from the English and force you from our shores, or bury you where you stand!'

Sir Reginald shrugged. 'You may think so. But God is on our side.'

'God will be with the Jacques.'

23

Gadiffer broke down when they found the little manor and saw the bodies of the families lying in the dirt.

Auffroy felt the same devastation at the sight. This was even worse than he had expected.

'Why? Why do the English do this?' Gadiffer moaned.

'They are evil,' Auffroy responded.

'But they didn't do this to the town. They didn't do this in other villages – why here?'

'Perhaps they thought the people here were re-sisting them? They were drunk? Who can tell what those murderers and felons are motivated by?' Auffroy said. He hefted his pack. 'Come, we need to try to catch up with them.'

'*Why?!* What is the point? Look around you, Auffroy! We can't fight this many men, and they're used to murder, where we are just workers. We can't go against them!'

'I will not give up until I have it back, and I can take it to her,' Auffroy said, his face white, and he grabbed Gadiffer by the collar of his shirt, shouting into his face. 'You hear me? I will *not* give up until I have justice for Juliot! I will find that murderer, and I will get it back for her and kill him!'

* * *

William left the room before they killed him. He had seen enough death in the last days already. He just hoped that Peter would be quick; he had the look of a man who would not feel the need to make a man suffer. William hoped not.

He was still standing outside the little building when Sir Reginald strolled out. 'So, esquire William, what do you think of that?'

William considered. 'If he's right and the whole area is rising, then we will have trouble going much further into the countryside. We should turn back, I suppose, go and find other English companies to join with for our own defence.'

'And leave prime lands to these damned Jacques? Nay, I don't think so. You miss the key point.'

'What is that?'

'He already said that the Duchess d'Orléans has fled her castle to escape to Paris, didn't he? Think of all the other castles waiting to be taken, the wealth that they hold, the manors, the forts, the rich towns – all these, and their garrisons are flying to the next town to escape their own peasants!' The knight laughed. 'It is perfect. Magnificent! If we don't make a fortune in the next weeks, I'm a leper!'

'I don't...'

'William, think about it. We are a military force to reckon with, if we get into a fight. But most Frenchmen seeing an English company like ours will run immediately. They know what happened at Crécy and Poitiers. Even in a siege, like that of Calais, we always prevail. Noblemen who fear for their lives because of a few unruly peasants are hardly likely to wish to tangle with us, are they? No! So what we can do is march fast, capture as many places as possible, and when we have taken enough to fill every wagon we can take, we make our way homewards, and I will build the biggest castle in Devon. I've always wanted to make the de Courtenays jealous. They may have their castle at Okehampton, but I will build a bigger, better castle at South

Tawton. We have a small market there already. A castle overlooking the town and the road to Cornwall – that would make them sit up and listen to me!'

His enthusiasm glittered in his eyes like the diamonds he planned to pilfer from the rich hoards he could see in his mind's eye.

William had one concern. 'What if he was right, and this Guillaume Cale has men who are experienced in war too? Could he have amassed an army large enough to become a danger to us?'

The knight chuckled. 'An army of peasants? You haven't seen these fellows, William. I have. When they first meet English clothyard arrows on a battlefield, they soon change their minds about fighting us. They will be no threat to us, no. But when they run, they'll leave behind everything of value, they'll be so keen to save their own skins. We shall be rich beyond our dreams!'

* * *

William was glad to hear that the knight was so bullish about the opportunities in the immediate future. He left Sir Reginald watching as the men brought out the Jacques' body and left it lying by a low wall, and he went to find Perkin.

His mind was whirling. The French were turning against each other. They were growing desperate, perhaps, but how could the peasantry think that they had any right to assault noblemen in their lands? The sight of the families at the little manor was shocking, but to see these nuns also slaughtered, raped and tortured was even worse. It meant the peasants were waging war on two equal pillars of society – the nobles and those praying for their souls. The labourers were rising against their lawful masters. That was unthinkable.

'We have found one of them,' he said when he found Perkin sitting with Dogbreath and the others.

'Yes?'

'He was lying in the house, dead drunk. Peter persuaded him to speak.'

'Can his words be trusted?' Robin asked.

'If it was me,' Dogbreath said, 'I'd lie and say anything.'

'You wouldn't have to,' Robin said. 'Your breath would make them all collapse.'

'Don't test me,' Dogbreath said, scowling.

'Why? Will you blow in my face?'

'Sir Reginald thought he was telling the truth,' William said, and told them what the man had said.

Robin sat back. 'He thinks we might be able to

make that much from the rebellion? That would be good, if he is right, and the guards and garrisons all decide to save themselves.'

Fulk was scowling.

'What is it, Fulk?' Hawkwood asked. 'You have a concern?'

Fulk stared into the campfire for a long moment before responding. 'You men, you are all English. Do you hear of my land of cantons?'

'What of it?' Dogbreath demanded. 'You tell us it's a place with mountains and valleys.'

'Yes. The men of the mountains, we grow strong. We are fighters, warriors. We hold our pride in our freedom. We have no peasants like these in France. We have no noblemen.'

'Who protects you, then?' Perkin asked.

'*We* do! We free men of the free cantons.'

'What of the knights? How can you survive without knights to defend you?'

'We have no need of them.'

Robin laughed. 'You had best pray that others don't decide to invade you. They'd walk all up your mountains and take your homes if you don't have—'

'They have tried.'

'Really?' Dogbreath sneered.

'Since forty years or more, the Habsburgs sent an

army to conquer us. An army of knights who wanted to steal our lands. The men of the confederation met them in the valley outside Morgarten, and we had a great killing that day.'

'You beat them? Knights?'

'Yes. And then, oh, almost ten years since, there was another battle with the Habsburgs at Dättwil. We won. They have not dared try to conquer us since that.'

'I see,' Robin said.

'How did they do it?' Hawkwood asked.

'The same as you English. We dismount and use pikes, lances, halberds, with the men in formation. The Habsburgs cannot break into our lines, and ride around until we break forward. At Morgarten we lured them to a valley, and there we rolled rocks into them, we ambushed them with tree trunks in their path, and blocked their escape, and then we attacked. We pulled them from their steeds, we hammered them until they were deaf and not mobile, and we stabbed with spear, halberd point, sword, up under their armour. They died easily.'

'Not good, then,' Hawkwood said. 'I have heard the same of a battle some fifty years ago, at a place called Courtrai or something. And the Scottish do the same, don't they?'

William looked from Hawkwood to Robin and back to Fulk. 'What? I don't understand.'

'What Fulk says is right,' Robin said. 'When we go to battle, we dismount. Even the knights stand on the ground, and we form a line many men deep in every battle formation. Archers and gonnes at either flank, usually with a river or marsh on one side, a thick forest on the other, so we can't be attacked from the side. And the French charge us at speed on their destriers. And what happens? As soon as the horses get close to our lances, they pull back. They aren't stupid enough to want to impale themselves. And their riders can't get close enough, even with lances, to do us much damage, so they're kept away while men like Archibald pour stones into them from their sides, and archers loose arrow after arrow at them. It has worked for the last forty years for us.'

Hawkwood continued for him: 'So, what would happen if the French peasantry decided to do the same? Even peasants who had far less training than us, peasants who were hardy, strong, determined, and had access to military minds who could pick the right ground to fight on? That would be more of a threat. If the Swiss could do it, who's to say the French couldn't as well?'

'But they would be fighting us as well as their own knights, from what this prisoner said,' Robin continued. 'If that's the case, then we may well have an opportunity. While the peasantry fight the noblemen, they won't be looking for us, will they? Perhaps that would be the time when we could hurry and take a fort or town, and escape while they're still engaged? If a host of knights is attacked, they will not be able to help themselves. They'll have to take up the challenge, especially if it means a load of peasants who're determined to revolt and throw over the government of the kingdom and take it for themselves.'

'Better than that,' Hawkwood said. 'If that's the case, and the peasants succeed, the kingdom will be like a goose ready to be plucked.' He smiled broadly. 'Think of it! We could all become rich. The peasants kill the nobles and leave the country ready for us to come and take it over.'

The men laughed, apart from Perkin. He looked anxious and fretful.

'Are you all right?' William asked him.

'Yes. I just... I hadn't expected to see so much death over here.'

Hawkwood slapped him on the back. 'You'll see. A couple of strumpets at the next town, a merchant's house where we can win his strongbox, and then a manor somewhere near Paris, where the land is good for growing or for cattle, and you'll see the world from different eyes. This is going to be glorious!'

24

The castle was still smoking when they came through the trees.

William leaned back against the cantle of his saddle, staring at it with astonishment. It had obviously been a great building, with towers still standing, and the walls clearly delineated. Houses and the main buildings were gone. They had been built of wood and wattle and daub, no doubt, with all the stone saved for use in the castle itself, and fire had taken them all. Only the outline of the castle itself remained, but even that was severely damaged.

'What happened here?' he asked of anyone listening.

'The brigands have been, I imagine,' Robin said

doubtfully. He had already unhitched his bow from his pony's saddle and dropped from his mount. He strung the bow ready to nock an arrow in case of danger.

The company had halted in the plain before the castle, and all the men were gazing at the ruins with frowns of surprise. The older men – Robin, Hawkwood, Dogbreath, Fulk and Saul – were looking about them with keen, wary attention, rather than directly at the castle.

Sir Reginald lifted his hand and gave a languid forward motion with his hand, and the group set off at a cautious walk. It took them some time to cover the mile or so between the forest and the castle, but as they approached the outskirts of the collection of buildings that had surrounded the keep, Sir Reginald slowed, turned and pointed to Peter, Hawkwood and Robin. 'Vinteners, have your men dismount and let the boys take your horses. Approach on foot and keep your eyes open for a trap. If the Jacks are here, we'll need to defend ourselves.'

* * *

Fulk smelled that hideous odour again. It reminded him of that night when he had woken to find the house ablaze, the screams of his wife and son up in the bedchamber over the cattle, and he down lying on a bench to sleep off the burned wine he had been drinking with the other men. He woke with the sluggish drink head, the incomprehension at the sight of the flames, the bellowing of the cows, the big, black dog whimpering at the door, and Fulk, still drunk, had gone to the door and thrown it wide to save himself, and all the while he could hear his family shrieking for help, and he grabbed a bucket and went to the trough and threw it at the flames, went to fetch more, stumbling and tripping as he went, throwing more water in, and all the while knowing he could not save them, that they were already lost, and then the cries were stilled, and he was alone in the world as his house burned, with his family and his cows all gone. He had nothing.

He turned in his saddle and peered back at the boys. There was something about Rat that reminded him of his own little Jacquet. A desire to please, to show he was a man, to be accepted. Perhaps Rat was a form of comfort sent to him, to give him companionship?

But then, maybe Rat was sent to remind him of his failure.

* * *

William watched the archers stringing bows, taking quivers and setting them over their shoulders. Some were grumbling about having to walk while the knights continued on horseback. The boys were soon scampering about, taking reins and leading the horses back to the rear, where Archibald sat on his wagon, an amiable expression on his face. Ed, beside him, was more alert to the situation and the dangers.

'Come along, esquire,' Sir Reginald said, and the trio walked up the roadway, watching every building carefully.

The household of the castle had been deposited in a heap at the side of the old gateway. Men and women lay in a tangled mess of bodies and limbs, and blood had pooled beneath them all, making a foul mess on the cobbles that reeked. Sir Reginald dismounted at the gateway, and William and Perkin followed suit, walking with him into the courtyard.

All was destroyed. Stables, storehouses, kitchen – all were demolished and burned. Whoever had decided to take the castle had also taken it apart. Rocks that had stood in the walls were tumbled to the ground; slates and stone were cracked and broken on the cobbles. The main keep itself had been fired, and now it looked like a giant chimney with smoke rising. When William peered in through the doorway, it was clear that the fire had taken the flooring, the various levels and the roof in one enormous conflagration. All that remained were the cinders and the heat.

'This is serious,' Sir Reginald said. His expression displayed his shock at seeing such destruction. 'If they are capable of taking a castle like this, and then destroying it from pure hatred, that is a sign they are a force to be reckoned with. Did they storm the walls, or do they have a siege train of artillery? How could they have achieved this?'

'Was this just a wilful desire to demolish a symbol of noble authority?' William wondered aloud.

'No. It was simple jealousy. And hatred. It is the trouble with the lower classes,' Sir Reginald said. 'They will so easily fall into this kind of simple thinking. They see a nobleman on a horse and think he is just a slave driver, forcing them to do all the work, while he idles away his time. They don't see the years of work that goes into training a man-at-arms, nor the sacrifices he must make to reach the state of perfection, when he becomes a honed machine of war.'

'No,' William said doubtfully.

Sir Reginald slapped his arm with a grin. 'I was

joking! The peasants cannot reason like you or me. They are simple folk.'

William stared at the heap of bodies, then at the rubble and destruction all about them. 'They may be simple, but they managed to capture this place and wreck it.'

'Ah, well, destruction is easy,' Sir Reginald said comfortably. 'That is why they are so suited to their tasks, labouring in the fields and creating the food that men like us need in order to protect them.'

William's eyes went back to the pile of corpses. 'They weren't well protected.'

Sir Reginald allowed a little testiness to enter his voice. 'No, well, they were members of the household here, I imagine. As servants to the men of the castle, I suppose they were considered fair game. What a waste, though. Look at this place. It must have been quite a strong point before they attacked it.'

'Yes,' William agreed.

'Still, nothing good to be taken, sadly,' Sir Reginald said with a mournful little shake of his head.

* * *

William was sure that he saw a movement. It was in the edge of the village, where there were a number of shaws, each used to provide the essentials of different types of wood for tool handles, for weaving into baskets or for firewood, and William felt certain that there was a figure there. He thought he caught a flash of colour moving quickly between the trees, although it was difficult to be sure.

He tapped Sir Reginald on the shoulder. 'A man, I think, up there in the trees.'

'Get him. Take three men with you, but don't let him escape,' the knight said.

William nodded and mounted his horse again, speaking conversationally, in case his voice carried and the watcher was warned. 'Follow me,' he said to Dog-breath and Robin. 'I think there's a man up there watching us. It could be a Jacques, so be on your guard. Perkin? Will you join us too?'

They climbed back into their saddles, and William led them back down the road to the right of the shaw, and spoke quietly to the men. 'Perkin, you ride at a gallop to the far side of the trees when we are through the other side of the hedge, and Dogbreath, you go more slowly at this side of the trees in case he tries to cut this way. Robin, keep your bow at the ready in case there are more men to support him.'

They rode on, Dogbreath halting and waiting while the other three rode through the gap. Then, he set off at a brisk trot along the front of the little wood, while Perkin suddenly lashed his mount and sprang off to cut off any escape. William cantered after him, in case the spy tried to double back, and Robin dismounted, his eyes fixed on the distant trees in case of an ambush.

Perkin thrilled to the feel of the wind in his hair, and the ripple and snap of his shirt in the wind as his horse thundered along the grasses, around the stand of trees and bushes, and over to the farther side, all the while watching the undergrowth for any sign of the man or other men trying to break out and escape. He saw none, but then, as he rounded the farther side of the shaw, there in the trees, he saw a flash of pale colour, and he reined in, sword ready in his hand. Dogbreath appeared in front of the man at the same time, just as William arrived at the rear of the treeline.

With a man at each apex of a triangle, the man slowly stood. He was clad all in pale linen, which was once dyed green, but that only showed as faded yellow now. As he rose, he allowed his hands to drop to his sides. 'Come out here,' Perkin said, and the man stared like a deaf mute, but finally he nodded and stepped out onto the grass. It was plain enough that he expected to die, but he stood defiantly enough.

'Come with us,' Perkin said, and motioned forward.

* * *

Perkin and William were both unsettled, and that night they walked about in the silver-grey light of the moon while the others muttered quietly at their campfires.

'The violence here is worse than I had expected,' Perkin said.

'Yes. It leaves me cold, to think of the injustice,' William said. 'I had anticipated, I don't know, some battles with small armies of Frenchmen, but I hadn't thought we'd find the peasants turning against nuns and their noblemen. How could they do that? I would like to think our king could bring some kind of peace to the land.'

'So much death,' Perkin said. 'It's hard to imagine the anger that could lead the people to rise against all their castles and destroy them.'

'I suppose they see them as symbols of the power held over them,' William said. 'It's hard to believe, isn't it? Not only that they would dare destroy them, but that they have the ability! And it will cost them dearly. Whoever rules France will need those castles rebuilt, and it's the local peasants who will be forced to pay for the works.'

'It makes me appreciate home,' Perkin said. He stared out south and east, gloomily. 'I miss the moors, the open spaces. Even the miners.'

'I want to see justice return here,' William said. 'I would like to have a property here, somewhere for people to live and thrive, without all this death and misery.'

'You think this land will ever see it?' Perkin said. 'All I can see is more and more violence and death. And much of it caused by us.'

25

It was less than a league to the next castle. The following morning they followed the river, which they had learned from their captive was named the Nonette, and which led the way to a small city called Senlis. They took their prisoner with them to this castle.

'You live here?' William asked the man as they walked along the path.

'Yes. I farmed up there,' the man said, jerking his head to point with his chin back the way they had come. He was a sturdy-looking man of perhaps three-and-twenty, a dark beard and slightly thinning hair, with grey eyes that were narrowed in concern. His hands were bound before him, and roped to Hawk-wood's hand.

'There were several men came by here,' Hawk-wood said. 'Who were they?'

'Men from Senlis, and some from other towns about here.'

'Which is this next castle?'

'Courteuil. It's a strong place, but... I doubt it's still there.'

'What do you mean?'

'You passed Chantilly, didn't you? I saw that two days ago. They sacked it, set it ablaze, and tried to pull down all the walls.'

'You think they did the same to this... Courteuil, you say?'

'I saw the smoke yesterday rising from that direction.'

Hawkwood frowned, and William knew why. The man was determined to make money from this journey, and if people were setting fire to these castles, that did not bode well for any valuables. Either they were already plundered, or they had been destroyed in the fires.

'Damn their souls to hell, if they've just destroyed everything,' Hawkwood muttered under his breath.

The castle was destroyed as a functioning stronghold. As before at Chantilly, walls were broken, the uppermost storeys of keep and towers were tumbled to the ground, and the whole mess set on fire.

Sir Reginald gazed about him, glowering with discontent. 'What is the point of this? I could understand them firing one or two castles, but to ruin them all? What will they do if a strong force comes here to punish them? They have destroyed the very places that they could run to for protection! This makes no damned sense.'

'Sir Reginald,' Perkin said, and pointed. He had seen another column of smoke rising south and east of them. 'Surely that can't be another castle?' He had grown at Crediton, which sat between Okehampton and Bickleigh castles, but here the landscape appeared to have a castle at every league or two.

Sir Reginald turned to the captive. 'Well? Is that yet another castle?'

'I think so. There is little else in that direction.'

'And this city, Senlis. Where is that?'

The man pointed with his chin more or less eastwards. 'Up there. Perhaps another league or so.'

'So the people are burning all the castles that lie about their city?' Hawkwood said. 'Perhaps they feared being surrounded and enclosed by these various castles, were they to be taken by the dauphin's men or

English companies. They could be blockaded, I suppose.'

'I expect it was more from pure devilry,' was Sir Reginald's view. 'These peasants just decided to take whatever they could and destroyed the buildings behind them. It is how peasants behave. You can't expect intelligence or planning or forethought from such as these.'

* * *

There was a subdued atmosphere among the men that evening. William and Perkin were fully aware of the way that the others ate and stared into the fire more soberly than before. The sight of the two castles destroyed so close together, and the suggestion that a third had also been burned, had given them all reason to consider their position and the dangers of the road ahead.

Their prisoner they had kept alive, since he knew the land about here. He was still bound and viewed with distrust, but William thought him fortunate, recalling the other man they had captured and killed on the way here. This one they might be able to use. The fellow sat back now, his arms bound before him, staring at the fire. Close by him, Fulk sat with his back to a tree, Crespin and Henri lying together beside him, Rat asleep at his other side.

'Aye, well, we've come this far,' Dogbreath concluded after deep thought for some while.

'You content to continue?' Peter asked.

'What's the point of going back? We don't have anything yet to show for all the leagues we've travelled.'

'We have to keep going, you think?' Saul asked.

Hawkwood answered, his eyes still fixed on the dancing flames. 'There could be some opportunities to be had here.'

'Opportunities?'

'I think so,' Hawkwood said, turning to William. 'Just think about it! The peasants are on the rampage; all the nobles of the area know it. They will have seen or heard of castles being destroyed, burned to the ground, the stonework taken down, all the inhabitants slaughtered. You think they'll want to wait to be hanged? I'd wager that all the garrisons will have deserted their smaller forts and outposts and made their way to larger cities for protection. They'll head south to Paris, or maybe north to Amiens. They won't want to be left stranded in a fortress when these Jacques have demonstrated that they can be besieged and starved out to be murdered, will they? And what of the folk of the small towns without real defences? What will they do? I would gamble that they would already be packed and ready to leave, just waiting for the smoke to start rising from nearer their homes. And they'll take to the roads to flee from English, Jacquerie or noblemen, because the knights won't want to let this get out of hand. The dauphin will already be mustering his forces to come and take back control, won't he? He cannot allow peasants to get a feel for power over his nobles. They will have to come here, and when they do, there will be even greater fire and slaughter. For us, that means opportunities.'

'Aye, to be killed,' Dogbreath sneered.

'Or to take a town with ease. Think! If we march through the night, silently, and reach a town just as dawn breaks, how do you think the townsfolk would react, if they suddenly hear the commotion of hundreds of men-at-arms breaking into houses, setting a couple afire, hearing the women and children of those houses screaming, the men crying out for help? How would a Frenchman react to that?'

'Go to help his neighbour?'

'You think so? If he thought it was just a fire, he would go help, to protect his own property. But if he thought this was the Jacks attacking, I'd bet the inhabitants would be out, over their town wall and into the fields and woods faster than you could say *knife*!'

'You think so?' Peter said. He had a pensive look about him now.

'I'm sure so. Who would wait to be slaughtered, when they could hear the company of murderers had already broken into their town?'

'And they might have had their valuables packed and ready,' Peter said, nodding with a contented smile on his face.

'That is the beauty of it. I'd bet that several of them will have packed all their best, ready to grab it as they leave.'

'So, what's the point, if they're going to have it all with them, eh?' Dogbreath said.

'The point is, my friend, that most won't. They'll grab their children and perhaps a wife will take her jewels, but many will just bolt. What, run away with a stone of added weight in silver and pewter? Hardly likely. No, more likely that they'll grab what is light, immediately to hand, and flee. But if you're concerned, we could have men at the other side of the town, ready to stop anyone leaving, and take their bags from them all.'

* * *

The town was some miles north and east of Senlis. William had no idea what its name was; he just followed along behind the others as they left their horses behind with the boys in woods close to the place in the chilly predawn light.

It was a calm, serene-looking collection of small houses, with three larger buildings at the centre. Those were to be the target of the men's interest. A rather pathetic effort had been made of constructing a wall about the town, but it was a poor start. There were several piles of rock, which masons had been working into the correct size and shape, but the walls themselves were less of a barrier than the thick hedge that had been thrown up about the place. However, when William studied it even now in the gloom before dawn, it looked less like an obstacle planted to become a serious protective screen; rather, it was a collection of branches and bushes that had been uprooted and piled together to create the impression of an impenetrable thicket.

William and Perkin were to go in with the first forces. Theirs was an easy task: to silently infiltrate the town, and then spring mayhem on the unsuspecting and sleeping inhabitants. The only concern was whether or not there was a sentry or two set to raise the alarm.

William and Perkin, with Dogbreath, Saul, Nick and Fulk, darted quietly over the pasture outside the town. A dog barked somewhere at the farther side, and close by a horse shook itself, almost giving William a brain fever. He swallowed hard, tightened his stomach muscles, and continued on, trying to ignore Dogbreath's sniggering. He always reacted to violence with the same giggling.

The hedge was easily crossed, the men stepping onto the thicker branches and making their way to the other side, while others made their way to the road, where a collection of beams had been laid across the earth surface. These were lifted quietly from their path.

William didn't stay to watch. He was, with the others, trotting towards the nearer houses. The wall here was only three courses high. William and Perkin sprang over it, landing easily on the other side. There were three houses nearby, and William, Perkin and Fulk went to the left-most, while Dogbreath, Ingram, Nick and Saul took the middle. All stood outside the main doors, staring at each other, panting slightly after their exertions. Then Fulk hefted his great halberd with its heavy steel cap at the bottom, and slammed it into the timbers of the door. Once, again, and a loud shriek was heard from inside. Perkin had brought a small axe, and now he used it to attack the door, and although the wood was strong and firm, he managed to strike between the fibres of the panels, and by levering and striking again and again, he broke the top open. The halberd struck again, and the timbers cracked. William kicked with all his might, and the door gave way with a loud clatter.

The three bounded inside. There were more screams from the upper storey, and then a woman's face appeared at the top of the ladder to the chamber upstairs. She squealed at the sight of the men, and William rolled his eyes. She should have already left! He grunted to Fulk to strike a fire from flint and tinder and set the place alight, and went to the ladder to get the woman down.

She was at the rear of the chamber, alone, her arms about her, the screaming reduced to a terrified whimper now, and she moved away as he approached.

'Woman, this house is going to burn,' he said. 'Come, descend the ladder and save yourself.'

She moved away again, as if trying to squeeze herself in between the beams of the wall. William could have cursed with frustration, but then he lunged to grab her and save her.

He had expected to grasp soft, pliant flesh, but she darted away even as he reached for her, and when he turned, it was in time to see her throw herself from the platform, head first to the floor of the house. Her neck cracked with a wet crunch.

William stared down at the body, her head sitting at an extreme angle compared with the rest of her body. He wanted to speak, but no words came. He looked over and as his eyes caught sight of Perkin, he saw his friend look up at him.

But in Perkin's eyes William saw only horror.

26

The rest of the day was spent ransacking the town, and the company went about their business with many a merry jest at the expense of the townspeople.

As Hawkwood had predicted, the inhabitants had fled as soon as the first screams were heard and the fire of the first two houses had taken hold. They grabbed what belongings they could, babies and children too, and took to their heels in the opposite direction. When full daylight dawned, the company found itself in full control of an empty town, and they could go through every house at their leisure.

Although it had been tempting to stop all the refugees in order to confiscate any valuables, the men had decided it was too much of a risk. A small force could be overwhelmed by panicked evacuees, while a larger force would denude the men assaulting of the numbers necessary, so in the end Sir Reginald agreed with Peter that it was best to keep the men all together. They might lose a few trinkets, but it would give them greater freedom of operation and minimise the risk of a concerted effort to reject the company's assault.

William slouched along the streets, that woman's face imprinted on his mind. After they had started the fire to destroy the house, he had picked up her body and taken her outside, so that she might be buried honourably. He had been tempted to make a grave for her, but instead he knelt at her side and said the *paternoster*, begging God to watch over her, and pleading His forgiveness for being the cause of her death.

Perkin had left him there, and after William had finished his prayer and crossed himself, he made his way into the town himself.

It appeared to be a thriving little community, with a good-sized market square, a large church, and a number of stone houses to demonstrate the wealth of the burgesses who owned them. The men rifled these first, convinced that there must be untold wealth in each, but all they managed to find was a number of casks of good wine. For many, that was riches enough, and many were broached.

William went through the town. It was full of the sound of cracking timbers as the men used axes and mattocks to open cupboards and strongboxes. Anything that might conceal coins or jewellery was broken open and investigated.

William found the tavern and sat at a bench outside it with a pint of wine he had poured for himself, listening to the destruction all about him. Another building had been set alight, and the smoke and flames rose high into the sky. The odour was choking, and William drank deeply.

Peter saw him as he walked past, a heavy sack over his shoulder. 'What are you doing? There's furs and pewter plates – all sorts to collect!'

'I'm just resting.'

'Where's Perkin?'

'I don't know,' William snapped, and turned away.

* * *

Auffroy trudged on. His determination to win revenge was a white-hot brand burning in his brain. It encompassed his entire soul, consuming all emotion and weakness and driving him onward. But how to do it? The two had watched as the company overran that town, and since then the English had remained inside the walls. There was nothing the two could do to try to track down the man. Instead they were forced to try to find somewhere that might have a little food for them – crusts of bread, old meat, even just a pottage. They had to find food.

Behind him, Gadiffer stumbled on sore feet. His shoes' soles were thin, so every stone and pebble hurt his feet. They had covered many miles on this wild goose chase, trailing after the company of English murderers. Yes, Gadiffer wanted revenge, just as Auffroy did. His sister was dead, and her son. And the English may not have killed them, but it was surely their depredations that had taken away her will to live. It was their appearance that made her kill her child and herself. And then it was the English who had seen to it that both were buried on unhallowed ground, without the benefit of a priest, she with a stake through her heart to pin her in the ground so she could not rise again. Even on the Day of Judgement, she would remain rotting in the earth. Auffroy would never see her again.

And this English devil had stolen her last possession – the cross on her necklace. It might have given her some protection, given Auffroy and Gadiffer a little hope that she might be gathered up by an angel and taken to Heaven.

To steal that last, remaining hope was terrible, sad, shocking.

But what good could come of chasing down the English? Vengeance was fine, but what was the true likelihood of avenging her? If they caught up with the English, it was more likely that the pair of them would die before they could draw their knives. These English were most competent fighters and murderers. There was little chance that two men from a remote village could overwhelm them.

No, Gadiffer was convinced that they were marching ever onward to their deaths.

He could not help it – a short sob escaped from him.

'Be quiet,' Auffroy snapped.

'Why? You think the trees will listen to my misery? Auffroy, what do you expect us to do? What, you mean to attack them? You have seen how they fight! They will kill us, just as they killed the people at that manor! Just as they went into that town!'

Auffroy spun around, his mouth set in a line of resolution, and Gadiffer was petrified. He thought his friend was about to attack him. 'Auffroy, please!'

That was when the first men appeared, surrounding them both, weapons raised and ready.

* * *

William left the others to their rampaging and walked back to the horse lines, where he saw the boys grooming the mounts, Rat and others so exhausted that they could barely keep their eyes open as they brushed.

'Boy, leave that. Give me the brush,' William said roughly.

'You, sir? I have to...'

'Go and rest. I'm an esquire, and I know how to treat my horse well enough,' William said firmly. It was true. One of the first rules his father had always imposed was that any man who aspired to knighthood must know his horse to be his most vital asset. It was the horse that would conduct him to battle, the horse that would carry him safely away from battle. The horse was the knight's first responsibility, his first and most important responsibility at all times, as well as his most valuable.

'Have you water?'

It was the prisoner they had taken before, and William glanced at him as he brushed his mount. The man was tied still, his hands bound behind him now, uncomfortably, around a pillar in the stable.

The Rat had not yet left, and William sent him to

fetch water. Rat brought a leather flask and the Frenchman greedily gulped the water while Rat held it to his lips.

'Why were you watching us that day when we caught you?' William said. 'You aren't one of the Jacquerie.'

'No. But there were Jacques about, and I didn't want to be caught by them any more than by you. Then your company arrived, and I didn't dare show myself.'

'You failed. I saw you moving among the trees,' William said.

'I was lying still.'

'I saw someone moving from one tree to another.' William smiled.

'That was the other men.'

William's smile faded. 'The other men? Which other men?'

Rat felt this news like a stabbing in his breast as the Frenchman continued.

'The one in the trees wore a grey tunic and russet cloak. I never saw his face, but he appeared just after your companions, and I was lying still because I thought he might attack me. Then you caught me. The other stayed back there, in those woods.'

William continued with his grooming. The fellow

was plainly telling the truth, and it made him wonder who the second man might have been, but it was no real concern to him. Why should it be? Just another man watching their company and wishing them to hurry away, no doubt.

One of the other boys, he saw, was frowning at the prisoner. 'What is it?' William asked.

'Nothing, sir.'

'Tell me.'

'Well...' It was the boy called Garnot. 'It was before you joined the company, sir. Rat there thought he saw the Devil kill Arn, but others saw a man, all dressed in dark clothes with a russet hood and cloak. It just sounded strange, that's all, to think that there's another man watching us all these miles away, looking the same.'

William shrugged. The boys were all bone-weary, yawning and almost incapable of keeping their eyes open. He was dreaming, no doubt. No one would have followed the company all the way here. It was ridiculous.

But when he looked at Rat, he saw terror in the lad's eyes.

* * *

'It was an accident,' William said again.

Perkin said nothing. It was that evening, and the two were sitting near a campfire, with Perkin keeping purposefully away from him. William was distraught to see how his friend was responding.

'I went up the ladder to get her down, so she wasn't hurt when the cottage was burned, but she wouldn't let me close, and then she killed herself. I was trying to get to her to rescue her.'

'I see. The poor woman must have thought you wanted to rape her, I suppose,' Perkin said.

William huddled into his cloak. He felt miserable. The whole reason for coming here to France was the lure of treasure. He had never truly thought that it might involve the death of women. Yes, he was no fool, he had known that women were likely to suffer during war, when their husbands and fathers were slain by other men, but it had not been a significant thought to him when he had been sitting in the hall at his father's home at Furnshill. He had always believed in chivalry and the rules of honour. There, at home, he had been brought up to treat even peasant women with respect, and while his father had bawled him out when he had visited the women in the stews at Exeter, he had treated them fairly. He had not mal-treated them or bilked them of their fees. Yet she had thought him so evil that death was preferable to capture.

Here in France, he was learning that other men did not treat women with the same scrupulous regard. They treated all women as chattels and objects of lust, and nothing more. And now even his best friend and companion considered him to be no better than those: a mere ruffian who was determined to find and swyve the first woman he could capture.

In his mind's eye, William saw again the long greensward leading to his father's home at Furnshill, the horses cropping the grass before the door, sheep in the farther field, the three cows in their byre, the dogs barking in excitement, and his father, tall still, although white-haired now, the scar on his face standing out against the darker flesh, his new wife, William's mother, Alice at his side. It was some years now since Baldwin's first wife, Jeanne, had died from a fever, and Baldwin had remarried. To see Alice and his father together was to see satisfaction. They truly loved each other, and it showed. That was how William had been brought up, to see women as equals to be cherished. But then, he saw peasants as humans, too. The way that the peasants here were being slaughtered was repugnant to him.

He made his way to the lines where the horses

were being kept and walked to the prisoner. The man stared up at him with sudden fear as William drew his dagger. He cut the bonds binding him. 'Go! Find your way home again, and keep safe from English and ruffians,' he said gruffly.

'You will let me go?'

William nodded and pointed back the way they had come. 'Go now; before the others realise.' As the man scampered away, William sat down heavily and watched the man disappear. At least he had managed one kind act here, he thought. Just now, he only wished he had remained at Furnshill and had never come here to this land of horror and pain.

27

They were shoved, and Auffroy fell on his face. Gadiffer stumbled, but managed to keep his feet.

'Who are you?'

The leader of the ruffians was a short, mousy-haired man of some thirty years or so. He had the thin skin of a man who had rarely had enough to eat, and he was missing several teeth from the scurvy. He scowled at the two captives now, while his men stood about fingering their weapons.

'We come from over to the west. Our village was attacked by the English, and we have come to try to fight them,' Auffroy said.

'You came to fight the English, eh? With what? A dagger and a long knife?' the man said scornfully.

'We will do what we can,' Auffroy said.

'You'll be killed. You were so stupid – you let us walk up to you without you noticing,' the leader said.

'We have come a long way to find them and win justice.'

'And you think you can do that? I ought to have you killed for your stupidity,' the man said. 'But I am feeling generous. I will allow you to join us. You can become *Jacques Bonhommes* and fight with us against the knights of France as well as the English.'

'We want to find the men who...'

'You will join us or you will find your own graves.'

* * *

In Paris, Thomas de Ladit had been in the chamber when the delegation arrived some days before.

It was a strange gathering in many ways: the richest men of the city meeting with representatives of the rebels, all clad in travel-stained and shabby clothing, many mud-stained, while more had clothing stained with blood.

Étienne Marcel and other leaders of the community met them in the Châtelet, where the Provost of the Merchants had his new chambers, and the rich tapestries and decorations themselves highlighted the contrast between the two groups. Before the uprising, this had been the building housing the chief civil authority in the city, where the courts were held and the officers of the law directed. Now Marcel had taken it over for his own purposes as he began to realise his own ambitions.

He was a curious man, Thomas considered, watching him. Pompous, arrogant, he had married money when he'd snared Marguerite des Essarts, the daughter of France's richest native-born banker, but that was before Crécy, the battle that impoverished so many bankers who had loaned money to the French nobility to purchase armour and weapons for themselves and for their households. When those knights didn't return, many bankers lost their all, her father as well as the others.

However, Marcel did not suffer. He had risen up the ranks of his own profession, until he reached the pinnacle of Parisian society, undisputed leader of all the city. As Provost of the Merchants, he was the man who controlled the administration and all legal affairs. Now he was also the leader of the rebellion against the king and his son. Paris was the crown of the kingdom. He who possessed Paris possessed all authority in the kingdom.

'You come from the Jacquerie?' he asked the delegation.

'We have come from Guillaume Cale. He commands nearly five thousand armed men, but we need assistance. Cities like Amiens have supported us with food and money, but we need more. We have come to ask that Paris also aids us.'

'And Paris will be proud to do so,' Marcel said. He threw out his arms in a demonstration of open admiration and affection. 'You are doing us a service, and France too. We shall overthrow these *nobles*' – it sounded like a curse – 'and then destroy the English and come to a more just and fair society. It will not be long.'

'There is much to be done,' one of the delegation said. He was a shorter man with the build of a boxer. 'We have so many castles about us, and all hold men-at-arms who would be glad to destroy us all. Those garrisons need to be killed, the castles and fortresses levelled. We have achieved much, but there is much more to be done.'

Marcel indicated that all should take their seats. 'What would you have us do?'

'You have men here. The Jacquerie has been successful north of Paris. We have taken the Beauvaisis, and comrades in Montdidier are razing the castles owned by the Crown near them, but there has been no uprising south. Can you not send men to foment the same uprisings there?'

'Send men south of the Seine?' Marcel rested his chin on his cupped hand, eyes narrowed. 'Yes, that should be possible. All the peasants must know that their nobles do nothing to protect them. It is the perfect time for us to persuade them to take up arms. After all, the nobility has simply withdrawn behind their own walls and hidden away, like the cowards they are. No peasants are going to be keen to honour them.'

That had been the start of it. Marcel had sent men to the lands as asked, but at the same time he began to raise his own army. The kernel had been the officers of the law, the *chevaliers du guet*, who were used as the primary building block of the force. Now, it was a powerful little army, and Marcel hurled it at the properties of those against whom he held a grudge, those who he felt were his enemies.

Thomas watched it all from King Charles's palace with a feeling of increasing anxiety. He held the position of ambassador from King Charles of Navarre, and Marcel valued his advice and support. Marcel knew that he could not take on the dauphin's army himself, but with Charles of Navarre and the men he commanded, even the dauphin must tremble. Charles wanted to topple the throne and take power for himself. Perhaps Marcel would be able to retain control of Paris under Charles – but then again, if Charles was to help overthrow the Valois dynasty, there was the possibility that Charles's own power would be diminished. A battle between his host and the dauphin's must lead to an uncertain outcome, but one possibility that gleamed in Marcel's eyes was that he himself could become the ruler of the whole kingdom.

From provost to king? That was the result that Marcel cherished.

Yes, Thomas thought, it was time that he returned to King Charles in Normandy to let him know what was happening in Paris. The king needed to know what Marcel had in his mind for the future of the city – and the realm.

BOOK 2

THE JACQUERIE

28

'He's a fool,' King Charles said heavily.

Thomas said nothing.

'He has truly raised his standard against the dauphin? That means he rebels against his king! Does he really think he can overwhelm all the knights of France? He could hold Paris and support the citizens, I suppose, but when he had the dauphin's advisers cut down in the presence of the dauphin himself, that was a *fatal* error, the fool!'

'And now he sends his men to exact justice on all his personal enemies. He has them flatten and burn the most valuable properties of any of those who have served the king and his son. Already five great mansions have been demolished.'

'Stupid, stupid behaviour,' King Charles said. 'He'll turn all the nobility against him – and us!'

'What will you do?'

'I am an ally of Paris and Étienne Marcel,' King Charles said. Then he smiled wolfishly and his eyes took on a shrewd look as he reassessed the situation. 'However, I am also a nobleman, and other nobles will recognise that in this time of conflict and distress I am the one man capable of bringing some semblance of order to this sorry kingdom. They will flock to my banner.'

'They have asked you to...?'

'I am asked to take an army and destroy the Jacques,' King Charles said, adding with satisfaction, 'They wish to crown me as the head of all noblemen in France.'

'What will you do?'

'Don't be a fool, Thomas! What do you expect me to do? Remain allied with Marcel? That fool decided to rebel against all France, for the nobility *is* France. If I remain with him, he will probably turn against me at the first opportunity. If I turn against him now, per-haps I can win a greater victory. Think! If I destroy these Jacques, I will be the Hector of the nation, and the nobles will be forced to recognise my leadership. They will flock to me as the only man who has demonstrated skill against these peasant ruffians. And once they are with me, it will become easier to achieve my own ends.'

'And what will they be?'

'What do you expect? King John's father the Valois stole the crown when I had the better claim through my mother. It is only right that I should claim the title I am owed. God is on my side, and if I destroy the Jacquerie, I will have all the nobles on my side as well. And then I will own France. I will collect my forces, go to meet the Jacques, and slaughter them.'

Fortunately, no one had thought to blame anyone for the escaped man. It was assumed by all that he had managed to wear away the cord binding him and make off on his own.

'Aye, well, what the hell?' Dogbreath said. 'Good luck to the bastard. There are plenty of other French here to attack us, what difference will one more make?'

William discovered that he was starting to hold a grudging respect for the men of the company. They were a vicious, brutal collection of mercenaries, but they were good at their trade, and their trade was killing. They would cut a throat or stab a man in the heart for the most minor reason, such as a real or imagined insult, but they were reliable, orderly and militarily obedient. When Sir Reginald gave a command, they obeyed, and when it came to a fight, they knew their jobs. Archers, footmen, cavalry – all knew how to command a battle, and after years of warring, they were not even fazed by the sight of armies much larger than their own forces. They were convinced that four Frenchmen could not defeat one Englishman – and so far they had been proved right.

William was relieved that Perkin was with him. He was William's oldest friend and companion. The two had grown up together, they had played together, hunted and journeyed here in each other's company. But now, he was realising, this adventure of theirs was more dangerous than he had expected.

He was tempted to leave, to ride back with Perkin as quickly as he could to the English territories, and from there to get to Calais and make his way homewards. The lure of his home, the lush fields and pastures, his brother, his father – all came to his mind wherever he was, whether riding along or sitting at the fireside. It was so appealing, to leave this land of woe and misery and ride back to Calais, to take a ship home.

But to do that would be to accept defeat. If he went

back, it would be to shame. Besides, it would mean deserting the company. He had taken an indenture; he was committed to the service of Sir Reginald. To merely reject that contract and return to Furnshill would be seen as cowardly at best, at worst an act of petty treason. If he gained a reputation of that sort, he could never rise to knight; he would never own his own manor. Even if he could, he would forever be subservient to a lord or banneret, a mere esquire and servant to his master, and that rankled. He wanted to show his courage, demonstrate his ability as a fighter, and collect his due reward as a knight.

William stopped his horse, allowing the column to walk past, until the wagon train appeared. First were some food carts and the wagons with their plunder, and then the trudging camp followers, a mixture of women and children, and Archibald and Ed with their great wagon drawn by oxen, Rat and Henri in the back of the wagon with Berthelot, Crespin and Garnot.

Oxen were not the fastest beasts, but creatures capable of hauling the great gonnes were never going to be speedy. They needed brawn and stolidity, not the ability to gallop.

'Master William, I hope I see you well,' Archibald said, ducking his head respectfully.

'I am well enough, I thank you. And you?'

'Oh, we are healthy – and a man can ask little more than that in these hard times,' Archibald said. He pulled off his cap to display his bald pate, which he rubbed vigorously before returning the cap to cover it. 'I just wish I could have an opportunity to show off my toys. All this travelling is giving me a headache. I need the smell of brimstone and rotten eggs to keep my cheerfulness up.'

'It has not been a *chevauchée* to your liking then,' William said.

Ed shook his head. 'If there ain't a decent bang, Archibald's not happy. He likes his gonnes to fire regularly.'

'And you don't, I suppose?' Archibald said sternly, but then he grinned mischievously. 'I would give much to see my gonne fire at a castle, but there are all too few to be had, aren't there?'

'I think the peasantry has decided to remove them all for you,' William agreed.

'Perhaps we'll find our way to one before long.'

It was as he said this that the column stopped moving, and hand signals passed along the line indicating that all should be quiet.

Archibald stared, frowning. 'What is this, do you think?'

'I don't know,' William said. He took a deep breath. 'I will speak to you later. Godspeed!'

And so saying, he lashed his mount's flanks and took off at a slow, quiet canter.

* * *

When he came level with the front of the column, William allowed his horse to slow. Hawkwood turned to him and gave an angry gesture to halt.

They were riding at the edge of a great forest, and just now the vanguard had almost reached the topmost corner of the trees. Beyond it the land fell away slightly. In the distance William could see another forest, with hills rising far beyond. The company had plodded on towards this corner of the woods carelessly, while riders were sent on ahead and to the sides to see that there were no ambushes or other risks.

'Sir Reginald?' William called.

'Hush!' the knight said quietly.

He was sitting on his horse, and up ahead, at the tip of the trees, William could see Perkin, leaning around the farthest trunks, peering ahead.

'What is it?'

'An army, apparently. We have stumbled into an entire damn force of French noblemen!'

William felt his stomach flip in alarm. He asked, 'Can I go and see?'

'Very well, but be careful! Keep your head down and don't let them see you. And be quick! I have to think what to do,' Sir Reginald said, frowning as he contemplated which action would serve for the best.

'Yes, sir,' William said, and dismounted quickly, trotting to Perkin's side. There he stopped, staring through the trees, and took in the sight.

It was an army. There were thousands of men, and the company had all but ridden into the midst of them. Flags fluttered, and men-at-arms milled about, all in a wide space. If Sir Reginald and the vanguard had plodded on any further, they would have marched straight into the flank of an army of thousands.

'What is this? Are they all French?' he whispered to Perkin.

'That is likely. But there are others too,' Perkin said. He pointed. 'See that? I'm sure I recognise that symbol.'

'The thistle and the dragon?'

'Yes. It is familiar.'

He was frowning as he and William rejoined the column.

'Well?' Sir Reginald demanded. 'Who the devil is it?'

'They are clearly men-at-arms,' Perkin said. 'They wear armour, and it is well maintained.'

William looked from him to the knight. 'Who are they – could they be the Jacquerie?'

Perkin looked at him with a pained expression. 'Do they look like peasants? You say they are men-at-arms: I doubt peasants will have mail or armour, and if they did, it would be brown with rust!'

'I think these are noblemen,' Perkin said. 'I saw several coats of arms, and one, I think, was familiar: a thistle and a dragon. Do you know that, Sir Reginald?'

The knight glanced over at his esquire. 'What do you think?'

'If it is a dragon atop a thistle, that sounds like Sir Robert Scot, sir.'

'By God's pains, I think you're right.'

'Is that good?' William asked.

'Yes. He's as good a knave as me!' Sir Reginald said with a broad smile.

Sir Robert Scot appeared to validate Sir Reginald's opinion of him. A smiling, thickset man with arms like small oaks and shoulders as broad as one of

Archibald's oxen, he welcomed the company and had them camp close by him.

'Don't trust all these Frenchmen – they'd cut your throat soon as look at you,' he said. 'Not that they don't have reason, after what we've been doing here, but just now they are glad of our help.'

'What are we to do here?' Sir Reginald asked. He gazed about their camp at the French flags and the suspicious glowers of the knights and men-at-arms all about them.

'They need us, whether they like it or not, and they know it. The Jacks are all over the place, and they've killed plenty of innocent women and children in castles and strongholds up and down the Beauvaisis. The nobles have tried to destroy them piecemeal, but it hasn't worked, so the King of Navarre has united them and raised this force. He intends to meet the villain churls in battle and destroy them entirely. Apparently there are some hundreds of men at Silly-le-Long, up ahead. They have plundered Ermenonville, and they're likely still flushed with their winnings there. They'll be drunk after that victory. But they don't know we're on our way. We outnumber them, but it wouldn't matter if we didn't,' he added, shrugging. 'What good are peasants against trained men-at-arms?'

29

Auffroy and Gadiffer had been marched to meet the main army, and Auffroy stood and gaped at the sight when they came nearer.

'There must be thousands!' Gadiffer breathed, awed by the sight.

Auffroy was for a moment lost for words. He felt as clumsy as a hippopotamus trying to sew tapestry. 'What can we do among such a force?' he wondered.

'Stand and fight with them,' their commander told them, chuckling as he led the way to the men gathered in the field.

* * *

It was the next day, the 7th of the month, that they marched forward, and there, on the plain in front of them, William and Perkin got their first view of the peasant army that had been causing such devastation.

Ranged before them stood two lines of footmen on the plain of Mello. They were being cursed and pushed into combat order by a number of men, who William felt sure must be trained soldiery. They were clearly men of some experience, because they had already taken a good defensive position for their camp, and more men were arriving all the time.

'What now?' William wondered. He was not left in doubt for long. Navarre had his men drawn up in battles before the peasant army, footmen to the front, and his cavalry behind, from where they could attack through the main force, or ride around either flank.

William and Perkin were given their positions and told to wait, and wait they did. All the rest of that day. The cavalrymen sat on their mounts, until in the late afternoon it grew obvious that there would be no battle that day, and the men dismounted to leave their horses to crop the grass and rest a little.

'How long before we fight, do you think?' Perkin said.

William didn't answer. He found that his belly felt as weak as a babe's. The idea of charging into a fight against such a huge host of men was as appealing as jumping into a well wondering what might be at the bottom.

* * *

The next day, the peasant army grew, and the men watched and waited. It was clear that the Jacques were led by someone with good military training. 'Must have been at Poitiers and seen how we fought,' was the impression gained by many about William. The day after that, they stood about and waited again.

It was the day after that, the 10th, that they had their battle at last.

William was with Sir Robert when he saw a small company riding slowly towards Navarre's lines. In front was a man with a white flag bound to a lance, with a small contingent of guards behind him.

'Who is that?' William asked.

'That, my friend, is, I think, the leader of the enemy,' Sir Robert said.

William watched as the party trotted through the lines of the Navarrese army, and out to where King Charles sat on his own horse. The party was permitted to pass, but then, as William watched, there was a flash of steel. Their leader was grabbed by men-at-arms and pulled from his horse, while the bodyguards with him were slaughtered on the spot. The commander was bound, and led away to the rear of the camp, while King Charles drew his sword and bellowed to his men, and the cavalry began moving through the lines.

William found himself in their midst, alongside Sir Robert. The older knight had an open-faced bascinet, and as he rode at a trot, he pulled his sword free, moving his wrist to relax the muscles and prepare for the clash. William had his own bascinet with a visor, and pulled it down, but it restricted his vision sorely. He had to lean forward to peer through the eye slots, and it was hot and claustrophobic in that unnatural, enclosed space, but he felt it was preferable to having a lance hit him in the face.

They trotted forward. The din sounded extraordinary to William inside his rattling armour. The thick, padded war coif deadened the noise, but he could clearly hear the squeaks and bell-like tinkles from thousands of mail shirts, and then it grew louder as the men urged their beasts into a canter – and the thunder of horses' hooves pounding, the whistle of the wind in the air holes of his helmet, the panting and whinnying of horses was all deafening. But then there were a series of bellows, and they were riding at a gallop, and Sir Robert was pulling away from him, and others were in front of him too, and then William could see the peasants through the eyeholes.

He was only yards from them, and he could see the distress on some faces, fierce resolution on others, and a thicket of lances facing him, shining tips gleaming evilly. Then he was in among them.

It was a rattling clash of metal on metal, an appalling cacophony of shouting, screaming, cursing, praying, weeping, and William found himself in the midst of them, his horse wheeling, trying to find a path through, and William hacking at any figure he could see through the limited vision of the visor, missing with that blow, the force almost toppling him from his saddle as his heavy sword's momentum pulled at him, and then he was back up, and his left arm was slammed with an axe or mace – he couldn't see – and it felt like his arm was cut off, with no feeling below the elbow, and he cried out, muffled, slashing and stabbing furiously, trying to keep these damned peasants away, but knowing that they were like fleas on a hound, always more of them, no chance of resting, and his arm was tired, and he could barely breathe, the helmet was so enclosed, and the breathing holes inadequate, and suddenly he felt sick, and dared not vomit inside the visor, and he pulled it up and free, and found that he was at the edge of the battle, and even as he gazed about him, dazed, he saw the enemy was fleeing.

Men threw aside their weapons in terror and panic, running as fast as they could from the field. They stood no chance against the men on horseback. William knew what he must do, and he spurred his mount on, but this was not bloodlust. This was the honourable duty of chivalry to chase down those who sought to upend the rule of law and the natural order. Cavalry were there in the battle to chase the enemy and kill them as they fled. And so now William gritted his teeth and set off after the peasants running from him.

* * *

He was exhausted. When his mount had taken him almost a mile, he reined in. His destrier was panting hard after that race. He shook his head and mane, and William felt the brute was as weary as he himself.

How many men had he killed? There were seven fleeing whom he had run down. How many he had killed in the mêlée, he could not tell. While his visor was down, he was effectively blind. Many, judging by the regular thump as his sword struck a head or a shoulder. He must have killed ten or more men today;

he had ended their lives. Boys and men, husbands and fathers. Perhaps some like the men on his father's manor: peasants, yes, but still men. They looked just like any other men.

He slumped in his saddle. If this was war, he was not sure he wanted to experience more of it. Yes, these peasants were rebels, but they were the enemies of the French king, not of him. He, William de Furnshill, was a knight's son from a different country. How would his father view such killings?

His father would be distressed. William knew that. Sir Baldwin had always sought to be a good master to the peasants on his own lands. He had their interests at heart. Yes, he would punish those who infringed the laws, but he was always keen to show that his punishments were just. If a man killed another, his crime would be dealt with as the law demanded – but Sir Baldwin could also show mercy when a crime was perpetrated by a man with a justifiable cause. The slaughter of men like this would not be to his taste.

Turning in order to head back the way he had come, William saw a young peasant hiding behind some bushes. He looked about twenty, a lad with a shock of tawny hair and wide, terrified eyes, his grey tunic all bespattered with blood, his russet hood torn, his cloak frayed. William looked at him for a long moment. He could kill no one else this day.

He shook his head. '*Allez!*' he said, and rode back to the camp.

* * *

There was a riotous party that afternoon. The peasants had raided several cellars and collected barrels of wine, which were enjoyed by those of the king's army. By the time William returned to the camp, most of the foot soldiers were already several pints down, and although he tried a cup of wine, his stomach was too unsettled. It made him feel sick. Instead he walked back to the camp of the followers, and found Archibald and Ed.

'You're safe, then,' Archibald said.

Ed was drinking slowly, staring back towards the field, where the scavengers were walking amid the bodies, searching for rings, purses, quality daggers, or simply to finish off those with wounds. Archibald sat with his back to the scene.

William looked up at him. 'I live.'

'Your first charge and battle?'

William nodded.

'It's not as easy as it sounds when you're instructed,

is it? Your next will be easier, and the one after that easier still. After a few, you'll forget you ever found it difficult,' Archibald said, and then his eyes hardened. 'But if you find yourself uncaring, if you learn to laugh at a dead body, or mutilate one, go back to England and find a priest to shrive you, because if that happens, you will have lost your soul to the Devil. Remember that.'

'Did you find it hard? Your first battle?'

'Yes. And most of the time I remain human, and don't forget myself or that the other poor devils I'm killing are only peasants told to come to stand against me. But at least with my gonnes I can give them a quick death.'

'What of the knights?'

'Ah, well, I feel little remorse for them,' Archibald said, and there was a harder note to his voice. 'They dedicate their lives to war and ending other lives. Against them, I feel entitled to use my toys. It's the others, the poor folks pulled from the fields, I feel sorry for. Not that it stops us fighting them. A man cannot help but fight when a host is launched against him. Yet, most of them are uneducated and foolish.'

'Except today they were fighting for themselves,' William said.

'Yes. But where would the world be, if they were to

succeed and overturn the natural order of things? Society depends upon the three legs. Warriors like you,
peasants to support us all with food and their labour,
and the religious, who support our souls. It is like a
stool. If you have three legs, the stool is solid. But cut
away one leg, and you cannot sit on it. You will inevitably fall.'

'I feel guilt for all the men I killed today.'

'You should not. You had no choice. You merely
helped leave the third leg on the stool. Besides, if I had
been there, I would have killed many more. My little
toys can kill many more than one man with a sword,
and do it faster.'

'That must be kinder.'

'Perhaps. But even I can lose myself in battles.
When a friend is killed in battle, I can lose myself in
the red mist, in bloodlust. And when that happens, the
Good Lord only knows what I do. So, I try to avoid
such fighting. You should do the same, William, else
you will gain a stain on your soul that cannot be
washed away.'

* * *

Auffroy had not stopped running. He felt himself
staring about him at every squeak, every snapped twig,

every animal's movement. Here, deep in the woods, he could stop, sit, allow his frantically beating heart to slow and find a little time to rest.

He had seen Gadiffer. Even now, he could not bear to recall that moment. When the demons in armour suddenly thundered towards them all, those with swords raised, some wielding maces, others with their long lances, all seemingly aiming at Gadiffer and him, and the way that the men in front of them in their battle moved back, compacting the whole line, while others behind him threw down their weapons in terror and fled.

Then the sudden eruption of lances through the backs of the men in front of him, and the coughing as men's lungs were spitted on those foul spikes, and other men screamed as they were kicked, trampled, bitten by the fierce warhorses of the knights, and the man before Auffroy had suddenly disappeared, and another beside him was cut down, a great sword cleaving his skull almost in half.

It was that which saved Auffroy's life, because the sword became stuck, it was so embedded in the man's head. The knight twisted and turned his blade, but it was trapped, and Auffroy saw Gadiffer try to stab upwards with the knife he carried, but his stabs met only the metal of the man's armour, and then Auffroy saw his friend stop and stand still, and then he turned with a slow, mechanical tread, and Auffroy saw that his mouth worked, but no sound came, and then the great tear in his throat where another sword had slashed him was opened and the blood erupted like waves in a storm, and Gadiffer crumpled before him, and Auffroy stepped back, one step, two, and then he turned and fled. He ran and ran, and while others about him were spitted on lances and flung high into the air, wailing, he had managed to escape the field and make his way here, into the woods, even as he heard the rattle and clank of the men in their armour riding about.

Why had that knight left him? He recognised the man from following the company, but while he had expected to be slain there when the knight turned and saw him, he saw only weary defeat in the man's eyes, as though the knight himself had lost the battle.

He had not. Auffroy had; even his best friend, Gadiffer, was dead.

Eyes tightly closed, Auffroy covered his face in his hands and began to weep silently, rocking back and forth on his knees, begging forgiveness of Gadiffer, and praying for his friend.

30

It was later that evening that William was called to see Sir Reginald.

He was sitting on his stool at a trestle table, a cup of wine holding down one edge of a scroll, while a clerk scribbled frantically on sheaves of paper. Sir Robert was with him, pointing a dirty-nailed finger at a line of writing. 'There, see?'

'Yes, I know,' Sir Reginald said testily.

'You called for me?' William said.

'Yes, esquire. I need to send a message to the dauphin's wife and her bodyguard. They are at the fortress outside Meaux, the Marché. Will you take it for me?'

William thought again about the scene of devastation so close to the camp, the bodies and the reek of blood and excrement, which reached even here to the camp, and nodded with enthusiasm.

'Good. I will have a message for you to take. It seems that the Jacquerie here were not the only force they had. More men under a different commander, John Vaillant, have marched towards Meaux, and it seems they are determined to capture the city, the fortress, and the dauphin's wife and daughter. I would like you to hurry there and warn them. I will send a vintaine with you, and a guide, but try to avoid battle on the way. We don't want to see you slain before you can give her the message. Is that clear?'

'Yes, Sir Reginald. Can I take my friend Perkin, too?'

'Yes, yes,' the knight said, with an impatient wave of his hand. William waited while the scribe finished his efforts, and then, with the scroll carefully wrapped and held in his purse, William walked out to the horse lines.

* * *

It was there that William saw Perkin, who asked, 'What are the orders now?'

'We are to ride to a city called Meaux. A guide is to

join us, and a vintaine, and we have to ride there swiftly,' he said, and explained about the dauphin's wife and child.

As he was speaking, he saw Dogbreath and Hawkwood appear, leading the rest of Hawkwood's vintaine, Rat with them. The men all gathered while William explained what he had been told, and Dogbreath spat into the dirt with his face pulled into a sour grimace. 'Ach, another long ride, then?'

'It should only be a few miles, I think,' William said doubtfully. 'The way should be five leagues or so, no more.'

'We should get there before nightfall, then,' Hawkwood said, glancing at the sun.

They did not reach Meaux.

Perkin was the first to realise the danger as they passed a small village. They were riding briskly, their senses alert to the risk of an ambush, through moderately open country, with a scattering of woods about the small farmsteads and villages, all deserted.

'It feels like the plague years,' Perkin said quietly.

'I can barely remember them,' William admitted.

'Even in the cantons, we suffered,' Fulk said, shaking his head.

'It was like this, whole villages deserted,' Perkin said. 'From farms and simple hovels all up to villages. When it struck Crediton, I remember it well. Families destroyed, all of them. Parents, grandparents, children, servants... all dead. We thought it was God's judgement.'

'In Furnshill, we saw many die, of course, but it wasn't like the towns,' William said. He had a memory of the great grave where so many bodies had been buried, it was a sight that had returned to him in nightmares for months afterwards, but that was all. And today he had seen more bodies in the hours of the battle than he had during the plague.

'There were many here,' Hawkwood said. He shook his head. 'So many died, we all thought it was the end of the world, but it all stopped and life went on.'

'I thought I would die,' Dogbreath said mournfully.

'You? No. You'll outlive Sir John de Sully,' Hawkwood said.

'Him? He's over fifty,' Dogbreath guessed.

'He's over seventy,' Hawkwood said.

'Nah, he can't be! At Poitiers he was fighting, same as a man half that.'

'Aye, and this year he'll be still older,' Hawkwood said.

'Well, if I can beat that, I'll die happy,' Dogbreath said with a wistful smile.

'You're bound to,' Seth said. 'They say, "Those whom God loves die young." You'll live forever, Dogbreath.'

Dogbreath smiled broadly, and then the import of Seth's words struck home and he scowled. 'You...'

That was when the trap was sprung.

Perkin was in the lead on the left, and he saw a moving shape at a wall ahead. He was about to yell a warning when he was grasped by the foot and pulled over the wall.

'No!' William yelled, and grabbed for his sword, but even as he did so, he saw the knife at Perkin's throat, and the men began to swarm about the vintaine, sixty or more, some with crossbows, more with long knives or billhooks.

And before them stood a man with the twisted smile of someone with a scarred mouth. 'So, my friends, who do we have here?'

* * *

Rat saw the men captured, and slipped back into the verge before he could be taken. He waited, watching, terrified, as the company was held, looking as Fulk was bound along with the others, and then, as they were led away, he rose and bolted.

It was panic, nothing more. He believed that it was Fulk who had saved him, Fulk who had kept the hag and her curse at bay. Arn's death had been so dreadful, so terrifying, that he was still convinced that the hag had sent the Devil after him. The temptation, the incentive, all came from evil. And now his saviour, Fulk, was to be killed, because he had no doubt that the French captors would soon slaughter the entire company.

He ran at full tilt; he ran without pause; he ran without purpose, just to be away, anywhere, so he would not have to witness the company being murdered. He ran because running was the only meaning to his life. It was the reason for his existence. He was all alone again. His mother, his father, and now his protector – all gone!

He ran and ran, head down, uncaring about the direction, just running to escape, until he ran almost headlong into the force riding towards him.

* * *

They were bound harshly, dragged to a small chamber in a farm's hall, and held there.

'Who are you?' the leader demanded.

He was a tall fellow, with a shock of tallow-coloured hair that hung in rats' tails about his head. The scar at his cheek and mouth showed as a livid line. It must have been inflicted some time before, but it had healed well, without the swollen signs of past infection. He had pale eyes that took in much, and an expression of mild disappointment. The room was full of his companions, all of whom held weapons pointed more or less determinedly at the vintaine. Some, William saw, were scarcely old enough to be employed in a town's jury.

William glanced about him at the rest of the vintaine. Hawkwood stood glowering furiously, while Dogbreath was hunched over as if trying to make himself small and insignificant. The only indication that he was angry was the dark brows and fierce gleam in his eyes. The rest of the vintaine behind them was more anxious than angry, although Perkin's face displayed his bitterness. One thing made him give a short frown – there was no sign of Rat.

'Well?' the man snapped.

'I am William de Furnshill of Furnshill in Devon,' he said.

'And what do you do here in the land of the Jacques?'

'We were not aware that this was, as you say, the land of the Jacquerie,' William said.

'It is France, is it not?' the man said, and then he sighed. 'We should just execute you all out of hand. That would be the right thing to do, but hardly civilised.'

'Who are you?' William asked.

'Me? I am nothing,' he said with a sour tone. 'I am only the servant of the Duke of Orléans. My name is Colet.'

'Whom do you serve?'

The man looked at him with his eyebrow raised. 'I am a Jacques. We serve *ourselves*! Our lords and knights have deserted us, lied to us, robbed us, and now they kill us! Why, whom do *you* serve? Since you are English, I suppose you serve your king, the enemy of my people.'

'We serve our king, yes. But not against you. We fight the noblemen of France and the man who calls himself king,' William said with such courage as he could muster.

There was an angry muttering at that, and the men in the room gripped their weapons more firmly. For a moment, William felt sure they would launch themselves upon him and the other men of the company, but the moment passed, and he breathed a sigh of relief when he saw Colet shake his head to the others. There was a slight lessening of tension.

'By what authority—' Hawkwood began, but William spoke across him. 'We have no argument with you. We would ask that you release us to go about our business.'

'And what of this?' Colet said, holding up the message from William's purse.

'I don't know,' he said. 'I cannot read.'

Colet held his gaze firmly then, staring at William. 'So, it would surprise you to learn that the message is for the dauphin's wife, warning her of the arrival of a force of Jacques determined to capture her?'

'All I know is, I was to give that to the garrison at Meaux,' William stated stubbornly.

'I see,' Colet said. He glanced at the paper and then threw it aside. 'It means nothing now.'

'What do you mean?'

'Oh, she is taken – and the fort, and the garrison slaughtered and left in the burning rubble of the place,' he said with a cool smile. 'Your message is of no importance now.'

31

The men were left with their hands bound behind them in the chamber, and three men stood about the room watching them. Two were swigging wine from a skin, while the third, a younger man with an expression of jealousy, kept his eyes on the vintaine.

William and Hawkwood were close to each other, and William leaned towards him. 'What can we do?'

'Little enough.'

'But we must escape here somehow.'

'You think so? I believe he will see us executed in the morning. It's a miracle he didn't top us all this evening. It would save those three losing their sleep.'

William shivered, and not from the cold. 'You mean that? You think they'll kill us?'

'What would we do in their shoes?'

William was about to speak when the younger guard snapped, 'Shut up!'

Instead William began to twist and pull at the cords binding his wrists. The leather thongs were too strong for him. He could feel them cutting into his skin, the needle-sharp pain starting to spread.

'Don't bother,' Hawkwood said. 'You won't get out of them.'

'There must be something we can do to escape!' William said.

His voice was higher than usual, he knew. He could not believe that this was how and where his life would end. His father would probably never learn what had happened to him. Instead he would be mourned and missed, and then forgotten. When his father died, and his brother took over Furnshill, that would be the end of all memories of William – and of Perkin, he re-alised. It was his fault that they had come here, to France, and it was his responsibility that Perkin was going to die here.

All because he had wanted to make himself a repu-tation, and perhaps win some land. It was his avarice that had brought them both to this pass. He looked over to Perkin, and his friend lifted a corner of his mouth in a wry grimace, as if to say he was forgiven, but before William could speak, there was a sudden clatter and rush of noise and confusion.

* * *

For a few moments William sat on his haunches, his wrists still working at the thongs binding him as the noise grew. The younger, alert guard ran for the door and out, while the other two men were transfixed, one with the wineskin still held aloft, the other holding his gaze as though petrified, frozen in an instant.

That was when William realised that the noises he'd heard were shouts and screams, the clatter of hooves on the packed earth of the roadway, and the clash of steel against steel. William rose, and the others of the vintaine followed suit. The two guards also stood, but they looked unsure what to do. Both had long knives, but neither looked as though he was competent in its use. The man with the skin dropped it, and the wine began to leak from the mouth. Both men exchanged a look, and Hawkwood knew what it meant.

'Vintaine! Form a line. They're going to try to kill us!'

The men stood and their discipline showed as they grouped together. In the face of the sixteen or more men, the two guards bolted from the door, and shortly afterwards there was a loud scream, then the clatter of boots in the screens passage, and a man appeared in the doorway. But this was no Jacques. This was a man-at-arms, who leaned negligently against the wall and asked laconically, 'Ah, good evening. Are you English?'

* * *

'I am the Captal de Buch,' the knight said.

He was a thickset, powerful-looking man, with the firelight dancing in his dark eyes. He had a force of fifteen with him, and they were sitting now at the fire-side in the hall where the vintaine had been held, but now all their wrists were released, and the men were being given wine and bread.

'My name is William of Furnshill, presently indentured to Sir Reginald de Tony,' William said.

'You are fortunate. Your boy here told us you were all held here.'

'The boy?' William said. Then: 'Rat?'

'Yes. When they attacked, I hid,' Rat said. 'I saw them take you, so I ran and ran to find someone to help, and met these. I heard them speaking English, so I knew they were safe.'

'You did well, boy,' Hawkwood said. He was

chewing some dried meat and bread, and cast a side-long glance at the men of the captal's force. 'Where have you come from?'

'We were part of the garrison of the Marché fortress outside Meaux.'

William froze. 'You mean it has fallen to the Jacques?'

The captal drew his head back as if shocked at the thought. 'Fallen? Christ's pains, no! We held it while the Jacques from Meaux and the surrounding area came to attack, and when they did, we rode out to them. We had twenty-four with us, and we slaughtered them. They had formed up into battles, but such groups were not capable of defending against a force such as ours. We are only recently returned from cru-sade with the Teutonic Knights, and we are vastly better skilled than a gathering of peasants and towns-folk. We went through them like steel through water. They fell on all sides, and when they turned to flee, we harried them all the way. And because so many came from Meaux, we went to the city and fired many of the houses as a sign that they should never again dare to take up arms against the dauphin's wife.'

'She is safe?'

'She is still at the fortress with her bodyguard. It is safe enough for her there. The Jacques have been destroyed all about the city, and I doubt any will survive for long. We have hunted down all the survivors for the last day. It is weary work, but it is essential to make an example of these fools who thought they could thwart their own prince.'

'What now?'

'There is to be a gathering of nobles at Gerberoy. They will march on the remaining rebel forces who are besieging the castle at Plessis-de-Roye, and I plan to join with them. Then we shall have ended the whole of the uprising, I trust.'

William nodded. Hawkwood, he saw, was grinning with delight. He was plainly keen to join this latest march. William did not understand how a man could thrill to think of joining another slaughter like that of the previous day. It made him shiver, a sour taste in his mouth at the thought.

Dogbreath was also pleased, William saw. The man sat with his head low on his shoulders, a wolfish grin fitted to his lips and a keen, speculative look in his eyes as if he could already see the treasure he was going to collect from this latest venture, fingering the silver cross at his throat. Others in the vintaine were as eager, nodding with glee, and only Gervase seemed less than enthusiastic.

When he peered over, he saw that Perkin was

frowning at the ground. He was, like William, thinking of the dead bodies they had already seen, the souls they had liberated. And like William, he was not happy to repeat the experience.

* * *

Two days later, they had joined with the main force of noblemen about the village of Gerberoy.

'Where are they?' Hawkwood demanded as they searched for Sir Reginald's men.

William had hoped to find Sir Reginald there with the noblemen near Montdidier, but there was no sign of him and the other vintaines. Instead there was this mass of tents, troops and horses all gathered together in the pastures outside the village.

'I don't know any more than you,' William said heavily. He felt as if he ought to be the commander of the vintaine, since he was obviously the more noble by birth, but since the last battles, and especially since leading the men into an ambush, he felt less than competent. Hawkwood, on the other hand, was capable, experienced, and every part the professional. William was happy generally to defer to his judgement, but here, in the midst of these hundreds of men, with companies of knights and esquires from as far away as Hainault and Flanders, he felt completely out of his depth. It was hard to maintain the stern attitude he felt appropriate to a man of his standing, whereas Hawkwood rode about like a man born to the army. He glanced about him at the others in the ranks with the casual eye of a warrior assessing those with whom he must fight.

The Captal de Buch had ridden on ahead as soon as they reached this extended camp, and now William was nudged by Hawkwood. 'There's the captal's man.'

It was the captal's esquire, who trotted to them on his mare.

'The captal asks you to follow me.'

William and Hawkwood rode between the camped men. Some looked up from their fires at the newcomers, but none with any great interest. It was apparent to William that they had all seen plenty of new soldiery appearing. One more band of rather tatty-looking warriors was more or less irrelevant to them all.

Soon the captal's man had pointed them to a clearing. 'Wait here and the captal will soon let you know what is happening.'

32

'Eh, I'm famished, me,' Ingram said.

He sat with his back to his saddle, a grim scowl on his face.

Hawkwood nodded and reached into his saddle bag. Inside was a fine linen cloth filled with oatmeal. He passed the bag around the men, and each took a handful of the grains, pounding and grinding them between two stones until all were crushed and broken. These the men mixed with a little water, forming solid cakes, which each of them carefully placed on their flat stones beside the fire, toasting the biscuits.

'Our old vintener, he said he'd never let a man go into battle or start a journey without food in his belly,' Saul said.

'What happened to him?' William asked.

'He got religion,' Dogbreath answered. He shook his head. 'Imagine him, old Frip, kneeling on the stones at Matins, eh?'

'Rather him than me,' Gervase said.

'I doubt his knees will manage for long, not at his age,' Nick said.

'You? You wou'n't wake for Matins. I've never knowed a man so lazy about getting up.'

'That is because I don't foul my bed.'

'You sayin' I do?' Dogbreath demanded.

'No, but the odour can sometimes lead a fellow to believe it might be so.'

Dogbreath was scowling like a demon now. But then he tilted his head in agreement. 'Aye, that's fair.'

Saul shook his head. 'I just wish the explosion from your bowels didn't force the blanket from your arse.'

'Yes, it's the trump of doom; the trump of despair; the last trump any man will hear, if he smells it after-wards,' Seth said gloomily. He had mistakenly slept beside Dogbreath one night.

'You're all jealous,' Dogbreath said with staggering confidence.

The others winced.

'What of the morrow?' Gervase asked.

Hawkwood sniffed and wrinkled his nose, considering before responding. 'The Jacques are all about the little castle called – what is it? Plessis-de-Roye. They are besieging it, and the guards fear for their lives. I estimate that the good noblemen all about us here will determine what the numbers are, and where they are all deployed. They'll form a plan of attack when they have that information, and probably send us in as hobelars to ride close enough to lay down some arrows, and then they'll ride in to the charge.'

'Will they survive? You remember what Fulk said? That the cantons where he lived had a battle and destroyed the army of the Habsburg. And the battle at Courtrai, where the peasants broke up the assault?'

Fulk nodded. '*Ja!* This is the way of things now, yes?'

'Aye, and the battle of Bannockburn, too. Yes, but this will be different. This is a peasant army, broken in pieces while it tried to take a castle. They aren't in fighting formation; they're only peasants, and they're besieging a castle. They'll be sitting on their arses staring at the castle, wondering when they'll be told to go and storm the walls. A sudden attack from behind them, led by a strong force of knights, with arrows falling among them, that will break them like twigs. They'll be driven off.'

'And then we can go into the city,' Dogbreath said.

'Perhaps. I think we can expect some form of reward,' Hawkwood said, and leaned forward to turn his oatcake.

* * *

'We've been given our directions.'

The archers listened as the captal's esquire loftily explained their dispositions, Dogbreath sneering under his breath at the esquire's arrogance. He was little more than twenty, but appeared to think that he could patronise men who had fought in battles since before he was old enough to wear a sword and belt.

'The captal expects you to go down there,' the fellow said, pointing with a riding crop towards a track. 'When you see the enemy, try to restrain your animal tendencies. The knights want a free rein to slay as many of them as they can. Afterwards, you can go in and cut the throats of those still breathing. It's not a hard job, so try not to be difficult or foolish. Keep out of the way of our knights, else you are accidentally taken for the enemy. It's not easy to tell the difference from one group compared with another.'

'Did he just say we look like French peasants?' Dogbreath demanded, and his head sank truculently as he glared at the esquire, who peered at him from atop his horse as if suddenly realising that there was a wasp in his salad.

'Dogbreath,' Hawkwood breathed. 'Enough!'

'Did he say we look like French peasants?' Dogbreath repeated.

'No, fellow. I said when a knight is riding at speed, wearing an all-enclosing bascinet, it is hard to see anything. The sight holes are very restricting, you understand. A knight seeing a group of men might think that they are all little better than a number of enemy. That is all. You have no insignia, no armour, no obvious signs to show you are men from his own company.'

'Oh,' Dogbreath said, mollified.

And then they were off, moving through the trees along the narrow track, their bows ready strung, quivers at their backs, Rat pushing a handcart loaded with more arrows, until they reached the edge of the trees, and could see before them the little castle of Plessis-de-Roye.

'We will wait here,' Hawkwood said, and the men took their places in a rough arrowhead formation, Hawkwood at the front, the point.

William and Perkin remained on their horses. They had not been asked to join the force being gathered to charge the peasant army, and William for one was glad. When he looked at Perkin, he felt sure that his friend felt the same. This was not their battle. It was a fight between French nobility and peasantry, and they were both happy to be observers and not participants.

There was an increasing noise on their right. This was the main force, approaching through the trees. William felt the stirring in his blood, a sense of rising anticipation. It was mingled excitement and disgust. He had been involved in a battle now. He had experienced the joyous release of pounding over the soil towards an enemy and the thunderous liberation of the charge itself as the knights met the enemy, crushing their victims; but he had hated the aftermath of the charge, the sense of guilt at pointless slaughter, the sight of mangled bodies, limbs hacked from torsos, guts opened, the shame of reducing his soul to mere passion. It was so shocking, he would not be disappointed if he never again experienced such a tawdry mixture of emotions. Yet he could not deny that there was a glory in it, too.

There was a clattering of armour. In the past, knights had relied on their mail shirts, and the rattling was still loud, where mail protected exposed necks, where it hung in skirts over some men's thighs. For the most part, these French men-at-arms were enclosed in steel. From their metal skull caps to their arms, to their breast plates, most were armoured in the modern style. It was natural. Since the arrival of the English, these men had been forced to rise to the occasion and defend their lands and people. They were determined to be encased in the best armour money could buy, lease or borrow. It was, after all, their lives at risk.

There was a shout, and the knights moved into a line abreast, and now the first of the peasants recognised their danger. Shrill cries went up all along the men outside the castle, and some few turned to face the unexpected challenge. The knights raised their lances until all were up in the air, and as the lances dropped, the horses began to move, a solid phalanx of metal, bone, muscle and blood, all walking forward. A knight began to trot, and as soon as the others saw him, they too trotted to keep pace with him; another urged his beast into a slow canter, and the pennons began to flutter about the lance points as they were aimed at individual peasants.

The peasants were gathering, trying to form a line of defence, some few halberds and spears set here and there, but it was not enough, not against the tons of combatants riding at them.

A shout, then another, and the horses moved from fast canter into a gallop, and the knights were pounding along, leaning into the attack, lances held outstretched, while behind them rode their esquires and, behind them, the grooms with the remounts, all in sequence, the air filled with the thunderous drumming of the hooves on the soil. William could have sworn that he could feel it through his mount's bones, through the seat of his saddle. It was an arrhythmic beat, like a thousand drums being beaten by demons, deliberately avoiding any tune or melody.

It was, William felt, a glorious sight.

And then...

The *crash*!

William felt the lurch in his stomach as the first lances pierced the enemy. Horses thundering into men, their breasts knocking the men from their feet, slamming them to the ground. It was the same all along the line of horsemen as the riders and mounts hurtled into the enemy, and the screams and shrieks as lances stabbed, as bodies rose, flung high into the air, as swords rose and fell and men fell: heads crushed, pates cut asunder, exposing brains, arms lopped off like pruned branches, men trampled and kicked, men bitten and butted...

William looked away, sickened. This was not what he was made for.

* * *

'Basically, we are to ride about the whole area, and if we see peasants, we must kill them.'

The battle was mostly over. The knights and their support had ridden over the besieging forces, and now the bodies lay broken, stabbed, crushed on the field. The knights had no deaths, only one, or men who had strained their arms in the battle. The esquire had trotted to the archers and was giving the men their instructions.

'How can we tell which men were involved in the Jacquerie?' Perkin said.

The captal's esquire rolled his eyes. 'You can't. That's why you have to kill all of those you see. Just kill them and leave the bodies to rot where they fall. We can't carry them to a gravesite. The objective is to show that peasants cannot rise against their lawful masters. A waste, of course, but it's what the Captal de Buch has ordered, and we can't ignore him. Right, any questions?'

Quietly, the men mounted their beasts. Dogbreath slouched along in his saddle, but for once there were no comments and complaints from him or the others. All were consumed by their thoughts. Rat himself was silent, his face betraying his alarm at the thought of joining the men in a fight. William himself rode slowly, his mind rebelling at the thought of the task in hand. As they passed over the field before the castle, he was aware of the bodies lying about the grasses. Hundreds of men, each with a broken skull, or a foul stab wound in the back; one he saw decapitated, others had broken lances in their chests, and several had their throats slashed wide. It was a scene from hell.

But as he went, the sense of sympathy that he instinctively felt for them began to dissipate as he remembered the convent, the villages, the castles, where these men had gone. Did they show mercy to those they slaughtered? No. And they deserved none themselves.

They left the castle behind them and continued on their way, trotting along at a swift pace, following the signs of the army fleeing. Weapons had been cast aside, along with many blue and crimson hoods, as though the peasants could cast aside all guilt along with those symbols of rebellion.

The bodies continued. This was the route the knights had taken while following the men running from the battle, and they had cut down many a young man on their way. Here was a man with his head almost cloven in two with an axe; there was a man with a great hole in his back where a lance had spitted him.

Then there was a boy, surely younger than Rat, who lay on his back, his head so violently crushed by a mace, William could only guess how he would have looked before the blow.

Their path took them between bushes of gorse and wild berries, and then they were through and into open lands. There were some houses on their right, which billowed yellow smoke from their thatch, and William saw some parties of men on horseback directing others to the destruction.

He was joined by Perkin.

'Are you well? You don't look good,' he said.

'I am healthy enough, but coming here to kill those fleeing a battle doesn't sit well on me. You?'

'My body is fine. My soul...'

'Yes, I resent killing peasants who may have had nothing to do with the siege or the Jacquerie.'

'You too?' Perkin looked over at him.

'Is it such a surprise? Back at the walled town we took, it was exciting, to rush the walls, to take the place. That seemed *just*! When we took the town, and that woman died, that was different, and this was different again. At the town... I feel guilt to have slain so many. I could not believe how many men I killed. And now these... they were only men, like the men near

Furnshill. Men who cut the pasture, harvest the corn, see to the horses and cattle... just farmers.'

'I know,' Perkin said. 'I did not expect to feel so distressed. I thought it was just – well, just enemies. After the castles we saw, the atrocities they committed against the people living there, I didn't expect to feel this... this *shame*.'

A farm a mile farther on was also in flames, and there were more bodies here; one had a crimson and blue hood, but the others were merely poor folk. Women, an ancient crone, and three children, all slaughtered together, perhaps because the husband had gone to join the men fighting against the castle. The next village contained more bodies, then there were two ruined houses, which had been fired before, and William was sure that these were the homes of members of the nobility which had been destroyed.

'This is madness!' he said. 'Two mutually dependent groups in society, and they have gone to war against each other! What is the point? What could either side gain from this? Murdering each other, and at the same time knowing, surely, that each needs the other? The nobility will starve without the efforts of their labourers, and the labourers must know that without the knightly classes, they will be lambs to the slaughter with free companies and English fighters coming to take their lands and wealth!'

'They don't see it, though, do they?' Perkin said. He puffed out his cheeks. 'They only see the latest insult, the latest foolishness from the other party, and decide to avenge it. And much of it based on misunderstanding, like the lies pushed saying that the nobles want to maintain the war.'

'The nobles treat their peasants with disdain and contempt,' William said.

'Aye, and arrogance,' Perkin agreed.

'The question is,' Hawkwood said, 'what is there for us in all this?'

'Our duty,' William said.

Hawkwood sniffed. 'Aye, well, my indenture is with Sir Reginald, not the Captal de Buch. I wonder whether we ought to be here. Shouldn't we try to find our way back to Sir Reginald's company?'

Hearing his words, Dogbreath called out, 'Aye, I mean, where's the treasure here, eh? I didn't join the vintaine to ride the countryside and murder peasants. I wanted treasure, and the peasants aren't likely to have much in that way, are they?'

William glanced at Perkin. His friend was contemplating the landscape ahead. When Perkin turned to him, there was a grim certainty in his eyes. 'Look at all that! All I can see is houses ablaze for miles ahead. What's the point of us riding after the men who have already passed by here and set all on fire? We may as well turn about and find Sir Reginald. As John said, our indenture is with him, not the Captal de Buch.'

William was about to argue when he saw another body lying amid the ruins of a little hut. The feet were those of a child, filthy and blackened where the fire had scorched her flesh. It decided him.

'Yes, we will return.'

33

Auffroy tottered. He was famished, and the road seemed to swim before him as he went.

His shoes were gone. Both had collapsed after so many miles, and just now he was oblivious to the pain in his feet. Gadiffer and the other men who had died in his pursuit of the evil man were all he thought of now. Gadiffer did not deserve to die like that. He was a kind, generous soul, and a good friend. But he had been slaughtered, like so many others. Unnecessarily killed.

It was all Auffroy's fault. He had been the cause of bringing Gadiffer across the country to his death. Auffroy carried that guilt in his bosom. It tore at him, and he felt it like a demon with razor-sharp teeth attacking his heart. There was little he could do. All he had loved and known was lost to him, even his best friend.

Ahead of him he saw a rising pall of smoke in the air, and he bent his feet towards it, recognising it as a city. And as he approached, he realised that this must surely be a great city, with enormous walls encircling it, and a mass of tight-packed buildings inside.

At the gate, he was almost refused permission to enter, but a priest saw him and berated the porter until the man relented and permitted Auffroy inside, slipping open the wicket gate for as long as it took Auffroy to stumble in.

'My son,' the priest said, catching Auffroy's arm as he almost collapsed. 'Come with me.'

'You are here to join us?' the man said excitedly.

William looked over his head. The fellow was younger than William, and looked as though he could never have fought in a battle before, but he was not alone. Behind him, ranged along the road, were thousands of others, men of all ages, some with the coat of arms of their heredity, other men-at-arms with a mixture of tunics and armour. It looked a motley group of mercenaries. 'Who are you?' he asked suspiciously.

He could feel that, behind him, the vintaine was spreading out, the men moving to get a better view of the men ahead in case this was some form of ambush, but from all William could see, there was less of a martial spirit and more of a carnival atmosphere. Men were resting, laughing and drinking.

'We are the host of King Charles of Navarre,' the man said. He was fair-haired, with a serious face that was almost unmarked by moustache or beard, and he smiled very easily. 'He is riding to defend Paris.'

'Against whom?'

'Against the dauphin, of course! The dauphin has shown himself to be faithless and dishonourable, so we're riding to the city to protect it. And King Charles has need of all the trained men he can hire.'

'I don't know, we are on our way to join our company,' William said.

'We could see whether Sir Reginald is with this force,' Hawkwood said. 'He might well have taken a contract with this King of Navarre.'

William nodded, although doubtfully. It would be the sort of group that the knight would want to join, so long as there was money in the contract. 'Very well, we need to find our commander. Do you know of Sir Reginald de Tony?'

'Sir Reginald? Yes, of course. We had him join us only yesterday! I will take you to him.'

William glanced behind him to Hawkwood. 'John, keep your eyes open and wait here with the men. If all is good, I will return myself to fetch you. If I am not back within an hour of the clock, you may assume that something has happened to me, and ride away.'

'Yes, esquire. We'll wait here.'

Perkin edged his mount closer. 'Let me come with you. My father would never forgive me if I left you to go on alone and you suffered injury because I waited here.'

'I think you should wait, Perkin. I thank you for your care, but if all is good, I'll soon be back to get you all, and if I'm not, at least you can send a message to my father to tell him I didn't embarrass him with my actions here.'

'You want me to perjure myself?' Perkin said with a grin.

'Of course,' William said, returning it. Then: 'Come, master. Take me to Sir Reginald.'

* * *

Dogbreath watched William following his guide. 'Ach,

where's he off to? Eh? Getting outside a nasty quart of ale or wine, I'd bet.'

'You must not judge all by your own measure,' Gervase said. 'He might be demanding two quarts.'

'I don't think he drinks heavily,' Saul considered. 'I have never seen him rising with a morning head on him. He always looks fit and happy.'

'Well, what does he do all day?' Dogbreath said. 'He sits on his horse and tells us what to do.'

'He joined us in battles for towns and villages,' Gervase reckoned.

'And he would be there to defend you, if you ever needed it,' Perkin said sharply.

'Oh, aye? A bold esquire coming to defend a low archer, eh? Our old vintener did. When we were riding from some French bastards, he came to help me. But William, I don't know.'

'Then learn,' Perkin said flatly. 'He is honourable and fair. I've known him all my life, and I've never known a better man.'

'Aye,' Dogbreath said, staring grimly after William. 'When he saves me, I'll believe you.'

* * *

Sir Reginald showed every sign of joy to see the vintaine. 'I had thought you were dead, or had taken a different contract.'

'We had our indentures with you,' Perkin said.

'That is true, but a man can sometimes forget to whom he owes his bread and meat. All too many mercenaries will come, take whatever they might, and then go on to another captain, ignoring the one who kept them afloat in previous months.'

'We are not so disloyal,' Perkin said. He was careful to avoid glancing at Dogbreath as he spoke.

The rest of the vintaine was in good health. They had remained with the nobles who had destroyed the Jacques, and Sir Reginald explained that, when the King of Navarre had heard that the dauphin was marching, he had ordered this small army to join him marching on Paris. With luck, this force would join with him and participate in the defence of the city. The dauphin was determined to take back the city, and had laid his plans accordingly. Paris itself, under the authority of Étienne Marcel, the provost, was equally determined to remain free and not submit to the dauphin and his father, the King of France. The city was paying for mercenaries to come and help defend it.

'What will we do there?' Perkin asked.

'Mainly show our faces. You think the dauphin will want to face us?' Sir Reginald said. 'We are not the only English marching to Paris. There are several companies there already. Sir James Pipe has been hired, and John Standen with his men. Another man called Jewel, I think, too. With their companies and ours, we could fight another Poitiers and win! I am confident of our strength compared with the forces the dauphin can muster.'

Dogbreath showed signs of interest. 'How much ransom would the dauphin be worth?'

'If we were to capture him, thousands! But we'd have to negotiate with Charles of Navarre. He would want to buy the ransom, and it would be a good deal. You don't want to have to feed and entertain a prisoner of his standard. It would be costly, but sell him to King Charles' – Sir Reginald chuckled – 'and you would be as rich as your wildest dreams.'

William looked over at Dogbreath, who was registering a sudden financial interest. 'My wildest dreams?'

It was Gervase who spoke gently, saying, 'I don't think his aspirations are a match for King Charles's wallet, Sir Reginald. He plans an alehouse – more than that would merely confuse him.'

Dogbreath glowered at him, convinced he had been insulted, but not sure how.

'I see. Well, Dogbreath, if you were to catch the dauphin, you could afford all the alehouses in Southwark,' Sir Reginald said, adding, 'and all the doxies too.'

Dogbreath frowned in an attempt to comprehend such wealth, but after some moments he had to give up. Wrinkling his nose, he spat at the ground. 'One tavern, that would do me. And three tarts to fill it. With that, and a cellar of ale, I could die happy.'

'With a barrel of ale, you could die happy.'

Dogbreath gave a beatific smile. 'Aye. That would be a good start, but I'd need some strumpets too.'

'You wouldn't manage them. I've seen you after a few pots of ale,' Hawkwood said with a scornful chuckle.

'Don't measure my tarse by your own,' Dogbreath snapped. 'You'd be disappointed.' Feeling this was answer enough, he turned his back on the vintener.

'Hold! Dogbreath,' Saul said.

'What?'

Saul held a small earthworm between thumb and forefinger. 'You dropped your tarse!'

* * *

They had reached Paris, and Navarre had his army encamped north of the city, making the abbey of Saint-Denis his headquarters. While there, the vintaine lazed a little.

'Why aren't we inside the city?' Dogbreath whined.

'Look in a mirror, and you'll see the reason for their reluctance,' Seth said.

Fulk was sweeping his small stone over the blade of his long knife, and now he looked up and over towards the city's walls. 'They do not want English or Navarrese soldiers in the city. They fear us.'

'Why fear *us*? We're only here to help defend the city! How can we do that sitting miles to the north?' Saul said. 'Do they want the dauphin and his men to just walk in and take the place? What are they planning?'

'I doubt they'd allow the dauphin in either. Think about it: all the leaders of the city have led rebellion against the dauphin – do you think they hope he'll forgive them?' Hawkwood said. 'They can expect a hurdle to the execution field, and there to be broken on the wheel. None of the ringleaders will be allowed to survive. What would the nobles think of the dauphin if he was to permit open rebellion to remain unpunished? And the people of Paris fear much the same. Whether it's us or the dauphin's army that enters the city, the people will suffer. They know it. So they wait, and hope for some miracle. And the dauphin lays siege to the east, while we remain here in the north.'

Fulk eyed his blade, nodded and slipped the stone back under his shirt. Rising, he said, 'These Parisians fear much, but without their help, we cannot protect them. We have one thousand men. We could man the city walls and save Paris from assault. But they refuse to let us in. So! We are held here, without the numbers we need to fight the dauphin's forces, and unable to save Paris. If they will not let us in, we must withdraw.'

34

PARIS

That was the same thought that exercised Thomas de Ladit. In the city the people were growing ever more restless and alarmed. Anyone climbing to the city's walls could see the smoke rising from the nearby villages. The dauphin's army was systematically destroying all in his path, and now he was camped before the city itself, and had blocked many of the rivers that kept the city fed. No boats could pass down to the city with food, and soon the dauphin would have a bridge built near Les Carrières. Everyone in the city knew it. Once it was constructed, that bridge of boats would mean that the dauphin would have enclosed the entire city in a ring of iron and steel. He had the men, and with the rivers blocked, the city must starve.

Thomas hurried to the meeting. There were still some men who were loyal to the King of Navarre, but they were countered by others who were terrified of the English he had brought with him. Almost all dreaded the dauphin and his nobles, for everyone knew that if the gates were opened and the nobles were allowed into the city, none would be safe from their vengeance. What was best to do?

Thomas met the emissary from King Charles near the Louvre.

'How are affairs in the city?'

'No one knows which way to turn,' Thomas answered. 'Every option holds risks for the populace.'

'Will they fight?'

Thomas shook his head doubtfully. 'They say they will, but whether that is the case when they are faced with the dauphin and his men with their rage at what Paris has done, who can tell? Many of them believe that they can hold the city against even the dauphin, but they are men who have not fought. They have never held a sword against a knight, nor seen a cavalry charge. Yes, there are many who could stand on the battlements of the walls and fight with crossbow or lance if the dauphin tried to assault the walls, but for how long? They have no true comprehension of the dangers.'

'Our king is to go to the dauphin. They are to hold a meeting.'

Thomas winced. 'He trusts the dauphin?'

'The dauphin is honourable,' the man said haughtily.

'But he will have men about him who will want to avenge the harm done by the Jacques, and they know that Paris is responsible for much of the rebellion, and that our king is now considered the captain of Paris. They blame him for much of the bloodshed.'

There was no answer to that. Both men knew it was true enough. Charles of Navarre would ever move with the wind. If he saw benefit in one alliance, he would drop any others in an instant.

'He has asked for you to join him,' the emissary said. 'It is your advice he craves, and your wisdom. You best know his mind and his needs.'

'Where should I meet him?'

'He is at Saint-Denis. If you could join him there, and go with him to the meeting, you may discuss matters on the way.'

Thomas agreed, and the two made their way along the streets to a stable, where Thomas hired a beast, and soon they were leaving by the Saint-Denis gate, and following the road north. It was only a mile up the road that they met the small force riding south.

'Good Thomas, my friend! I am glad to see you again!' the king said, his gratitude evident.

'My Lord, I am glad to see you healthy and strong.'

'I am strong enough,' the king said, and then launched into a series of questions about the garrison of Paris and the populace. The news Thomas brought him was enough to make him glower with bitterness as he considered his options. 'Your advice?'

'Make the best peace you can with the dauphin. He has the nobles on his side. Since you joined with Paris, they all believe you are on the side of the rebels.'

'But I have just destroyed them in battle! The Jacques are no more!'

'The rebellion began here, in Paris. The nobility view you as a traitor to them. Allying yourself with the city has destroyed any confidence they had in you. You must make your peace with the dauphin and seek the best terms you may.'

Thomas rode back to the city with a leaden sense of impending disaster deep in his bowels.

It had gone as well as it could have. Three prelates

mediated the talks. The dauphin for his part was a stern, fierce figure sitting opposite Navarre, who only rarely graced the king with his full gaze. He was still bitter about the treachery in which Navarre had involved himself. No matter that he stressed the battles he had held against the Jacquerie and that he had destroyed them utterly and laid waste to much of the lands where they had been rampaging. He was considered a traitor by the dauphin.

That was why Thomas was so taken with the final offer from the dauphin. It was astonishingly generous to a man he could hardly trust. If the king would depart and not bear arms against the dauphin again, he would be granted lands worth 10,000 livres a year, a payment of 400,000 écus, and he could leave in peace. As for Paris, they would be forced to pay the first instalment of the ransom of King John, but the dauphin would set aside the crimes committed by the populace. All their offences would be unpunished.

The agreement was astonishing. Thomas could barely keep the grin from his face on hearing the terms, but when he looked at the king, he was concerned to see that Charles of Navarre was hesitant and thoughtful, as though he was in two minds whether to accept or not.

How could he think he could win a better offer?

This was the best of all worlds. Yes, he was expected to persuade the people of Paris to agree to these terms, but then all the crimes committed would be remitted and the armies could avoid battle.

There was to have been a short ceremony, at which the Bishop of Lisieux was to ask both the dauphin and the king to swear on the body of Christ, but even as prayers were spoken, and the Host was brought to them, Charles rose to his feet, apologising, and explaining that he had not fasted that day so could not take the Host.

He hurried from the pavilion, Thomas following him, desperate to know what the matter was.

'You didn't swear! How can the dauphin have faith in you, sir?'

They had reached their horses and mounted, riding away briskly, Charles glancing over his shoulder every so often, fearing pursuit. 'It is easy! What is my best option? To take the dauphin at his word? What is *his* word worth? How can I tell whether or not he will keep to his promise?'

'Sir, he is the son of the King of France! If he gives his word, that should be adequate for any man,' Thomas said, and there was a rising desperation as he considered the affair.

'You don't understand,' King Charles said. 'This

dauphin is only a boy. We shall see what the people of Paris have to say, but I dare consider that my interests lie more in Paris than with the dauphin. Did you see the looks the knights about the dauphin were giving me? They hate me! As soon as they can, they will all petition the dauphin to have me executed. They don't trust me or love me. My life wouldn't be worth five sous if I was to give my word. You can have my word on *that!*'

And with that, he spurred his beast into a canter and rode at speed for the gate.

* * *

Fulk looked about him as they walked along the street from the gate. At his side was Rat, who was staring about him with the wide-eyed gaze of a peasant seeing his first great city, and this was the largest city in Christendom, so Fulk had heard. Not that he found it particularly impressive. It was just a place with more buildings than most, and a large fortification at the north-west, the famous castle of French kings, the Louvre. Apart from that, it was a place of streets filled with horse and human excrement, and a man had to beware as he walked so he didn't step into either of them.

The English and Navarrese army had been invited into the city at last. William and Perkin, walking their horses in and up the lanes, were bemused by the sudden agreement.

'Will, why do they want us in now, all of a sudden?' Perkin had said when they heard that they were to strike camp.

'They must realise they need the extra men, at last,' William said. 'They'd hardly invite us in to help deplete their food stocks, would they?'

The loud rumble behind them spoke of Archibald and his wagons. The Parisians watched the vintaine and the rest of the army with sullen resentment, but Archibald treated them all to his broadest smile. 'Smile, damn your soul,' he said to Ed.

'Why?'

'Because just now we are entering a massive gaol, boy, and when that gate closes behind us, we will be shut in with all these other prisoners, and we will have to hope that they are welcoming and grateful, because there are a lot of them, and only a few hundred of us. So if you want to keep your life, you had best show yourself to be the most amiable, gentlemanly, upright soul these fellows have ever seen. See?'

Ed began to smile and wave.

'Not that much, boy.'

* * *

The vintaine found itself a barn, which was large enough to accommodate the men, their horses, Archibald's oxen and wagons. Archibald himself spent considerable time turning the wagons so that they faced the door, and he fussed about them all the while when the other men were making a little fire and cooking a thick pottage.

Sir Reginald appeared sometime after they had settled themselves in the stable. 'You have made yourselves at home, I see,' he said, smiling broadly.

'What's happening?' Saul asked.

The men stopped whatever they were doing to pay attention as Sir Reginald squatted by their little fire.

'The good King of Navarre was offered very gracious terms for peace,' he began. 'However, some of those terms involved the people of the city. They must surrender their city and much of their wealth to the dauphin, and they refused to accept those terms. With the whole populace, they reckoned they could hold the city against a force three times the strength of the dauphin's army. It will be,' he said thoughtfully, prodding the fire with a stick, 'interesting to see whether they are right. The truth is, I don't know any better than they. Still, there are a thousand of us English here, with Sir James Pipe and his men, as well as other companies, and the Navarrese are hardy fighters. So, we do have a good chance of winning.'

William looked at the men. There was a general feeling of confidence, almost. Perhaps it was more acceptance. They all knew why they were there in France: they were there to fight, and hopefully to make a profit.

However, many of the English and Navarrese were to forget who was the enemy, and who were their friends and paying their wages. Two nights after Sir Reginald came to speak with the vintaine, there was a loud ruckus in the street outside their stable, and when Perkin and Fulk went to investigate, they found three Navarrese fighting a group of Parisians. It was, so it seemed, a dispute over the possible professional engagement of a young Frenchwoman, whom the Navarrese wished to employ and whom the French populace wished to defend. The battle was quickly curtailed by William and the vintaine separating the two groups. One Navarrese, drunk, tried to push past Fulk, who lazily swung a fist the size of one of Archibald's biggest stones and sent the man flying, unconscious, to a wall three feet behind him.

Sending the Parisians on their way, with the woman (who was eyeing Fulk speculatively in a manner that spoke of the Navarrese having been correct in their assumption of her trade), the vintaine closed the stable doors. Archibald was pensive as he did so, and then had a low conversation with Ed. The two set about their wagons again, and although the rest of the vintaine watched, they did not interrupt.

It was only when Archibald completed his tasks and sat down once more that William nodded towards the wagons. 'What are you doing?'

'I have two small toys under the wagons. If anyone wants to come into the stable to start a fight with us, they will have a surprise,' Archibald said. He rolled himself into his blanket. 'Master William, I would suggest that we keep a wakeful guard through the night. If there is a reason for alarm, make sure that I am woken first.'

35

Four days later, the dauphin's bridge blockading the river was almost completed, and it was clear to all in the city that it must lead to a complete encirclement of the south and east of the city. That spelled disaster. The whole city was anxious in the face of the threat to their food supplies, and it led to desperate measures. To William's and Perkin's concern, the company was to ride from the city to attack the bridge.

It would not be them alone – a second force would attack from the other side of the river, while a third would make its way by boat. All three converging on the bridge should lead to the destruction of the guards and the bridge itself. At least, that was the plan.

'We will ride out from the Porte Bordelle. Others

will ride from the Porte Saint-Antoine, and more will use the river on fortified barges. We will make our way swiftly to the bridge. There we shall kill the guards, drop a small barrel of Archibald's powder, set the bridge ablaze, and return. It shouldn't take long, and then the bridge will be destroyed. Any questions?'

The men stared at Sir Reginald without speaking.

'No? Good.'

William took a deep breath. 'Sir, how many men are there in the dauphin's army to the north of the river? I mean, how many will we meet on the way to the bridge?'

'Oh, I wouldn't worry about that. It's only a short distance and we'll have three forces attacking simultaneously. They'll be hard pressed to defend themselves, especially with our archers all behind us. I doubt any of the French will be able to hurt us. Make sure you have enough arrows.'

'Enough arrows, he says,' Dogbreath said after the knight had left. 'How many is enough? Ten thousand? Twenty? Get ready, Rat. You'll be carrying a lot this day.'

'I can't carry that many,' Rat said, perplexed.

'Don't worry, Rat,' Fulk said kindly. 'You only need to fill a cart and bring that.'

The plan was simple enough. Hawkwood's vintaine, along with Robin's and Peter's, were to ride their ponies out through the gate to a short distance from the bridge. There, while William and Perkin rode with the men-at-arms for the bridge, the archers must deliver a withering attack on any men sent to try to prevent the force from reaching the bridge.

It seemed easy, William thought to himself as he tightened the girth on his horse's saddle, testing it for position and firmness.

Sir Reginald was two horses further along the lines, and William caught him looking over. 'Yes?'

'I know you were unsettled by the attack on the town, and you have not been happy since, with the attack on the Jacques rebels. It shows in your eyes. But today, esquire, remember that we are here to protect the people of this city. We are not here to harm peasants and farmers; we go to battle against a strong force of armoured men. It is a glorious, honourable thing we do. But it will be a serious fight, so remember to grip your sword tightly, keep your point up, and come back safely.'

'Yes, Sir Reginald.'

'The same goes for you, Master Perkin. This is not going to be an easy walkover for us. The archers will unhorse and loose their missiles at the French, but we must ride amid them and set our charge on the bridge to destroy it. When we reach the bridge, we must choose whether to ride over and reach the farther side, which may offer an easier route back to the city, or we may return by the same route we take to reach the bridge, back to this gate. We shall have to make that decision when we see which way will be safer. So, keep your eyes wide and your way back firmly in your mind.'

'Yes, Sir Reginald,' they said, and soon they were on their horses and trotting to the gate.

'How shall we know when to ride?' Perkin said.

'I imagine there will be a signal,' William said, but he was unconvinced himself. A horn blast from the other side of the river would not carry so far as this, and it would not be possible to see a flag waving or a man trying to signal some other way.

He was still wondering, when Sir Reginald gave a bellowed command, and the guards lifted the gate's beams and opened the gates wide, and they were cantering out into the open land before the city.

* * *

William had his visor open as they left the city at the Bordelle gate, and he could understand why so many knights and their men-at-arms fought without a visor.

It gave a far better view of the battlefield, admittedly at the risk of an injury to the face, but it was worth that risk, he decided, to have the chance to see where enemies stood, to be able to breathe without restriction, and to lose that sense that a man was sitting in a steel coffin ready to be thrust into the ground.

There was a group of men about the entrance to the bridge of boats, he saw, perhaps a hundred or more, and as he rode, he saw a large number of them throw aside their tools with which they were finishing the construction, and bolt back for the dauphin's lines. Men on the bridge itself gaped as the men rode briskly towards it, and then the first of the arrows appeared, sleeting through the air like hawks flashing down on their prey.

William bent over his mount's neck as the group increased their pace and began to gallop. There was a howling as the wind soughed in his ears with the speed, and his world was taken up by the snap of tunics, the clattering of armour, the jingle of mail, the thunder of hoofbeats, until he could hear little else. All his concentration was fixed upon the bridge and the great supports that rose high over the construction itself. That was their target, and he could pay no attention to anything else.

But when he looked over the river to the far bank,

where he should have been able to see the second company of mercenaries pounding along in the same way as his own – there was no one there. When he glanced at the river, the third assault was sailing up against the flow, with crossbowmen and men-at-arms brandishing their weapons, but of the last group from the Porte Saint-Antoine, there was nothing to be seen. It was only when he looked back over his shoulder that he saw the second group appear at the gatehouse and begin their own charge, under the command of Sir James Pipe, but it was already too late. The men would not be able to reach the other side of the bridge in time to support William's company or the men on the barges.

He spurred his horse, and he and Sir Reginald with the men reached the bridge quickly. William directed his horse at a group of three, with Perkin behind him, and although a sword was aimed at his face, it struck the edge of his face guard, and then he and Perkin brought him to the ground, immediately moving to the next men, their swords ringing and clattering on mail and armour alike. A second French knight was unhorsed, and the third, hemmed in by the English, submitted reluctantly.

Amid the fight, William heard the alarm being sounded. Fighting through the men set to guard the bridge, William and the others could approach the bridge only slowly. The men from the barges did their best, but trying to reach the shore was difficult with so many French men-at-arms defending the northern bank, and the men at the southern bank fought back resolutely and with determination, preventing the bargemen from landing. Even as William watched, French horsemen were cantering over the fields to the northern bridgehead, and a large contingent came on steadily, reaching the bridge, half immediately charging the English and Parisians from the Porte Saint-Antoine, while others crossed over the bridge to assault William and Sir Reginald's force in the flank.

The coordination of the plan had failed, and that meant that their ride to the bridge was in vain. Already, he could see that more French were forming up, with knights and men-at-arms mounting hurriedly, grabbing weapons from their servants, and setting off towards the bridge and the English.

They were hopelessly outnumbered, and only the archers could save them now from the reinforcements crossing the bridge. He crouched lower as the next volleys of arrows flew towards the French. It was too far for the clothyards to be able to penetrate armour, but many horses were unarmoured, and the arrows struck them with hideous efficiency, some few maddened by the sudden pricks and trying to turn and bite the irritant, two beasts unhorsing their riders. One took an arrow in the head and slid on forelegs on the grass, already dead.

William saw a man in full armour heading straight for him, and he pulled his sword free, ready for the clash, waving it to free muscles tightened by fear and the gallop, and then they met in a cacophony of metal, swords striking armour, striking swords, lances punching at and through armour, the hardened steel tips puncturing steel and mail and stabbing deep into breasts.

A sword struck the side of William's helm and he reeled in his saddle, but then punched out. His sword missed the vulnerable point beneath his opponent's chin piece, but it flashed up and clattered against the man's sights, and with the appearance of the sword point so close to his eyes, he recoiled at speed, but then William was past him and hammering at a smaller figure, who ducked and tried to avoid his attack, almost falling from his saddle.

'William!' he heard, and when he turned, he saw, to his horror, that he was alone apart from Perkin and one other – Sir Reginald and the rest were riding back for the city, a number of prisoners with them.

'Perkin! With me!' he shouted as a sword clanged

on his shoulder. He whirled his sword about him to deter another assault, but then they were off, galloping like kings' messengers straight towards the gates. More arrows, and he heard someone behind him fall, but then he was only some hundreds of yards from the gate, and even as he realised how close he was, he saw the wagon appear and turn, so that the side of the wagon was facing him, and he saw Archibald on the wagon's bed, blowing on a match to set the ember glowing. He waved a hand imperiously at William to get out of the way.

'Perkin, 'Ware Archibald!' William bellowed urgently, and swung his horse away from the river and the city gate, leaving a clear view of the pursuers for Archibald.

He had almost reached the archers, who stood to one side of the wagon, when he heard the blast and saw the devilish smoke erupt from the barrels of the ribauldequin, which hung beneath the wagon. A number of small stones were flung from it towards the riders following William and Perkin, and the effect was immediate.

Horses, shocked and terrified by the unexpected explosion and smoke, reeled and reared, while three were stabbed by the vicious hail of stones. Lacerated, one set off at full speed for the river, leaping in, his rider falling into the water and drowning under the weight of his armour. William looked behind him at the carnage, and once again thought to himself that such new weapons were more appalling than swords and lances. At least a man could see an approaching sword and deflect it. A gonne was a different matter. There was no defence against such devices. It was little surprise that the men felt these were the weapons of the Devil himself.

36

'What happened to you and your men?' Sir Reginald was shouting. 'We could have been slaughtered without your support! As it is, we didn't destroy the damned bridge!'

They were at the road outside the main stables, and while Rat rubbed down the horses with the other grooms, Sir Reginald was standing before Sir James Pipe, leaning forward with his face as purple as a ripe plum, enraged.

'I lost three of my men thanks to your *slowness*! Was it simple stupidity that meant you delayed, or something else? Did you mean to see us all slain?'

'I was out of the gate at the appointed time.'

'You were *late*! I was there at the agreed time – and

so was the third group, the men attacking by the river – but where were you?'

'I don't know,' Sir James said. He had a grim expression, like a man who knew that this was a stain on his character. 'We should have been there with you.'

It was an argument that had continued, going in circles for the last hour since the parties had returned to the city, and William felt sure it would continue for a lot longer. He caught Perkin's eye, and the two left the knights to their wrangling, and went out.

At a tavern a little further up the road, they saw Archibald and Ed, and William crossed to them. 'I am very glad you were there today.'

'Ah, well, my little toys can have a wonderful effect when used correctly. I am glad you saw my intention and moved from the path of the gonnes.'

'It was devastating to see how effective they were,' William said.

'One ribauldequin, with seven barrels all ignited in sequence,' Archibald said, draining his cup. 'There are few horses who could stand that kind of noise and alarm. Not many riders, either,' he added thoughtfully.

'I am glad that my horse didn't panic like the French's,' Perkin said. He had heard the whistle and howl of the stones passing close by as he followed William from the path of the gonnes, and the memory of the sound made him shudder. That was a noise that would stay with him forever, he felt.

'There isn't much that can beat the impact of my little gonnes,' Archibald said smugly. 'But if you are so grateful, I wouldn't refuse a fresh pot of ale or wine.'

Although Sir Reginald had complained bitterly to Sir James about the tardiness of his assault, William learned that his own force had suffered numerous casualties. The fact that the dauphin's men had seen the barges and the southern attack develop meant that they'd had ample warning. Where Sir James should have met with a small defensive group at the bridge, instead he and his men were to meet a cavalry charge, which was formed of men-at-arms well practiced in the exercise. They were all men who had been tested in multiple battles against English knights as well as the Jacquerie, and their sudden onslaught was devastating, the more especially since Sir James had a supporting host of Parisians who had followed his lead. These, both those on horseback and on foot, were easy prey for the dauphin's regular fighters, and many had died.

'It will have an impact,' Archibald commented as

he and Ed walked back to their stable with William and Perkin. 'The Parisians have just come to appreciate that fighting expert fighters requires more than mere élan. They must have experience and skill as well as simple courage.'

'You mean they will want to learn how to fight?' William said and gave a humourless laugh. 'It would take many months to teach this rabble.'

'I think it means they might seek another accommodation with the dauphin,' Archibald said. 'And if so, we must see to our own defence.'

'How so?'

Archibald glanced at him. 'First, I have set up my wagons with my ribauldequins facing the two doors. The gonnes are loaded. If anyone tried to break into the stables, they would receive a warm welcome. That should deter them. In the second place, if we have the opportunity, we should seek to find as many other English as possible to join us, so that we may all stand together. Smaller parties would not be able to hold out for long. And third, we should discover any suitable routes of escape from the city, in case matters develop that look unhealthy for us.'

'The Parisians rely on us. We cannot leave them.'

Archibald said nothing, merely lifting one eyebrow cynically.

* * *

One week later a second negotiation took place. This, as though to rub salt into the wound of their failure, was held at the middle of the bridge of boats over the Seine, which so many men had died trying to take and destroy.

William, Perkin and Hawkwood's vintaine were there with a large group of other English and Navarrese warriors, and William was surprised to see the dauphin appear with only a small number of unarmed knights. He was confident of his position, and he took his place on the bridge opposite King Charles with the demeanour of a man prepared to listen to a servant's petition. For Paris, Jean Belot, who had a reputation of being loyal to the royal family, and who had not supported the rebellion, was the chief spokesman.

The dauphin washed his hands methodically, drying them on the laver's towel. King Charles did the same, and then both took goblets of wine as the discussions began.

It was clear to William that the three men were arguing their corners with energy. King Charles wanted to list all his grievances, while Belot for Paris wanted to agree the original terms that King Charles had agreed with the dauphin two weeks before.

The dauphin listened intently, and then looked at Belot firmly. 'You ask that the rebels should be unpunished? I promised that I would remit all penalties for their insubordination and rebellion, but since then your citizens have again betrayed me and my trust in them. They have tried to attack this bridge of mine, and they remain in Paris in defiance of my rule. This cannot continue. I will not promise to remit all penalties.'

That was the beginning of the lengthy discussion that ended with the dauphin agreeing to consider individual cases on their merits, in conjunction with the dowager Queen of Navarre and King Charles. That was agreeable to those representing the Parisians on the bridge – although it was obvious that the rest of the city may find fault with the offer. The dauphin agreed and suggested that Belot could have five days to secure approval from the city.

William returned with the others to Paris, and he didn't like the atmosphere. It was febrile. 'These people are terrified,' he said to Perkin.

Sir Reginald overheard him. 'Aye, and why wouldn't they be? They have taken arms against the dauphin, aye, and he might demand some compensation for the harm they have done him. That will cost the city dear, I have no doubt. He still expects the city to pay for the first month's ransom of his father.'

'They could hardly expect better,' William said.

'No, but there is worse for them,' Sir Reginald said. 'Think on this. The dauphin came to the bridge just now without a weapon, and his knights were all unarmed, too. Just think what might have happened if they all came bearing arms? Those knights all know of the atrocities committed by the Jacquerie. Some, perhaps, have lost friends, sons, wives to the rebels. If they were all armed, a fight could have broken out, and what would have happened?'

'It would have ended badly,' William said.

'That it would. Now think, once the city agrees to submit to the dauphin's rule again, they will have to throw open their gates to him and his men, won't they? To an army of men-at-arms who all have a grudge against those who raised the flag of rebellion against the dauphin – but also, by extension, against them as well. What do you think will happen when they all enter the city and are faced with the rebels who were responsible for slaughtering noblemen, destroying their castles and homes?'

'Do you think they will let the army into the city?' Perkin asked. In his mind's eye he could see streets teeming with fighters, with men in armour clamouring for vengeance, swords and lances dripping with the blood of the citizens.

'I do not know. I fear that whichever decision they take, this city will suffer for their actions supporting the Jacques and open rebellion,' Sir Reginald said. 'So beware!'

* * *

The situation began to alter almost immediately. The vintaine had gathered together several other men and formed their own company in the stables, with men from Wales, England and Normandy as well as the Navarrese, and they were soon to be glad that they did.

It was not long after the conference at the bridge that men on the walls cried down that the dauphin and his army were pulling back. When William ran up to the battlements, he saw that the mass of men and beasts in the dauphin's camp was dispersing. Long wagon trains could be seen withdrawing, and soon he saw that the men-at-arms were pulling down tents and packing them.

Later, when scouts were sent out to look, they discovered that the camp was deserted.

'What's he doing?' Dogbreath demanded.

Saul was grinning. 'The dauphin must have given

up! He knows he could never beat Paris! Look at the walls here!'

Fulk nodded. 'He has retreated. But for how long?'

The hotter heads in the city began to swagger with the thought that they had succeeded in toppling the royal family, where all others and the English had failed. Others, William heard, took a more sanguine approach, declaring that the dauphin was simply showing good faith and generosity of spirit. They thought that it was obvious to the dauphin that the city would never open her gates to an army such as the dauphin's, which was full of men desperate to see retribution for the harm done to them, their friends or families. By telling the army to decamp, the dauphin had shown the citizens that they had nothing to fear from him. He would rule them fairly.

In a tavern, William overheard some men discussing the disappearance of the army. These sounded like diehard rebels, who rejected the dauphin's proposed agreement out of hand. They saw no reason to submit to the prince, and instead muttered angrily about having their vengeance on those who wanted to. It was only a short time afterwards that properties owned by the dauphin and his associates were attacked. Many were broken into and plundered. William chose not to mention it when he noticed that suddenly Dogbreath's pack, and those of Ingram and Saul, grew in weight and size. He considered it more diplomatic not to ask where their new-found goods had come from.

In the midst of this tumult, Étienne Marcel and his closest companions holed themselves up in the monastery of St Eloy on the Île de la Cité and planned to fortify it and protect themselves.

That was when the climax struck.

37

It was a terrifying evening.

Auffroy had been staying in the priest's house since arriving in Paris, initially sleeping and praying with the kindly religious, but then a horrible reaction had set in. He began having nightmares, and saw Gadiffer appear in front of him, horribly beslubbered with blood, accusing Auffroy of deserting him, leaving his body on the field of battle, after taking him all that way, just to try to avenge Juliot. It left Auffroy weakly and exhausted, feverish and desperate.

That evening was the first that he had begun to heal from his experiences. The priest, Father Marc, had nursed him through the worst of the fevers, and at last, that evening Auffroy had felt strong enough to tell him all about his journey: about the death of Juliot and their son, the decision by the village to see her buried at the crossroads, the mutilation of her body and, finally, that last cruel indignity and the proof of his own eyes as the mercenary Englishman came back from burying them both. Then the long hunt, trying to catch the mercenary responsible, trying to take back what had been stolen, and seeing so many of his friends slain in the attempt.

'My poor child,' the priest said, with tears of sympathy in his eyes. 'These English devils are monstrous, I know, but you can do nothing more. You have tried your best.'

'I cannot stop now! That would mean all those deaths were pointless!' he burst out, desperately.

'It is difficult, I know, but you cannot continue. Who else must die for your attempt at vengeance? You must return to your home and make a new life.'

Auffroy was about to respond when the first cries were heard out in the street.

Father Marc rose and went to the window, peering out into the street. 'What is this? Has the world gone mad?' he muttered.

'What is it, Father?' Auffroy asked.

'Men in the street. Nothing more. It is nothing for you to worry about,' the priest told him.

There was a scream, suddenly cut short, and then a series of cheers and cries, and Auffroy rose from the bed where he had been lying in view of the altar, and stood beside the priest.

'It is the end of things, perhaps,' Father Marc said. He drew Auffroy with him to the altar, and there the two knelt and prayed for God's mercy and forgiveness, even as they listened to the shrieks and appalling sounds from outside.

It was a warm evening, and the night promised to be one of those hot, humid, sweltering occasions when a man swore and threw aside any coverings as the sweat trickled and the flea bites itched. William had never known such a temperature at night, and he found it all but unbearable. He had been sleeping in only his shirt, lying on his blanket on top of a bed of straw, but he awoke, coming to with a strange sense of alarm.

In his childhood, he had regularly had a dream of a hideous town filled with ghosts and blood-drinkers, the *sanguisuga*, creatures who had died, and came back to drink from the throats of children and young adults. Those dreams had always woken him, and he woke now with a horrible feeling of foreboding.

It was enough to stir him from his makeshift bed and stand, rubbing his armpits, where the sweat was lingering. Perhaps it was largely the dream that had made him feel like this? But for whatever the reason, the anxiety remained, and he went to the doors, planning to slip outside and see whether the air was cooler out there.

Stepping carefully past the snoring men, he went to the doors and was about to slip the beam, locking it, when he heard quiet voices outside. He was almost tempted to call out to whoever was up this late in the day when some of the words came to him. Speaking in that rapid French, with the strong intonation of Parisians, he heard someone speak about surprising the men, breaking in and killing them all in their beds.

He stood still, shocked, thinking surely he must have misheard their words, that the people of this city must appreciate the English and the way that they had come here to protect the Parisians, but even as he had that thought, he saw the long blade of a sword appear in the gap between the doors, and it rose silently to the bar. There it paused, and he heard heavy breathing on the other side of the double doors, as men tried to prise the bar up and out of its retaining slots so they could pull the doors wide.

'*Archibald! Perkin! Hawkwood!* Attack! Wake up!' he

shouted, leaping over slowly waking men and grabbing his sword. Even as he grasped the hilt, he heard the bar topple and crash to the ground, and then the doors swung open. But even as they did, there was a fierce blast, a confusion of filthy smoke and flame, and William saw for the first time how a gonne could tear at a man's body at close range.

There was a hellish disorder as the men in the doorway tried to make sense of what had just hit them. It was not aided by the bellows of the company's men as they were woken from deep sleep, the whinnying and neighing of terrified horses in their stalls, the screaming of Rat and other boys.

Three of the attackers were shredded by stones from the first two barrels, then the second wagon also erupted in flame and death, and William saw the shocked men in the doorway as the latest stones flayed them, the powder burning their skin, the stones puncturing their clothing, one man losing his jaw, another having his arm almost detached from his body. Three men were already squirming in agony on the ground, and then another barrel was fired, and in the hellish flame, William saw the nearest man eviscerated, falling and screaming with a high keening that tore at William's soul.

He sprang towards the door, in case the others

tried to rush it and enter, but the rest of the gang had fled after seeing their comrades so mutilated, and after he had checked that Archibald could see him, he went to the remaining men. He had nothing to do for them, other than kneel and offer the *paternoster* to each as they died, but one could still talk, and Hawkwood went to him, kneeling beside him with his dagger in his hand, demanding to know why the men had decided to attack them.

'You are English! You attack our country, you defile our lands, you...'

Hawkwood slipped his dagger into the man's eye and pressed down.

* * *

Out in the street, William could hear more shouting, and then a lot of cries and screams. He peered up the street, where there were torches flaring and hurried figures darting about. A house was on fire, and he saw men dancing in front of it, gleefully celebrating their destruction.

'What is happening?' he pleaded.

'The people are rising against Navarre and the leaders of the city, I suppose,' Hawkwood said. He had gone to William's side, and now stood pensively gazing up in the same direction. 'I think it's time we left our lodging here, and found somewhere more congenial.'

'I agree,' Archibald said. He had already started yoking his oxen to the first wagon, but the beasts were dull-witted with sleep and he was forced to man-handle them into place. 'I'll never get them to work,' he muttered as he and Ed tried to get the first into the traces.

'Look to the horses,' Hawkwood said. 'You may find some heavy draught horses here. If so, we won't have to go too far, with luck. I say we head for the monastery where Marcel and his men have taken their refuge. That should not present a difficulty for a strong mount.'

But when they searched the stable, they found only palfreys and rounseys. There were no heavy-built draught horses capable of dragging Archibald's wag-ons, and even if he could find some, there was no har-ness suitable for horses.

'I'll have to leave them behind,' Archibald said mournfully, gazing at his wagons and the gonnes mounted below them, the great gonne on the bed of his own wagon.

'There is no choice,' William said. 'We have to leave. There are more men gathering down there,' he added, pointing.

Hawkwood peered. 'You're right.'

Sir Reginald joined them. While William pulled on his hosen and took a tunic over his head, the knight stared dejectedly at his armour, and regretfully pulled his sword belt about his waist. 'No time to waste, I fear. Company, with me!'

'Archers!' Hawkwood called. 'String your bows. Bring all the arrows you can carry. Rat, you bring as many as possible. We shall go right from here, and head for Notre-Dame.'

* * *

They scurried through the streets like rats in a sewer, crouching low, their eyes on the way ahead, all the archers with arrows ready nocked. Dogbreath and Saul kept their eyes fixed on the rooflines and windows overhead. Robin kept his eyes fixed on the roadways ahead. Fulk, with his halberd, glared and stalked like a lion, Rat at his side, scampering to keep up, his arms full of quivers of arrows.

Their path took them into a small square, where a nondescript group of wattle and daub houses surrounded an open space with an elm tree, and the men hurried almost past it before one of the men gasped.

William heard his exclamation and turned, and

only then did he see the tree's decoration. Hanging from the branches were seven English and Navarrese men, all hanged by the neck, faces swollen, eyes staring wildly.

'That's what they wanted to do to us, then,' Sir Reginald said calmly. 'Very well: Master Hawkwood, have your men at the front. Master Robin, your vintaine to bring up the rear. Master Peter, yours in the middle, and prepare to support either. Clear? Then, onward.'

Sir Reginald strode forward, and they passed many more trees, and even one house that had five men dangling, before they came to the bridge to the Île de la Cité. The garrison was at first wary, and a brief stand-off almost led to a sharp altercation, but then a sergeant appeared, and Sir Reginald was known to him. He cleared the bridge and allowed the company in.

Once on the island in the middle of the Seine, the company was confronted by a large number of English and Navarrese men.

'What's happening?' William said. 'There are a lot of men murdered out there.'

'It's a riot,' one man-at-arms told him. 'They suddenly rose up and they've already caught and hanged forty or so. They captured a number of our knights, too, and were going to mete out the same treatment, but Marcel managed to persuade them to let the prisoners into his custody. And us. Over four hundred of us were caught in our berths, and they were going to kill us too,' he added.

'What now?' William said, looking about him.

'We're going to a safer place, so they say. We're going to be housed in the Louvre, the castle to the west of the city. I daresay the walls are thick enough there that this rabble won't break in easily.' He spat at the dust at their feet. 'The bastards!'

38

After some argument, Archibald gained permission to go and liberate his oxen and wagons. The company went with him, but in addition they had ten knights ride with them, trotting loudly down the cobbled streets. Archibald and Ed managed to hitch the oxen to the two wagons, and soon the troop with wagons behind was making its way towards the Louvre, William and Perkin on tenterhooks the whole time, constantly fearing and expecting a fresh attack. William in particular was nervous of the wagons. Every bump and rattle, he now associated with the roar of flame and smoke from those barrels, and he feared constantly that the barrels containing that terrifying powder might detonate for no reason, and all the company would be obliterated.

He had not seen the Louvre before, and now, reaching the great fortress of Paris, he found himself gaping up at the massive walls as he rode in through the gatehouse.

'Aye, it would take more than my own gonne to destroy those walls,' Archibald said.

William looked at him with frustration. 'Do you only ever think of destroying places?'

Archibald shrugged, his eyes twinkling. 'No! Just now, I'm thinking that I'm glad I left my ribauldequins loaded before I took my rest. Without my little toys, we could well have been captured or slaughtered by the mob.'

It was a vast stronghold. William had heard that the grounds of the Tower of London were extensive, but he doubted they could match this. They had marched along the Quai de Bourbon into the grounds beside the river, and then turned right into the main fortress. They passed through a small gatehouse, and from there had to pass over the huge drawbridge under the towers of the second gatehouse, which was a massive defensive barrier, with portcullises, gates and a dedicated killing zone under the guardrooms where missiles and oil could be dropped on the heads of any men foolish enough to try to force their way inside. After that, they were in a huge space with stabling, barracks and kitchens that could cater for several thousand men.

Dwarfing all was the great donjon, which rose before them. It was a circular tower, rising six or seven storeys tall, itself enclosed within its own circular wall and moat, with a second drawbridge.

William stood and gaped. It was so tall, so clearly impenetrable, that he felt as insignificant as a fly on an elephant's arse.

'Now, *that*,' Archibald said, 'that would take more than all the powder I have ever made to make a dent in it.'

For once, William could not make any comment. He was so taken aback by this proof of wealth and power that he was utterly lost for words.

They were given housing in a large chamber to the east of the courtyard, but there was no space for Archibald's wagons. They must remain in the outer court, and he and Ed spent some hours covering his weapons with waxed linen sheets and carefully carrying their barrels of powder indoors, to where they could be stored safe from the rain and the risk of foolish sentries with torches. It was unlikely that anyone would try to steal his wagons, for the gonnes were too heavy, but Archibald would not risk his precious powder.

Sir Reginald appeared as dawn was rising, his face grim. 'Well, we survived the riots,' he said. 'I think the Paris mob is as reliable as that of London. They rise up with any damned grievance and blame others, and then set about trying to cause mayhem wherever they go.'

One of the younger men with Peter's vintaine asked with a slightly querulous voice, 'Are we safe here, Sir Reginald?'

The old knight gave a twisted grin. 'Did you not see the size of the walls? If this place could be taken by the Paris mob, don't you think we English would already hold both it and the kingdom of France in our hands? Nay, boy. This place is impregnable. We are safe here for as long as we choose to stay. For my part, I will choose to stay for quite some time. Now, vinteners, I want to have you assess your stores. How many bows, how many arrows do you still hold? Any weaponry in the company, I need accounted. We have to know we can defend ourselves, and for how long.'

'What is planned?' William said. 'If the mob remains outside these walls, where could we go?'

'Well, remember, we are here in order to protect this city from the dauphin. That is why the King of Navarre called us to support him, so that he can hold it and assist our king in his claim to the throne.'

Dogbreath grimaced and sneered, 'We won't be able to help him much from inside these walls, Sir Reginald. What'll he do to protect us, eh?'

'He will send help,' Sir Reginald said curtly, and then he grinned. 'King Charles has already sent for his brother Philip and his armies. He has sent to Normandy for aid from our king and his representatives, and the Captal de Buch, Sir Robert Knolles, Hugh Calveley and others are already marching to us. There is no need for us to fear.'

But he was wrong.

* * *

The sound chilled Thomas.

The meeting was being held at the town hall, the building surrounded by armed guards, who themselves were anxiously fingering their weapons in the face of the rioters before them. Étienne Marcel and the leaders of Paris were inside, trying to work out the best approach to calm the mob, but the shouting and chanting were rising even as they held their panicked discussions. It was one thing to quell a violent disturbance when it was a matter of a few hundred apprentices or complaining guild workers, but utterly different when the entire populace came out to protest.

Not that these were protesting. As Thomas stood near a window, he could hear the chanting: *Death to the English; Kill all the English at the Louvre; Death to the collaborators* and much more. The slogans were rising in volume and intensity, and even the usually placid Marcel was pale and twitchy. He knew that it would take little for a mob like this to break out into more violence.

'What can we do?' he was demanding of the advisers and business leaders in the hall, while the guards stood flinching as the sound of stones flung at the walls grew louder.

Thomas had no idea, but he prayed that someone would soon think of something. And, as usual, it was his master who showed himself to be the true leader of Paris.

'I will speak to them,' King Charles said. 'This is a foolish crowd, that is all. They are the sheep of the city and this flock fears the wolves under the dauphin.

They think that there must be a simple way to correct matters. They have no idea of the true situation. I will explain things to them. Without the English, the dauphin would already have retaken the city, and where would they all be then? I will tell them.'

And he did. King Charles went to the balcony over the Place de Grève and held up his hands for silence. Gradually, the shouting and sloganising died down, and the king could speak.

'My friends, you know me. You know that I, Charles of Navarre, have been your true and faithful friend for these last months. I am a loyal servant of France! But you must appreciate that without these English...'

The crowd erupted once more. Men had grabbed weapons from butchers' knives to lances, and they waved these in defiance of the king's words. Thomas watched, appalled, as the people overrode King Charles's words with more chanting of *Death to the English* and other, similar mantras. Never had Thomas seen such a response to his king's oratory. Navarre, speaking in gentle, honourable terms, polite, restrained, calm, could always control even the most violent of mobs, but today the people of Paris were defiant and rejected even his entreaties.

He tried again. 'These English you complain about

are our allies! They are our servants! Without them, the dauphin and his army would already have sacked the city! Is that what you want? Do you want to hand the city to the dauphin's noblemen? You know what they did to the Jacquerie! They slaughtered all in their path as retribution for the rebellion! What do you think they would do here? Your houses burned, your women defiled, you all slain! Do you really...'

The shouting was redoubled, deafening, and utterly drowning out his words. He tried three more times, holding his hands high for quiet, but this crowd would not be silenced. It had tasted blood last night when it hanged some English and captured others, and they wanted more. Now the demands changed.

The king glanced round and Thomas saw how his face had changed. It was not fear; rather, it was rage. He was being defied, ignored, and that was one response he would not tolerate. He gritted his teeth, glaring.

'Very well!' he bellowed. 'I will lead you!'

* * *

Thomas caught up with him when he was almost back in the town hall. 'You cannot do this! The English will be slaughtered!'

'They will not,' Navarre said. He threw open the doors to the hall and marched inside.

'Well?' Marcel asked. He was anxious, as were the other city leaders. It was one thing to rebel against a feeble government, which had just lost most of its leaders and guards in a battle against the English, but it was quite a different thing to have the entire population of Paris, as it seemed, laying siege to them inside a small building like this.

'They will not disperse,' King Charles said, walking to a chair and seating himself. He was very upright, his chin held high, the picture of nobility and calm pride as he surveyed the other men in the room. The bodyguards at the doors stood listening, Thomas knew, and their tension was expressed in their hands, white-knuckled as they gripped their weapons, more than one polearm shaking. No one in that room was unaware of the danger they were all in.

'If they won't, what shall we do?' Marcel asked.

Robert le Coq at his side frowned. 'Do they make demands?'

'They do. They wish you, Étienne, and me, to lead them to Saint-Cloud and Saint-Denis to find the English and kill them all.'

'You said no, of course?' Marcel said.

'Can you hear that mob?' Navarre shouted, half-rising from his chair. 'Do you think they sound like they'll listen to reason? Do you think they'll care what you or I think? There are three thousand out there, three thousand people of *your* city, who are prepared to defy us to get what they think they want! They blame the English for everything, and they do not care that without the English, the dauphin would be here already!'

'But we cannot lead them against the English,' Marcel said, aghast. 'We need them to protect us now.'

'You go and tell them! You think they will listen to you, go and tell them that! But I warn you, there are crossbows in that crowd.'

'What can we do?' le Coq demanded. 'You must have a plan, I think.'

'I do. We shall allow the crowd to consider all this day, and if they are still determined, we shall lead them from the city and head towards Saint-Cloud.'

'My God,' Marcel breathed.

39

It was as the sun was sinking past the walls that Thomas joined the mob at the gate leading north. The mob had not dispersed. If anything, it had grown, and now it surged about him, the men pushing and shoving angrily, all hot from their long protests, their ire fuelled by wine, until now they were ready to slaughter every Englishman in France without compunction.

Thomas was on his palfrey, the message he must bear carefully memorised, and he rode along with Marcel and the king in the circle of their bodyguards, although the mood had changed subtly. Since King Charles had acceded to their demand that he should lead them with Marcel, the crowd was more conciliatory. They applauded the king's appearance, and cheered to see Marcel. Soon they were on the move, a mass of two or three thousand, marching forward into the evening to destroy the garrisons at the two forts.

It was not long before the king called a halt and began to command the mob to form into three battles. Each to be of some hundreds of men. And as he did so, he loudly ordered Thomas to go and scout the land ahead.

Thomas trotted off towards Saint-Cloud with his heart pounding. As soon as he was out of sight of the Parisians, he clapped spurs to his mount and crouched low, galloping at full speed through the woods that led to the bridge at Saint-Cloud until he came across a vintaine of English archers.

'I must speak to your commander,' he gasped.

* * *

Thomas was already at Saint-Denis when King Charles arrived with his bodyguard.

'You did well,' he commented as Thomas passed him a goblet of wine. 'It was entirely successful.'

'What happened?' Thomas asked.

Navarre took a long pull at his wine and sat back, sighing with contentment, but it did not entirely erase his anger. That was still bubbling underneath his calm exterior. It showed in his eyes, unblinking, determined. 'What happened? All occurred as I had planned. The garrison at Pont Saint-Cloud marched straight to the woods after you took my message. I rode with the Parisians, but at the back, so I could see it all. The ambush was most effective. English archers blocked the road with wagons, and as we approached, they started to assail the Parisians with their bows. I do not know how many fell, but it was many hundreds, perhaps a quarter of all the men in the mob. And then they came on, shrieking, with swords and axes, and the Parisians fled the field. Me, I came here straightway with my bodyguard. Marcel, I think, returned to the city.'

'What will happen now?' Thomas asked. He felt as though the floor was tottering underneath him. It was tempting to reach for a chair, but he knew that the king would deprecate such disrespectful behaviour.

'Now? Now, my friend, we wait. My brother Philip should soon be here, as will the English and Normans whom I have called upon to support us against the dauphin. With them, we shall soon retake the city and punish those who seek to evict us!'

* * *

The shouting could be heard from all over the Louvre, and William felt the anxiety of the men. He felt it himself. Archibald and Ed spent their time testing their powders, cleaning and oiling their gonnes, and keeping busy, but for the rest of Sir Reginald's company, there was little to do. Wine was rationed, which was a good thing with so many men in the fortress. With their pent-up frustration and fear, minor disputes could soon lead to bloodshed.

Outside the walls, there were constant bitter protests against the English, and William began to hear slanders against King Charles and Marcel. It seemed that more and more people were coming to the same conclusion: that King Charles had deliberately led the men of Paris into an ambush, and that Marcel himself was responsible for the dire straits in which the city now found itself. With the dauphin to the south and east, and King Charles of Navarre to the north, the city was besieged, with little hope of food or drinks able to be brought in. The people must sit and wait to see which army attacked first, and since the ambush and the failed attempt on the dauphin's bridge of boats, more and more men inside the city were realising that they were incapable of military action against trained warriors. They had armour, weaponry, trained cavalry, and the resources to fight a lengthy battle. What did the people of Paris have? Enthusiasm.

William was himself fearful of what might happen. He felt safe enough here inside the Louvre, but they could not remain there forever, and while the mob remained outside, he and the other English were captives, and subject to siege, if the Parisians decided to stop food being brought. And that was likely to be soon, since the whole city was now suffering food shortages. Why would the Parisians allow food to support the hated English in the Louvre, while their own families were starving?

Although the grounds of the Louvre were extensive, after four days, William was already beginning to feel trapped. He walked about the inner court, his mind a jumble of different wishes and regrets, chief of which was ever thinking it was a good idea to leave quiet, peaceful Furnshill for this land of blood and terror.

'Are you well?'

William was walking along the upper battlements, gazing over the city, but his mind was far away in Devon. 'Perkin, you surprised me. I was thinking of home.'

'Yes, I have been, too,' Perkin said. He looked over the city towards the forests outside. 'I miss home and the moors. I could happily return today and forgo all the treasures others win here.'

'I am sorry I ever thought to come here,' William said, and he had to blink away unexpected moisture in his eyes. 'I am sorry I brought you here.'

'I came of my own volition. It was my choice. Besides, we're still alive,' Perkin said. 'Sir Reginald is confident enough that we will leave here secure.'

'I don't know what he bases that hope on.'

'No, but I will not give up hope while he remains optimistic. And Dogbreath, and Fulk, and even Hawkwood. They have all endured more fighting than us, and they know better what may be in store for us.'

'Perhaps,' William said.

* * *

It was another two days – then the miracle happened.

William was walking about the inner court when there were horns blown, and then the sound of marching boots. He glanced up at the walls and saw a number of guards running to the battlement nearest the city, men pointing, and then calling down to other members of the garrison, and then he himself ran to the steps up to the walkway on the wall.

Outside there was a large force of men, all in the

blue and crimson of the city, many with crossbows, some with polearms, and they were engaged in a lengthy conversation with the Louvre's porter.

It was enough for William; he ran down the stairs as quickly as was safe, and at the bottom, ran to the company.

'There are men from the city at the gates,' he shouted quickly. 'String your bows, grab some arrows, and prepare to defend the gates!'

The men moved with urgency on hearing his words, and in a short time the full company was standing behind Archibald's wagons. He and Ed were assiduously working at the ribauldequins, charging the barrels and carefully priming them with stone balls. When done, Ed lit two string matches and blew on them to keep them glowing before passing one to Archibald. The rest of the men stood, some nervously, some careless, but all of them thinking more of the gonnes and that evil powder than they did about the mob at the gates.

The porter and castellan were at the gatehouse, shouting down at the men outside, and William watched as they conferred, before one of them shouted down at the men holding the bars to the gate.

'Sir Reginald! They're going to let them in!' he called.

The knight looked over at him and nodded, calling out to the vinteners. Peter, Hawkwood and Robin commanded their men to nock arrows in preparation, but not to draw yet, and the whole company watched as the gates were unbarred and opened outwards.

Dogbreath muttered, 'God's cods, there's a lot of them.'

Sir Reginald strode forwards and stood before the archers, his sword in his hand, glaring at the force entering.

Seeing him, the man who appeared to be the commander of the Parisians marched to meet with him. William approached near enough to hear their discussion.

'What do you want with us?' Sir Reginald was demanding.

'We are here to protect you, sir,' the Frenchman said. He cast an eye over the archers standing ready. 'The provost of the city has decreed that you should be given safe passage to the north gate so you can rejoin the King of Navarre at Saint-Denis and his garrison. You are not secure here, and the provost feels you would be well advised to leave.'

'What if we do not?'

'There will be bloodshed. Not from us, I assure you. We are the bodyguard of the provost, and it is our wish to protect you. But the mob is revolting against the provost, and your presence makes the whole city endangered. I beg that you consider our offer and come with us.'

Sir Reginald saw William standing close by and jerked his head to beckon him. 'What do you say, esquire?'

William looked at the guards. 'Do we have his word on his honour that this is no trick to have us open to attack?'

'Well?' Sir Reginald asked.

The captain gave a humourless grin. 'It is something when allies can no longer trust each other. Yes, I offer my word of honour, and I swear by the Gospels and by my faith that this is no trick. I only wish to escort you safely.'

Sir Reginald snorted, looked up at the blue sky overhead, and then back at the company. 'Very well, I accept your offer of safe passage, and I will ask the rest of the men to join us.'

40

It took half the morning to collect their weapons and return the barrels of powder onto the wagons. The oxen took more effort than almost anything else, being recalcitrant by nature, but by noon, the English in the Louvre had gathered together and joined the company, ready to depart. With the French guards fanning out in the street ahead, their crossbows ready armed with quarrels, the English moved out.

Their journey was not long, but as they made their way, the horses' hooves clattering on the cobbles, the wagons and carts rattling and thundering, William was struck by the appearance of the people of Paris.

'They truly hate us,' he said to Sir Reginald.

'What would you expect? As far as these folks are

concerned we are a symbol of their desperation,' the knight said. 'They rose up against the royal family and nobility, supported the Jacquerie, and looked to Charles of Navarre and us to defend them, but then discover that the Jacquerie has failed, and now the dauphin and nobles will come and exact punishment. It will be a harsh retribution, I doubt not.' He shrugged. 'That is the cost of rebellion, of course. It is deserved when the folk rise against their lords.'

There were several men who stood at the side of the road without weapons, but one had a stone, which he flung at the party, shouting abuse. Two of the escort went to him and one struck him down. Other men moved forward, but so did the escorts, and the crowd backed down, pulling the groggy stone thrower from the road and away to safety.

He was not the only one. Others shouted insults, calling the English *butchers* or *murderers*, while others resorted to making the sign of the evil one, thumbing their nose or spitting at the street as the men passed.

One man in particular caught William's eye – a younger man, thin, with the deep chasms of fear and misery cutting into his cheeks and forehead. He stared at the archers, William thought, and then he realised that the man was staring most of all at Dog-breath or Fulk, who were riding together. William was tempted to point the man out to both of them, but then another stone was flung at them, and he had other matters to concern him of a more pressing nature.

For all that, the English and Navarrese managed to make their way along the streets and up into the northern reaches of the city, all the way to the gate, and soon they were outside the city and passing through the suburbs up to Saint-Denis. It was with great relief that William and Perkin rode under the gatehouse and into the monastery proper.

But this was no longer merely a convent for the religious monks of the order. It was a fortified camp for thousands of men. Here the King of Navarre had his headquarters, and the Captal de Buch, Sir James Pipe and others had congregated, and it was clear that they were preparing for another fight. As the company dismounted and began looking about for food and drink, the first elements of Philip of Navarre's army began dribbling in. This was to be a sizeable force to contest the dauphin's.

'We are to be ready to move into Paris,' Sir Reginald told them that evening as the company sat about their fires. 'The gate is to be held by guards of Marcel, and they'll open them for us. They're going to remove all the chains from the roads after curfew so we can pass straight through to the town hall and take the city.'

'The people did not look as if they would welcome our return,' William said. He recalled the stone thrower, the insults, the mood of grim resentfulness, the atmosphere of tension that could snap at any moment and lead to open combat.

'They're just citizens. Merchants and tradesmen, nothing to concern us,' Sir Reginald said dismissively. 'They cannot compare with trained Englishmen, can they?'

'When will this be?' Hawkwood asked.

'Four days from now. We shall enter the city, take it over, and then King Charles will declare himself King of France. The people will acclaim him, as any sensible citizenry must, and we can sit back and enjoy ourselves with wine and women while the dauphin chews his knuckles in frustration,' Sir Reginald said. 'It'll be easy. You'll see.'

* * *

He had heard the noise when he was out and enjoying a little rest in the priest's churchyard. There was a rippling of voices, then shouts and abuse, and Auffroy went to the gate, peering out. As he watched, men came from the houses in the street and stood, milling, watching as the cavalcade appeared.

There were the men of the city guard, their blue and crimson uniforms and hoods bright in the sunshine, all armed with polearms and cudgels, pushing the crowds from the roadway, guarding the murderers. A man hurled a rock and was immediately knocked down and dragged away, but even as he was pulled back, Auffroy saw him – the man. The foul, wizened little fellow was riding alongside a huge, blond man with a boy on the horse before him, a tiny figure next to the giant, and Auffroy saw the boy's eyes flit to him and stay on him, fixed with horror.

He should pull his dagger and launch at the man; he should run to that fellow on the horse and stab him repeatedly; he should not hesitate...

But he did hesitate. What good would it do to attack the man here? If he breached the wall of the escorting guards, could he possibly get past the giant? It was impossible. Even if he succeeded, and killed the man, how could he escape? He needed that item of Juliot's. Without it, he could not rest, but even with it, if he was cut down before he could take it to her, what was the point? Was there any merit in getting it and failing to deliver it?

The men rode on past, one man-at-arms staring at

him as his horse pranced, and then there were more men, and wagons, and the last guards protecting these English murderers. It was enough to make a man weep, but Auffroy did not break down. He stood watching the men disappear up through the streets on their way to the north gates and escape.

Only when they were out of sight did he return to the church, but now, when he knelt to pray, he begged God to allow him his revenge on the man who had robbed his Juliot of her cross.

Thomas was reluctant, but he was loyal to his master, and when King Charles said he must take a message to Étienne Marcel, he swallowed his unease and accepted the mission. It was his duty as a servant, and he was a man of honour.

The way to the city was empty. Even the suburbs had been deserted in recent days as people grew more afraid of the likelihood of more violence and fled to the countryside or took shelter inside Paris's walls. But all too few were going to be allowed inside. Food stocks were growing scarce, and with the near-complete blockade, the Parisians wanted no more useless mouths. It took some effort for Thomas to persuade the guards at the gate to allow him in, and then it was only after payment of a large bribe to their captain.

'Shouldn't let you pass,' he said gruffly as he took the coin. 'Now, fuck off before someone sees you and I get the blame.'

Thomas made his way along the Rue St Martin to the town hall, and was perturbed to see that the men at the doors were fretful. It took some arguing to be able to gain access, and when he had, there were more guards inside, and all were plainly nervous.

Marcel was in the hall itself eating a sparse breakfast. 'Ah, Thomas! You have news?'

'The king has asked me to tell you that his men will be ready to come and enter the city this evening. He requests that you be certain that the gates will be opened to his men.'

'We have it all prepared,' Marcel said. He affected confidence, but Thomas was convinced that he was as fearful as the guards. His eyes moved to the door with every sudden noise, and although he had barely eaten his breakfast, he pushed the plate away and threw his napkin onto the table, standing and walking about the room. The guards at the doors watched him, Thomas noticed. It was rather as if they were hoping to be told that they might soon be permitted to flee.

'We have painted the houses of all those who are

supporters of the dauphin, or known to be enemies of Navarre,' Marcel muttered. 'They will be taken and held or executed. The men at the gates will be mine this evening, and they will allow the king to enter without trouble. All the chains in the streets will have been taken down, so there will be no impediment to the king's passage, and I will have men to meet him here when he arrives, so that we can hold the city and declare his occupation of the throne. The city will obviously come to his support immediately. No one will stand against him. Against us, I mean. And then we can begin to bring food in from the north, which will soothe those who might otherwise baulk at the idea of changing allegiance. So, yes, all is well. All is in train. The plans are set.'

'You see no difficulty?' Thomas said.

'No. No, all will be well.'

He was trying to convince himself, Thomas felt, but it was natural enough. Attempting to depose a king was a hazardous course. King John, the dauphin's father, was the man anointed by God to the throne. If God Himself had allowed the royal family to ascend to the throne, which man could gainsay Him?

But the crown had been taken from Navarre unfairly. King Charles's mother had a full right to the crown, and had been forced to give it up. That was why

King Charles felt the right to claim it, and Thomas was
convinced in his own heart that the king was right.

There was shouting from the chamber outside,
and Marcel almost stumbled in alarm. He stood firmly
as the door opened, steadying himself on the table,
and staring with a wide-eyed gaze at the door as it was
thrust open. A man burst in, gasping, 'The city mob
has risen! It is attacking anyone to do with Navarre or
you, Provost! May God save us!'

41

It was Josseran de Maçon, the treasurer of King Charles, and while Marcel took a seat like a man suddenly drained of all his blood, and Thomas listened, appalled, Josseran told of the angry mob that had gathered outside his house how they were hunting down all those who supported Marcel's party or the Navarrese. 'They congregated at Les Halles, and were shouting their rejection of those ruling the city, demanding that the dauphin be allowed to enter. They have heard that there is a plot to allow the King of Navarre into the city,' he said.

'We must act!' Marcel said, but he remained in his chair.

'They are determined, Provost. My house has already been broken into, and I think they'll burn it to the ground. They want blood. Maillard and his men are leading them with ropes to hang any of your supporters or those of Navarre,' he added, glancing at Thomas. 'They missed me, but the mob is not to be satisfied with just taking and destroying my house.'

Thomas turned to Marcel. 'You must get to the gate and make sure that it is held by your men. This needs swift action, sir. The king is to come by the Porte Saint-Denis – is that held by your men?'

'No, not yet.'

'Then we must go. We can demand that they give up the keys and pass over responsibility to you and your men. Come! There is no time to lose!'

'I don't know,' Marcel said. 'Shouldn't I talk to the ringleaders first? Maillard was always a reasonable man, and I am sure he would listen to reason and—'

'Are you prepared to wager your life on that?' Thomas snapped. 'No? Then come!'

With Josseran's support, Thomas managed to bring Marcel to his senses, and soon they had an escort about them and were mounted, trotting briskly towards the Porte Saint-Denis. As they went, they could hear the rising clamour from the west as the mob moved about the city. The shouting and screams chilled Thomas, but the effect on Josseran and Marcel was even more pronounced. Marcel gazed about him with the terrified eyes of a hart hearing the hounds.

They hurried along to the main gates, and here Marcel summoned up his courage. Demanding to see the captain of the guard, he stood imperiously and demanded that the keys to the gate be given to Josseran.

'Why?' the captain asked.

He was a thickset man who looked more than capable of fighting off a bear, and he called his guards to his support as Marcel's men began to spread out, ready to attack.

'The garrison here is too large. I need you to take some of your men to Les Halles to quell the disturbance there. Listen! Can't you hear it? The whole district is in uproar, and you remain here, cosseted in your gatehouse! You have a duty to the city, and as Provost of the Merchants, I order you. Give up the keys, and take half your men to see to that riot.'

'I will not. I have my orders, and they are to remain here.'

'I am *provost!*'

'My orders came from Jean Maillard. I will wait to hear from him.'

'I *order* you!'

'What is the urgency?' the captain said, and now his expression was less bemused and more determined. 'There are rumours about plots to give the city to others. I won't allow my gate to fall to traitors.'

'You dare to call me a traitor?'

'If he won't, I will,' a man shouted, and when Thomas turned, he saw that Jean Maillard had appeared behind them with a force of men. 'What are you trying to do here, Provost? You want to take the gate? Why?'

'I just want the riots to be stopped before the city is destroyed, Maillard. Are they all your men? It is outrageous that the city should live in terror of your mob! You should be there, to calm them all and stop all this mayhem!'

'While leaving you in charge of the gate, I suppose?' Maillard said, and signalled to his men to move around Marcel and the others to join the captain and his men before the gate.

'If you will not do your duty by the city, I shall go and find someone who will act responsibly,' Marcel snapped.

'I wish you godspeed with that, Provost,' Maillard said. 'I doubt you'll find more than one or two people prepared to support you today. Your time is past. Your plots to supplant the dauphin and give the city to the English and the Navarrese have been discovered, and your end will be swift!'

Marcel was fit to burst, he was so angry, but even as he drew breath to damn the man and his guards, the noise of the mob grew louder, and he and the others quickly remounted.

'Where now?' Josseran demanded.

'I think the Porte Saint-Antoine has Navarrese guards at the gatehouse,' Marcel said distractedly. He spurred his horse, the others following suit. 'They will be more helpful.'

Thomas rode a short distance behind them. When he glanced back behind him, he saw Maillard running after them, and he could hear the man bellowing the war cry of the French kings: '*Montjoie, Saint Denis!*'

It was enough to make him urge his beast to greater efforts.

* * *

The gatehouse was a massive structure, but the guards were Navarrese, and Thomas was reassured by the sight of them.

'Here is a new guard for the gate,' Marcel said. 'The mob has risen and is doing untold damage. You must send half your men to go and put down this uprising! Give us the keys to the gate and go!'

The captain of the men at the gate peered at him. 'Who are you?'

'I am Étienne Marcel, the Provost of Merchants, in God's name! Give me the keys!'

'There are rumours of plots and counter plots. How do I know you aren't a traitor?'

Marcel flung out an arm. 'Look! This is Josseran de Maçon, your king's treasurer! You know you can trust him.'

'I don't understand why the guard should be changed. If there's a riot, use these men about you. I've been ordered to protect this gate with my men, and that's what we'll do.' The captain set his feet firmly apart and drew his sword.

'You fool! You stupid, dogshit-for-brains lunatic! You've given the city to the dauphin!' Marcel shouted, and would have ridden the man down, but just then there were a series of cries behind them, and suddenly a crowd appeared. Seeing Marcel and the guards, they set off after them.

Thomas dismounted. There was nowhere to ride to. All the approaches were full of rioters now, and he would never ride through them. Right at the front of them there was a man carrying a huge banner – it was the coat of arms of the dauphin.

The escort did what they could, but they were

hopelessly outnumbered. Most stood their ground, trying to hold the crowds back, but what could they do against the entire city? And that was what Thomas thought it looked like. The whole of Paris had come to slaughter anyone who was for Marcel or Navarre, or anyone who supported the English.

Men who had been fervent rebels, who had thought Marcel offered a route of safety, who believed him when he promised better times ahead, when he spoke of his vision of a new Paris, a Paris free from the depredations of the English, a Paris free from the whims and demands of an ever more acquisitive nobility who behaved much as the English mercenaries, riding out to steal and kill for their own benefit – these men felt betrayed. They had believed Marcel – but now they thought he had lied to them, and had brought them to this low pass where the citizens must pay for their own rebellion. The dauphin would exact a huge cost for the city's mutiny and support of the Jacquerie. They were distraught, furious, and they would take revenge on the man who had been the architect of their disaster.

The guards were swamped, slaughtered like pigs at the butchers, with knives and daggers and rocks, and three tried to escape, barging past the gatekeepers and Thomas, who had moved to the side of the captain of the guards. Now, as the last of the bodyguards passed him, Thomas cried out, '*Saint Denis! Montjoie!*' and took the last man by the arm. He spun the man around to face the rebels, whipped out his own dagger and stabbed the man quickly in the neck. Blood spurted over his hand, his arm, his face, and the man gave a bleating gurgle as he fell to his knees. As he did so, the first of the rioters reached him. The man held a large cleaver, and plainly considered Thomas a confederate, for he set about Thomas's victim with gusto, until only a foul, bloody mess lay on the ground before him.

That was when Thomas turned to Marcel and Josseran. Josseran had disappeared under the milling crowd, but he saw Marcel. He was already dead – a huge cut in his skull had almost broken his head in two – and now he was being held up, eyes staring into the distance, while the crowd cheered and bellowed their defiance of the city and of Marcel's government. Men stripped Marcel's body of all his rich clothing and jewellery and they forced the gatekeepers to open the gate, and took the naked body to the steps of the little church outside the city and dropped him there. Another naked body was set beside him, but Thomas could not see whether it was Josseran or one of the escort. Thomas was slowly and carefully slipping between the rioters, away from the gate as they pressed past him, until he was at the very back of them and could turn and walk slowly away, so as not to cause anyone to notice him.

He was just one more man who had been involved in the slaughter of the old regime, his arm and face clotted with blood. For now, he was safe.

* * *

William heard about the reign of terror in the city when Sir Reginald and he were called to a discussion with the leaders of the army at Saint-Denis.

All around, William saw the leaders of the English. Sir James Pipe was there, as were Sir Gilbert Chastelleyn and Sir Stephen Cusington, two of King Edward's advisers.

'What are they talking about?' William asked.

'How to split France,' Sir Reginald said. He was disapproving. 'I had expected that the wars would go on a little longer, but if these damn fools choose, we will have no more profit from France. Navarre wants Champagne and Brie, maybe Picardy too. King Edward will take the rest of the kingdom along with his existing French assets. Where can we go to charge our *pâtis* if this all comes to pass?'

'Perhaps it will fail at the last.'

'That is possible,' Sir Reginald said, brightening slightly. 'Who can tell what the dauphin will do, after all?'

Then King Charles of Navarre stood and addressed the gathered commanders.

'My friends, we have come to an arrangement. These envoys of King Edward of England have agreed that the lands of France will be separated. But in order to ensure this contract, we shall have to enforce it. That means we shall ally ourselves against King John and his son the dauphin. Yesterday, we hear, the leaders of Paris were set upon by the mob and murdered. It continues today. It is hard to believe that this city, the jewel of the kingdom, could be so devastated by violence, but I swear, I shall bring order and justice out of this chaos! I shall not rest until the city is subjugated. To this end, I shall lead the army tomorrow to the city, and we shall take it in the name of Edward, King of England and France. My friends, we are to raise our standards against the dauphin and his father. I shall reward richly all those who join us! So go now and prepare for battle on the morrow!'

William went to rejoin Perkin and the others of the company, his mind whirling with the thought of the day to come.

'Well?' Perkin asked. 'What was said at the meeting?'

'I think that tomorrow we attack Paris,' William said, and as he spoke, his eyes went to the south, as though he could see through the buildings and trees straight over to the city itself. In his mind's eye he was seeing again the small villages and towns he had seen on the journeys about France, the men and women slain and left in the streets, the burning houses, the poor wretch in her own house, who had leaped to her death rather than submit to a man she thought would rape her.

'God forgive us,' he said.

42

Thomas had found a cellar and remained in there while the murders went on up in the streets. Men who had been involved in the government of the city, men who had been loyal to Marcel, members of his family, the businessmen who had supported him, all were captured and executed or held for later punishment. Men whose guilt was that they had annoyed a neighbour, men who had nothing to do with the rebellion, but who possessed lands coveted by another, men who tried to stop the worst injustices, all were put to the sword or taken to Les Halles and beheaded in front of approving crowds.

All those who had proudly worn the particoloured crimson and blue hoods now bundled them up and hid them, or burned them, so that they would not be discovered in possession of such dangerous items.

The whole time, while he cowered in the cellar, he could hear the screams of the victims of this counter-revolution. And all the while, he knew that his own life was in danger. He dare not show his face. He had not been recognised at the gate, but that was because the mob knew Marcel far better than him. They had their target clearly in their minds, and once Marcel was spotted, the mob knew what it wanted to do. The fact that Thomas was seen cutting the throat of the guard had shown him to be on their side and had saved his life.

But he could not remain down here in the cellar for long. Already he could hear the sound of doors being broken open, shrieks as men were torn from their wives to be taken away, and Thomas knew it was only a matter of time before he was also taken, and then he would have no protection against the rabid fury of the mob. They would tear him apart if they learned that he was the man upon whom Navarre had depended for so long.

He must remain here for now, but when it was dark, perhaps, he could try to escape.

Thomas dozed off. He was exhausted after the last days, the panic, the terror, and now the failure of all his king's plans. It was impossible to keep his eyes open.

He woke to the feel of steel against his throat.

* * *

The priest knew the violence was coming. He had heard the rumours of the revenge that all the men planned to take on Marcel's supporters and the others who were keen to promote Navarre in the city, those who had paid for the English to come to Paris and prevent the dauphin from entering. Yes, the mob was enraged. Those who had believed Marcel's promises, those who had wholeheartedly cheered Navarre; now that the dauphin was in the city, all these men were keen to demonstrate their support of the old regime. Many were the counter-rebellion groups sent about the city hunting for those who were now on the wrong side of the law. Men who only days before had enthusiastically declared themselves for Marcel's new government, who had supported the Jacquerie, who had participated in the destruction of houses owned by the dauphin's advisers, now these same men sought to prove their loyalty to the crown by persecuting those whom they had sustained.

Father Marc found Auffroy in the church's nave, praying with his head bent.

'My son, you must leave the city.'

'Father?'

'You will not be safe here. The mob is seeking any man who could be accused of being a member of Navarre's party. You are a foreigner here, a stranger. It is easy to accuse a man such as you of being an enemy to the dauphin, and people will kill you if you remain. You must escape before you can be attacked.'

'Where can I go?'

'Go home, Auffroy. There is nothing for you here. Go home and find peace. Seek another woman, marry, raise children, and avoid the English demons. You can achieve nothing against them. Make your peace with God, and leave violence to those who seek it. Pray for your Juliot and your friends, and try to sincerely beg for their souls, and plead for yourself and your sins.'

'What of my duty to Juliot? The men who did that to her?'

'You must forgive them, my son. God will bring them justice as He sees fit. Speak the truth and leave it to God.'

It was not yet noon when the priest took Auffroy to the Saint-Denis gate and gave some coins to the porter.

He reluctantly opened the wicket gate to allow Auffroy to slip out.

'Father, I thank you for your kindness,' Auffroy said.

'Thank God, my son. And godspeed. Farewell.'

* * *

The army was moving.

William rode along slouched, not looking forward to the day to come. Perkin sat more upright in his saddle, peering ahead constantly, searching for any threats of ambush or assault, but all the way to the city appeared open and there were no men in the fields or the roads who posed any threat.

'What will we do, do you think?' he asked.

'I hope we aren't to assault the walls,' William said quietly. 'It is one thing to attack a town or a village, and another completely to try to climb the walls of a city like that.'

As he spoke, they rounded a corner in the road and the whole of Paris was laid before them, the city lying under a blanket of smoke from the cookfires. The walls showed clearly, their great turrets formidable, towering over the immense walls.

'Yes, it doesn't look like a couple of scaling ladders will do the job for us,' Perkin agreed.

'Even if we had enough ladders to climb those walls, the city doesn't need experienced soldiers to keep us at bay,' William mused. 'They only need numbers to push the ladders away, bowmen to hit the topmost men, and men with lances to attack those who reach the walls. It would be a fool's errand to try to take the city by storm.'

It was clear that the King of Navarre and his advisers were of much the same mind. The army rode slowly down the road to the Saint-Denis gate, but seeing the numbers of men holding the gatehouse, the army turned to the east, and assessed the defences at other gates, eyeing the men standing opposing them high overhead.

'What now?' Perkin muttered.

'A gentle amble all around the city, perhaps.' William grinned, but they were not going much further. The army moved east to the Senlis Road, and occupied the abbey of Saint-Laurent, where they heard that they would attempt to break into the city in the morning.

It was not to be.

It was early in the evening that scouts rode to the

abbey and shouted excitedly that there was a large force riding for the city. William and the company were called to arms by Sir Reginald, and they all prepared for an engagement, tense but confident enough of their numbers and strength to oppose even a strong host. However, soon the army learned the truth. The dauphin had arrived with a fresh army, and had been invited into the city. Paris had returned to the king and the dauphin.

King Charles was incandescent with rage, and gave the order to retreat. He led his army all the way back to Saint-Denis, and from there he decided to ride to Mantes, where he would nurse his frustration and anger and concoct fresh schemes.

Sir Reginald called the company together and spoke to the men. 'The good king has chosen to leave this field,' he said. 'And I am glad to say that we can continue our efforts here in France. The risk of peace has been averted, fortunately, which means that we can go wherever we wish. Does any man here have a comment about the best route to take?'

'I would return the way we came,' Hawkwood said. He had memories of the woods where Rat had seen Arn murdered, and he was still convinced that there must be a great treasure concealed in among those trees.

'I would be keen to avoid these parts,' Saul said.

'There must be richer pickings south and east. Our armies have been through Normandy and Guyenne so often, I doubt there is much to be won. But further south, I think there might be some towns and cities that haven't been assaulted yet.'

'That could be a good idea,' Sir Reginald said. 'If a man wishes to make a little money from this country, it would be best to do it swiftly, before any treaty is agreed between our king and Navarre – or King John of France. Either way, a peace treaty must demand that all we routiers must leave the country. No king will want us to remain,' he added sadly.

'Will Navarre want our support, then?' William asked.

Sir Reginald pulled a face. 'He may, but look at the way things are now. If there is plunder, he tried to take it all. If we stay in his army, what is the likelihood of our earning enough to feed ourselves? It is more likely that we will be forced to accept a mere wage for our efforts. But if we take Saul's advice, perhaps we can take a small town and charge our *pâtis*, or perhaps catch a rich abbey and make merry with the gold and silver we find? There are many ways of earning a good living here in France, but few involve working under a man like Navarre.'

* * *

It was on the second night that he found them.

Auffroy had no idea that the company was before him, but as he walked, and as the shadows grew, he saw a flickering ahead behind a small copse. It was natural that he should decide to avoid risking danger, and he had an inclination to bypass the fire and the potential of danger, so he moved around the copse with great care to make no noise, keeping to the shadows of the trees, but even as he tried to escape, there was a sudden blur, and then an immense blade was at his throat.

'Stand still,' Fulk said.

43

William found the sight of the man unimpressive. He stood before them in the firelight, his face pale, his figure slim, but his features familiar.

Of course no man would have more than the one suit of clothing, and this man's old, dark grey robe and russet hood and cloak immediately struck a chord. This was the man he had seen in the crowd at the side of the road when the company left Paris.

'I know his face,' William said, and explained when he had seen the man.

Fulk nodded, but he was surprised by the Rat's reaction. The boy was plainly terrified, and tried to keep away from the man's sight, shrinking back behind Fulk. The Swiss looked down at the boy, and then across at the man, and suddenly he recalled that day when Arn had died. The 'Devil' Rat had said had appeared, the colour of his hood and cloak, his dark tunic, and he realised that this must remind Rat of the man he had seen that day.

'He is not from here,' Fulk said.

Sir Reginald had been speaking, but now he glanced over at Fulk with surprise. 'What do you mean?'

'Robin, Peter, do you remember that day when Arn was killed? Rat described the man he saw in the woods, and Crespin too. A man with a dark tunic, with russet cloak and hood, just like this fellow's.'

Sir Reginald looked from Fulk to the vinteners. 'What does he mean?'

'There was a man who murdered one of our boys in the woods,' Fulk said. 'Rat saw it, and said it was this man.'

'I did nothing! I found a boy in the woods, but I didn't kill him. Why would I?'

'Then who killed him?' Sir Reginald rasped.

And that was when Fulk caught sight of Rat's face. The boy was glowering, but more, he was obviously terrified, not of a devil, but of something else. Fulk knew that the boy had been with Arn when Arn was killed, and it seemed natural to think it was the man who had found the boys in the woods – but this man did not seem to be lying.

'What did you do there? Why have you followed us?' Fulk demanded.

Auffroy wilted. His mission was over. These men would kill him, he knew, just as they had murdered so many others. They had no sympathy for men such as him. Yet the words of the priest came back to him: *'You must forgive them, my son. God will bring them justice as He sees fit. Speak the truth and leave it to God.'*

'I have been following you. In my village you found my woman and child dead, and you took them to a crossroads to bury them.'

'Yes?' Fulk said. 'What of it?'

'She wore a silver cross. I had given it to her, and when she died I hoped it would help her plead forgiveness from God for her self-murder. But that man,' he rasped, pointing, 'that man stole it from her. He wears it yet.'

All the men turned to look at Dogbreath, who looked from one to another. 'What? She didn't need it, did she? I just thought, well, it was pretty.'

'Show me,' Sir Reginald said.

Dogbreath glared at Auffroy, but pulled the little cross from beneath his shirt and looked at it, then passed it to the knight.

Sir Reginald studied it. It was a plain, simple cross, with the hammer marks denting the surface, hanging from a fine silver chain. 'This is far too elegant for you, Dogbreath,' he said. 'But you did not rob a living woman, did you?'

'She was already dead when we reached the village. And it was pretty. I thought taking it was better than leaving it under the soil,' Dogbreath said defensively.

'What of the boy?' Fulk said.

'I found a little boy's body, but he was dead when I got to him,' Auffroy said. He looked over at Rat. 'He was there, I think.'

Rat shook his head wildly. 'He did it! I thought it was the Devil, but it was him! He stabbed Arn in the back – I saw him!'

'I didn't see the boy until I got to him. He was already dead.'

Rat's eyes filled. Crespin was frowning. 'I saw you – you had a dagger in your hand.'

'I had heard voices. You English are everywhere. Of course I had a dagger,' Auffroy said to Sir Reginald. 'But why should I kill a boy? Besides, if I was to kill him, how could I? He would have seen me from a long distance away and run.'

Fulk nodded slowly. 'Just as Rat did.'

'He crept up on us, though, like a cat!' Rat said. 'He grabbed Arn before he could make a sound and killed him. He shouted. He said, "I'll kill you all!" before he stabbed, and that was why I ran!'

Fulk looked down at Crespin. 'Did you hear that, or anything like it? A man shouting?'

'No, only Rat. There was nothing else I heard. I just saw this man, and when Rat shouted, I ran back to the camp,' Crespin said.

'Why, Rat? Why did you kill him?'

Rat's eyes were full of tears now, and he dashed them away with an angry bitterness. 'He had stolen my spoon. I saw it on him. I thought I'd lost it in the straw, but then, that day, I saw it on him, hanging round his neck, and I realised he'd stolen it from me! I hated him; I still hate him! He took my only thing. I don't have anything else, and he took it!' He looked about him at the others, the men studying him with frank disapproval, Crespin and Henri looking scared as they heard his confession. The only man who seemed unaffected was Auffroy. He was gazing down at his feet.

Fulk went to Rat and put his hand on the boy's shoulder. 'Where is this spoon?'

Rat pulled it from his shirt where it hung about his neck.

Fulk took it and looked at it. Then he drew his

hand back and hurled it into the middle of the woods. Rat gaped, and then tried to scamper after it, but Fulk held him back. 'That spoon was not worth the life of the boy Arn. You killed him for a spoon? Your friend and comrade?'

'He stole it from me! It was *mine*!'

'And now it is gone. Was it worth the killing?' Fulk said harshly.

'I'll find it.'

'It is cursed. If you find it, you do not remain with the company,' Fulk said.

Rat scowled at him, and then jerked his shoulder away and ran off after his spoon.

* * *

The next morning, Rat was still scrabbling about in the undergrowth. Dogbreath went to him and attempted to persuade the lad to leave it and return to the company, but Rat ignored him and continued his searches.

They had bound Auffroy's wrists and ankles, and taken his knife from him the last evening. Now, he watched as Dogbreath returned to the main camp and sat down with a grunt. The wizened little man looked about him with a blank expression. 'What now, then?'

There was some dispute among the men about the best route to take. Whether to aim east, or to take a road southwards, and while they were arguing, Hawkwood went to Auffroy and kicked his feet to get his attention.

'That wood, where you saw the boy's body. You weren't protecting something there?'

'Me? No. I was following, hoping to get Juliot's necklace and cross back.'

'So there wasn't a cave there, a storehouse with treasure inside?'

Auffroy looked at him blankly. These English, he thought. All they thought about was murder and gold. And now they would kill him. He had no doubt about that. Why would they let him live? He was nothing to them, any more than any number of the other Frenchmen they had slaughtered in the last months.

Hawkwood dropped to his haunches and pulled out his knife. 'Well, I suppose that's all, then,' he said, and the blade whipped out like a serpent striking.

Auffroy felt his heart stop. And then he felt the odd warmth flood through his body as the tingling in his fingers began as the cords binding him were cut away. 'You will kill me?'

'Why?' Hawkwood asked. 'What will that earn us? No, you can go.'

'My cross and necklace.'

Hawkwood stared at him. 'You should be grateful to be able to leave with your life.'

* * *

Rat was still desperately searching when he heard the rumble of the wagon wheels rolling away. He would stay here just a little longer, and see whether he could find it. It was valuable, that spoon. His most prized possession. He couldn't just leave it here. Fulk should never have thrown it away; it was *his*, Rat's. No one else had the right to take it and discard it.

He thought there was a glint of metal in the undergrowth, and scrabbled through the leaves and twigs, but it was just his imagination.

High overhead, while he hunted, the spoon dangled from its string, caught in a branch. But Rat never looked up.

* * *

Fulk rode solemnly, today with Crespin on his horse with him.

'Are you well?' William said.

'*Ja!* Naturally. Why should I not be?'

'The boy.'

'He had a choice. He made his decision,' Fulk said. But he didn't look back. The boy had killed another. He was not like Fulk's son.

William let him ride on, and waited while Perkin caught up with him.

'We continue?' Perkin asked.

'What else can we do?' William said. 'There's nothing for us back home, and returning without anything to show for our efforts would be shameful.'

'And you want your spurs, you mean!'

'Well, I would like that, yes,' William said. He looked ahead. 'Perhaps we will make our fortunes, but I fear it will be a long and dangerous journey.'

'All journeys are dangerous.'

EPILOGUE

JULY 1358

Auffroy could not return to his town. The guilt about the lives of all the men who had followed him to try to ambush the English, the death of Gadiffer, all weighed heavily on his soul. But he returned briefly to the area.

He knelt and scraped away a little of the soil. They were both under here, the soil as dead and lifeless as their bodies where it had been disturbed earlier in the year. Only a few plants struggled to colonise the grave.

After planting the cross, the cause of so much death, he patted the soil over it. Sir Reginald had been gracious to him, placing the cross in his hands like the holy bread of the sacrament. 'Go, and I hope you and she find peace,' the knight had said. And to Auffroy's astonishment, the company had ridden slowly away, leaving only him, and the boy scavenging in the woods.

Now, kneeling here, Auffroy turned his face heavenwards.

'What now?' he asked, and then began to weep.

September 1358

Thomas de Ladit shivered.

The cell in which he had been held was not the worst in the palace, but he felt the chill nonetheless. He had been interrogated for weeks. At least, thanks to his priest's robes, he had not suffered the same fate as so many others. Many had been hanged, many beheaded, or broken on the wheel, but he had survived, and perhaps could still return to serve King Charles.

It had been a shaming experience. Forced to sign a full, and somewhat imaginative, confession, including many acts he had not been aware of or plots to which he was not privy, he had then been forced to read the full declaration before the dauphin, and a large invited audience there to witness his utter humiliation.

At least now, he was to be released from the palace into the custody of the Bishop of Paris, and held in his rather more salubrious prison. It was good to feel the sun on his face, hear the wind in the trees, and to be able to see the sky and the clouds overhead. Thomas was content for a moment just to stand still, eyes closed, face up to the sun.

The gate was opened and he was thrust through it by his escort. They set off at a fair pace, the guards about him, and made their way to the Rue de la Barillerie.

Thomas was hobbling slightly after his incarceration, and it was the pain in his left leg that slowed him somewhat, but it was annoying to see that the guards were walking more swiftly, and it made him frown. They ought to have stayed with him, after all. He was their charge, and it was their duty to look after him. But no matter, he thought. They were just the sort of men who could not be bothered to be held up by a man who was limping. Besides, they would soon be at the bishop's palace.

The first blow stunned him, but he remained upright, a hand to his skull. He turned, demanding, 'What the—'

That was when the second cudgel struck him, and he was knocked to his knees. A third blow hit his mouth, smashing teeth and nose simultaneously. He gave a cry.

'This is for your treachery to the dauphin and to France,' a man hissed, and then the blows rained down in earnest and Thomas de Ladit heard no more.

* * *

MORE FROM MICHAEL JECKS

The next instalment in Michael Jecks' epic Vintaine series is available to order now here:

https://mybook.to/Vintaine5BackAd

ABOUT THE AUTHOR

Michael Jecks is the author of over 50 novels inspired by history and legend. He is the founder of Medieval Murderers, and has served on the committees of the Historical Writers' Association, the CWA and the Detection Club. He was International Guest of Honour at the Bloody Words festival in Toronto, and Grand Master of the first parade in the New Orleans Mardi Gras.

Sign up to Michael Jecks' mailing list for news, competitions and updates on future books.

Visit Michael Jecks' website: www.michaeljecks.co.uk

Follow Michael on social media here:

f facebook.com/Michael.Jecks.author
X x.com/MichaelJecks
instagram.com/michaeljecks
BB bookbub.com/authors/michael-jecks

ALSO BY MICHAEL JECKS

The Vintaine Series

Fields of Glory

Blood on the Sand

Blood of the Innocents

Ashes of Rebellion

WARRIOR CHRONICLES

WELCOME TO THE CLAN ✕

THE HOME OF
BESTSELLING HISTORICAL
ADVENTURE FICTION!

WARNING:
MAY CONTAIN VIKINGS!

SIGN UP TO OUR
NEWSLETTER

BIT.LY/WARRIORCHRONICLES

Boldw**oo**d